I0766930

Their GRACES

A *New York Times*, *USA Today*, *Amazon*, and *Audible* bestselling author of award-winning Georgian historical romances and mysteries, Lucinda's books are renowned for their wit, heart-felt drama and a happily ever-after. She has degrees in history and political science from the Australian National University and a postgraduate degree in education from Bond University, where she was awarded the Frank Surman Medal. *Noble Satyr*, Lucinda's first novel, was awarded the $10,000 *Random House/-Woman's Day* Romantic Fiction Prize, and she has twice been a finalist for the Romance Writers' of Australia Romantic Book of the Year. Her novels have garnered multiple awards and become worldwide genre bestsellers. Lucinda lives a stone's throw from the beach, in a writing hut with wall-to-wall books on all aspects of the Eighteenth Century, collected over 40 years—Heaven. She loves to hear from readers (and she'll write back!).

lucindabrant@gmail.com			lucindabrant.com
pinterest.com/lucindabrant			twitter.com/lucindabrant
facebook.com/lucindabrantbooks			youtube.com/lucindabrantauthor

Their GRACES

SEQUEL TO HER DUKE

ROXTON FOUNDATION SERIES BOOK FOUR

Lucinda Brant

A Sprigleaf Book
Published by Sprigleaf Pty. Ltd.

Their Graces: Sequel to *Her Duke*.
Roxton Foundation Series, Book 4.
Copyright © 2023 Lucinda Brant, all rights reserved.
Editing: Martha Stites & Cathie Maud Cabot.
Art & design: Sprigleaf.
Original artwork reference: *The Declaration of Love* by Jean François de Troy.
Back cover 'postcard' crop art: *A Stag Hunt at Versailles* attributed
to Jean-Baptiste Martin.
Carriage returns fleuron design by Sprigleaf.

Typeset in Adobe Garamond Pro.

Also in ebook, audiobook, and other languages.

ISBN 978-1-922985-57-6

10 9 8 7 6 5 4 3 2 1 Casebound Library Edition   (ii) I

for
Martha

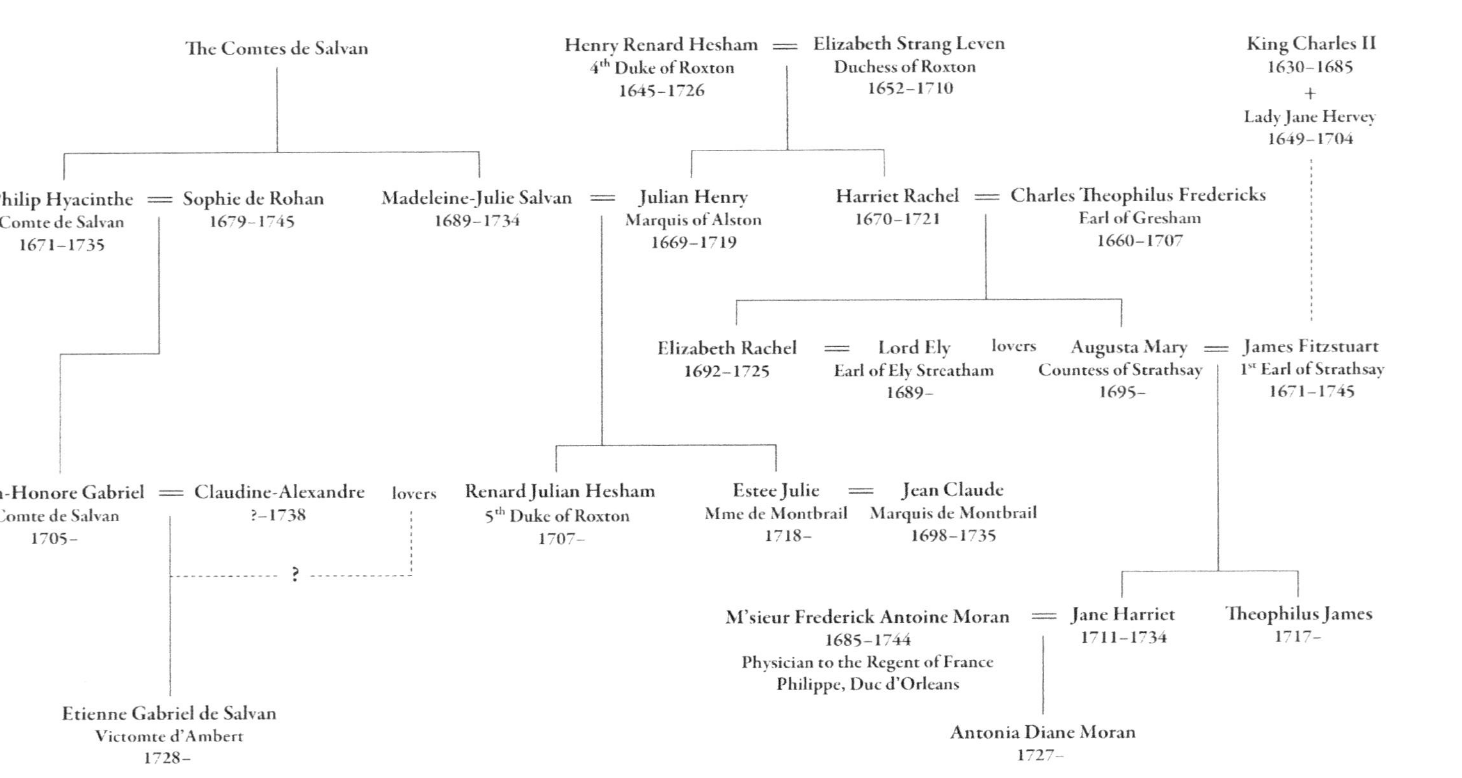

The Comtes de Salvan
Henry Renard Hesham
4th Duke of Roxton
1645–1726
Elizabeth Strang Leven
Duchess of Roxton
1652–1710
King Charles II
1630–1685
+
Lady Jane Hervey
1649–1704
Philip Hyacinthe
Comte de Salvan
1671–1735
Sophie de Rohan
1679–1745
Madeleine-Julie Salvan
1689–1734
Julian Henry
Marquis of Alston
1669–1719
Harriet Rachel
1670–1721
Charles Theophilus Fredericks
Earl of Gresham
1660–1707
Elizabeth Rachel
1692–1725
Lord Ely
Earl of Ely Streatham
1689–
lovers
Augusta Mary
Countess of Strathsay
1695–
James Fitzstuart
1st Earl of Strathsay
1671–1745
Jean-Honore Gabriel
Comte de Salvan
1705–
Claudine-Alexandre
?–1738
lovers
?
Renard Julian Hesham
5th Duke of Roxton
1707–
Estee Julie
Mme de Montbrail
1718–
Jean Claude
Marquis de Montbrail
1698–1735
M'sieur Frederick Antoine Moran
1685–1744
Physician to the Regent of France
Philippe, Duc d'Orleans
Jane Harriet
1711–1734
Theophilus James
1717–
Etienne Gabriel de Salvan
Victomte d'Ambert
1728–
Antonia Diane Moran
1727–

DRAMATIS PERSONAE

The Roxton Family and household

Roxton—*Duke of Roxton aka M'sieur le Duc*
Antonia—*Duchess of Roxton aka Mme la Duchesse
    aka Comtesse du Roucy.*
Vallentine—*Lucian, Lord Vallentine, Roxton's best
    friend and married to his sister.*
Estée—*Lady Vallentine aka Madame, Vallentine's
    wife and Roxton's sister.*
Martin—*Martin Ellicott, Roxton's former valet and
    Julian's godfather* (mon parrain).
Julian—*Roxton and Antonia's infant son aka JuJu.*
Gabrielle—*Antonia's personal maid, youngest sister of
    Yvette, Rose, and Giselle.*
Céleste & Cécile—*infant Julian's wet nurses aka the
    Morvan* nourrices.
George Geraghty—*Roxton's valet.*
Jean-Luc Levron—*natural son of Roxton's father the
    Marquis of Alston and his mistress, a* marion-
    nettiste.
Augusta Fitzstuart—*the Countess of Strathsay aka*
    Grand-mère. *Antonia's grandmother.*

The Salvan Family and household

The ancient aunts—*sisters of Philip, Comte de Salvan. Roxton's aunts through his mother Madeleine-Julie; Salvan's aunts through his father Philip.*

Tante Philippe—*Marquise du Touraine-Brissac aka Mme Touraine-Brissac. Mother of Alphonse, Duc du Touraine. Grandmother of Elisabeth-Louise and Michelle Haudry.*

Tante Victoire—*the Comtesse du Chavigny.*

Tante Sophie-Adelaide—*twin sister of Victoire. A nun.*

Madeleine-Julie Salvan Hesham—*youngest of the Salvan sisters. Marquise of Alston, Roxton and Estée's mother d. 1734.*

Salvan—*Jean-Honoré Gabriel Salvan, Comte de Salvan. Son of Philip, Comte de Salvan, Roxton's first cousin. Nephew of the ancient aunts.*

Chevalier Montbelliard—*aka Cousin Hugh. The Comte de Salvan's heir.*

Michelle Haudry—*aka Mme Haudry, daughter-in-law of a Farmer General, daughter of Alphonse, Duc du Touraine, granddaughter of Philippe, Marquise du Touraine-Brissac.*

Alphonse—*Duc du Touraine, only son of Mme Touraine-Brissac, Roxton's first cousin and best friend. Father of Michelle Haudry and Elisabeth-Louise Salvan Gondi Touraine.*

Elisabeth-Louise—*sister of Michelle Haudry, grand-daughter of Mme Touraine-Brissac.*

Thérèse—*Comtesse Duras-Valfons, Roxton's ex-mistress, wife of Baron Thesiger, sister of the Marquis de Chesnay, mother of the infant Robert.*

Gustave—*Marquis de Chesnay, Roxton's friend, brother of Thérèse Duras-Valfons.*

'Ricky'—*Richard Thesiger, Baron Thesiger, estranged husband of Thérèse Duras-Valfons.*

Giselle—*Elizabeth-Louise's personal maid, sister of Gabrielle.*

Historical figures appearing or mentioned

Louis—*King of France. Louis XV (1710–1774), known as Louis the Well-Beloved, King from 1 September 1715 until his death in 1774.*

Mme de Pompadour—*the King's* maîtresse-en-titre *(official chief mistress) aka Marquise de Pompadour, born Jeanne Antoinette Poisson (1721–1764).*

Comte d'Hozier—*the King's genealogist, keeper of* L'Armorial général de France *and* juge d'armes de France. *Louis Pierre d'Hozier (1685–1767).*

Marquis de Dreux-Brézé—Grand maître des cérémonies de France.

Joachim—*Marquis of Dreux-Brézé (1710-1781)*

Duc de Bouillon—*Grand Chambellan de France.*

Duc de Richelieu—*aka Armand, First Gentleman of the Bedchamber. Louis François Armand de Vignerot du Plessis (1696–1788).*

Marie Leszczyńska—*Queen of France (1703-1768), wife of King Louis XV.*

Marquis de Maurepas—*Minister of the King's Household. Jean-Frédéric Phélypeaux, Count of Maurepas (1701–1781) French statesman.*

M'sieur de Marville—*Lieutenant General of Police for Paris.*

ONE

VILLA ROXTON, RUE DES RÉSERVOIRS, PETIT PARC, VERSAILLES, NOVEMBER 1746

WHEN ESTÉE Vallentine arrived at her brother's villa, no family member was in the foyer to greet her. This despite her sending one of the postillions on ahead to announce her arrival.

It had rained all the way from Paris, making the journey onerous for one in her delicate condition. She did her best to bear it, keeping her spirits up with the knowledge she would soon be reunited with her husband, brother, and sister-in-law. And she could not wait to see how much her baby nephew had grown in the weeks since the family had left the hôtel to come here to Versailles.

Under the *porte-cochère*, a liveried footman handed her down from the big carriage, her ladies-in-waiting following up behind as she entered the house to be greeted by the porter and a handful of liveried footmen. Although they did their best to make a fuss, it was not the same as if her family were present.

Her spirits fell and she became disgruntled.

Divested of fur-lined travelling cloak and muff, she took a cursory glance about the entrance foyer with its black-and-white marble tiles, chandelier, and curved marble staircase, and her mouth set in a prim line. This was her first visit to the villa that had once been the home of her parents, before she was born. And while she had been warned that it was a modest townhouse for one of her noble birth, it was left to the sour expressions of her ladies to mirror her thoughts. After a lifetime surrounded by opulence on a grand scale, this foyer was depressingly restrained in décor and size. It did not bode well for the rest of the establishment and reinforced her belief that by taking up residence here the Duke was yet again indulging the whims of his much younger wife. That the house was surprisingly warm was small compensation.

"Is there a family emergency?" she demanded of the porter.

"Pardon, Madame? Emergency?"

"Is there one?"

The porter shook his head vigorously. "No. No, Madame. I assure you there—"

"Are my family in residence?"

"Yes, Madame. That is to say—"

"I do not need you to say anything. Take me to M'sieur le Duc."

"Unfortunately I cannot do that, Madame," apologized the porter.

"Then find me someone who will!"

"That is not to say I do not want to fulfil your every wish, Madame. But I have been ordered that under no circumstances is M'sieur le Duc to be interrupted while he has as his guest a very important personage."

Estée's eyebrows lifted. "Personage?"

"A very important personage, Madame."

"They must be exceedingly important to have prevented M'sieur le Duc from welcoming his own sister to his villa!"

"Yes, Madame."

"Who is with M'sieur le Duc?"

The porter took a step closer and said in awed accents, "I cannot tell you, Madame. All I can say is that there are none more important than those who come calling on behalf of *Sa Majesté.*"

Estée's blue eyes widened, and with a gloved hand to her embroidered velvet bodice she dropped her voice to a whisper. "A representative of the King is here, in this house?"

"Yes, Madame."

Like co-conspirators they spoke in whispers.

Estée took a step closer to the rotund little man. "Who? You must have a name."

"Sadly, Madame, I cannot tell you."

"Won't," she hissed.

The porter stuck out his bottom lip and appeared rueful. "It is as you say, Madame. I would if I could, but I do not wish to incur the displeasure of M'sieur le Duc. But—!" He smiled secretively and shrugged a shoulder. "What I can tell you is that I was *not* told not to divulge the position this nobleman holds in the King's household—"

"Yes?"

"*Monsieur le visiteur* is the King's *juge d'armes de France*."

Estée smiled knowingly. Every noble worth his coat of arms knew that the *juge d'armes de France*—judges of arms for France— was the King's genealogist, and presently that position was held by the Comte d'Hozier.

This nobleman was responsible for verifying claims of nobility and deciding issues regarding the use of arms by nobles. And as the King's genealogist d'Hozier was also keeper of *L'Armorial général de France*, the precious register that contained within it the names of every noble family, their coat of arms, and an ancestry that had to stretch back at least to the fifteenth century if one aspired to be included within its pages. If one's name was not inked in the register, then one was not noble, and that was that.

Estée was exceedingly proud that as the granddaughter of Philip, Comte de Salvan, she was in the register, and so, too, was her brother. But she had a notion that the King's genealogist was not here on their behalf, and presumed the visit must have something to do with Antonia's court presentation. She hoped there was no last-minute impediment to the proceedings, but quickly dismissed any worry, knowing her brother would soon set matters to right.

She took a step away from the porter, her superciliousness firmly back in place.

"We must not disturb M'sieur le Duc while he has as his guest M'sieur le Comte d'Hozier, so you may take me to my husband."

The porter threw up his arms.

"Unfortunately I cannot do that either, Madame."

"M'sieur Vallentine is with M'sieur le Duc?"

"No, Madame. M'sieur Vallentine departed the house at dawn for *La Grande Écurie*. He did not say when he would return."

Estée Vallentine's shoulders slumped. She felt abandoned. She was about to ask the whereabouts of Mme la Duchesse when a series of resonating thuds overhead startled her. She fell back into the arms of one of her waiting women, whose gaze had shot to the ceiling in alarm, expecting ornate plasterwork to rain down upon them.

The servants were unmoved and awaited her pleasure.

"Did you hear that-that—*noise*?" Estée demanded, gloved finger pointing upwards.

Before the porter could answer, there were more thuds and what sounded like a hundred running feet. This and muffled shouts of excitement kept the women gazing skywards. Estée Vallentine dropped her chin and glared at the porter.

"You cannot be deaf to that cacophony!"

"Yes, Madame. I am. We all are."

Estée frowned her incomprehension.

The porter was self-effacing in his explanation.

"You will forgive me for saying so, but we are also blind until told otherwise. *Madame comprend-elle*?" He bowed and indicated the staircase where one of the footmen waited on the bottom step. "Now please to follow Simon to the Nursery Gallery. Mme la

Duchesse requested you join her there." He bowed again and stepped out of the way. "Welcome to the villa, Madame."

ESTÉE ENTERED the long room to the astonishing sight of two sedan chairs being raced up and down its length, cheered on by all present.

Lifted up on poles and carried between two burly chairmen, the sedan chairs sped down the room as fast as the chairmen could run, their passengers bumped about on the ride and enthusiastically acknowledging the spectators through the side windows with vigorous waves and squeals of laughter.

Estée wasn't sure what horrified her more—that sedan chairs were being raced inside the villa, or that these particular sedan chairs were the transportation used by the masses. The liveried blue coats of the chairmen and their blue-painted boxes proclaimed them as public conveyances for residents of the township with coin to pay for their services. She doubted very much that these men had ever seen the inside of a nobleman's home, and never one belonging to M'sieur le Duc d'Roxton. As for the number and types of persons who had occupied the bench inside such common transport, she shuddered to speculate.

One of the chairs was set down at the far end of the nursery, whereby a couple of the maids dashed forward to open the door, lift out the child inside, and put in its place another, whose turn it was to enjoy the thrill of the ride. If the child was too young or too small to see out of the windows, an older child climbed in and sat on the bench, and the smaller child was placed on a lap, and there held securely for the duration of the ride.

When the occupants were settled and the door closed, both sedan chairs were lifted up on their poles. The chairmen then waited for the signal for the race to start. This was a length of blue ribbon waved from halfway along the line of spectators—nursery-maids with babies in arms or young children on a hip, and the other children clinging to their petticoats or holding the hands of an elder brother or sister or a servant.

And with the signal given, off the sedan chairs raced, passing the assemblage of laughing servants and excited children, all of whom waved and shouted and blew kisses. Reaching the far wall, the chairmen turned about without setting down their chairs and raced back up the room to start the process all over again.

Estée was fascinated and alarmed in equal measure, wondering if this was what a madhouse must be like if the inmates were in control.

No one took the slightest notice of her, not even when she was several steps into the room. And when the footman who had opened the door for her turned to leave, her instinct was to run out into the passageway behind him. She now regretted dismissing her ladies, sending them off to prepare her rooms and unpack her trunks.

But she was not as invisible as she supposed. A young maid scurried across to her with a wicker chair, set it down, bobbed a curtsy, and fled. Estée sat, doing her best to keep her features neutral while her senses adjusted to the heady atmosphere, one arm across the folds of her velvet petticoats in her lap under her growing belly, the other across it, as if her baby within needed protection.

Looking beyond the line of servants and racing sedan chairs, she took in the rest of the nursery. At the far end, tapestry screens had been folded away and leaned against a wall, exposing a row of unoccupied cots made up with bedding, and several wicker cradles on pedestals. A hipbath full of sudsy water before the fireplace did have an occupant. Two maids were leaning over a child, scrubbing him clean from the backs of his ears to between his toes. A heap of sodden dirty clothes to one side of the hipbath suggested he had been caught out playing in the mud in the pelting rain. A young maid—the one who had provided Estée with a chair—scooped up this soiled laundry and disappeared behind a servant door.

She wondered at the whereabouts of the Duchess and her baby son. It never occurred to her to give the occupants of the sedan chairs more than a cursory look. Her attention shifted back to the rowdy spectators, and how it was that these servants were so undisciplined without their mistress present, acting as if it were their day off and they at a saint's day fête. They would never have misbehaved when she was in charge of the Duke's household. Here again was another example of her brother's over-indulgence where Antonia was concerned. She had tried to warn him, but he had refused to take heed, and here was the result!

And then she noticed amongst the servants one who had until recently been one of them.

The Duke's former valet was in the midst of this madness, looking well-pleased with himself, cheering on just as enthusiastically as the others, and waving about that absurd blue ribbon as if he were the master of ceremonies at a circus. Why was she not surprised that he was encouraging Antonia's waywardness? Her prediction about him, too, had also come to pass! Give a servant an inch of freedom and they became unwieldy smug tyrants.

She was having none of it.

Up on her heels and shaking out her petticoats, she was about to cross to the other side of the Nursery Gallery and demand he explain himself. And then one of the sedan chairs careened off course and its chairmen set it down in front of her, blocking her way.

TWO

"M ADAME! You are here at last!"

It was the Duchess.

Estée heard her but could not see her. And then she realised the greeting had come from inside the sedan chair set down before her. A maid had swung wide the door, and there seated on its bench was Antonia, bright-eyed and smiling, porcelain cheeks delicately flushed, and her honey-blonde hair mussed. On her lap, amongst the layers of her embroidered, pale-blue quilted silk petticoats, was her baby son, gurgling with delight and flapping his arms.

"Oh my darling girl! There you are!" Estée exclaimed with relief.

Antonia kissed her son's rosy cheek and spoke to him. "JuJu," she cooed. "Your Tante Estée, she is finally here! Now the family is altogether again, which pleases your maman very much."

She held her son out to be taken by a maid, and then Gabrielle helped her alight. Once on firm ground, and stepping away from the sedan chair, another of Antonia's maids came forward to shake her mistress's silk under-petticoats and velvet over-gown free of creases, while a third adjusted her gauze apron, retying its ribbons about the Duchess's waist. Antonia then took back her son and went over to Estée.

The two women embraced in greeting as best they could with a wriggling infant between them, and lightly kissed each other's cheeks.

"We have had such a merry morning!" Antonia announced. "I had no notion chairs could be carried at such a pace!" She smiled brightly. "And now Julian he does not scream while sitting in a chair with me. Yesterday, I tried having him on my lap in my chair for the short ride to visit our neighbors, but no! He would have none of it, and so Celeste she had to carry him across while I went in my chair alone." She gave her son a little squeeze of delight. "But after our rainy-day races, he does not mind the inside of a chair in the least. But enough about our morning. How was your journey? Did it rain all the way? Are you feeling not so ill these days? You look very well. Pregnancy suits you, Madame! We have so much to tell you! But first coffee—oh!" She leaned forward, a frown between her brows. "I hope those are happy tears?"

Estée dabbed at her eyes and pinched her little nose with her lace-bordered handkerchief.

"Yes. Happy tears. *Bien sûr*! Always." She sniffed and smiled. "I have missed you all so very much."

When Antonia sat on the wicker chair a footman fetched for her, her baby son on her lap, Estée resumed her seat and took hold of her nephew's little clenched fist.

"He has grown so much, *ma très chère belle-sœur*. Is it possible he is twice the size since I last saw him?"

Antonia laughed behind her hand.

"He is such a fat, jolly baby and all because he cannot get enough of the breast. It is as well he has two *nourrices* at his beck and call. And since finding he has a voice, he makes more noise than a macaw in a cage!" Her green eyes shone as she confided, "Your arrival is most opportune, because he has had enough excitement for today and requires changing before he can be in civilized company again."

She looked about for one of his nurses or a nursery maid, but all were preoccupied shunting the children to the far end of the room or scooping up stragglers. And then Martin Ellicott came across to her, having left the chairmen in the hands of the footmen.

"They accepted refreshment?" Antonia asked him.

"Yes, Mme la Duchesse. They were exceedingly grateful for your offer of nuncheon in the kitchen, and even more so when I calculated their payment—"

"—on the number of races back and forth, yes?"

"As you requested. I sent a note with the sum to be paid upon their departure."

Estée sat up. She could not help herself and had to comment.

"Why are you paying them at all when they are being fed? They have spent the entire morning out of the cold and wet, and so should be grateful for the privilege of being permitted to enter the house of M'sieur le Duc d'Roxton! And once they brag to their fellows of their good fortune, that they had as their passenger M'sieur le Duc's duchesse, they will have paying passengers lining up down the avenue! All for the privilege of using the chair you were carried in! No. Save your deniers, my dearest. Roxton's steward will thank you."

Antonia and Martin exchanged a look, but neither commented, Martin making Estée Vallentine a bow of acknowledgment. If Antonia witnessed Estée stiffen and slight her son's godfather by turning her cheek, she pretended otherwise, not wanting to upset her sister-in-law in her first hour at the villa.

Kissing her baby son, she said to him, "Your very patient and understanding *ton parrain* will take you to Celeste." Holding him out to Martin, she confided in a low voice, "Please to have the fortitude to lose your sense of smell, Martin. *Merci.*"

Estée watched Martin Ellicott stroll off up the Gallery talking to his godson, a gaggle of children soon surrounding him, happily skipping alongside, chattering away in the most familiar manner. And when more than one child's fingers reached up to touch the baby's chubby fingers, she screwed up her mouth and forced herself to look away.

Antonia saw the look and said gently, "They are excited, as children always are, with something new and fascinating. Not only did they have the opportunity to sit in a sedan chair, but to ride in one, and to race each other. They will settle soon. It is almost nuncheon, and after they have eaten, they will nap, and peace will once again be restored—" She sighed happily and chuckled. "—if only for a few hours! And then we must see what can be done to run off their liveliness while it continues to rain, and they cannot get out of doors."

"My dear, I offer you this advice as one who loves you as a sister," Estée said with the fixed supercilious smile Antonia had come to know so well that it dropped her shoulders. "You would do well not to take such an inordinate interest in the children of those who serve us. Best to keep your distance. Better still, limit your time in the nursery. Your son's attendants should come to you, not the other way 'round."

"M'sieur le Duc apologizes for not being able to greet you—" Antonia began, attempting to change the subject, not wanting to be drawn.

"There is no need," Estée replied, brushing the apology aside. "One does not keep waiting *Sa Majesté*'s genealogist." And because she was still disturbed by the management of her nephew's nursery, returned to that concern. "Have you given consideration to the notion that children in your son's nursery are a distraction for the nursery maids, and a burden on their time?"

"They are the children of our servants, and of Julian's *nourrices*. These women are far from their homes—"

"And now, so too are their children. Would they not have been better off remaining amongst their own kind, where they could be of use, in the home and out in the fields—"

"Pardon, Madame, children should never be separated from their mothers until they are old enough for such separation."

"What a singularly novel notion, my dear, when one considers every noblewoman at court places her babies into the care of nurses from birth—"

"Your mother did not."

Estée's smile became fixed. "She did not for the simple reason her brother had forbidden her the court."

"Oh? Monseigneur tells me she did not give you both into the care of others because it was her wish, and the wish of your father, that you remain with them. That is our wish for our children, too. And having the other children here," she added with a forced bright smile, hoping to put an end to the discussion, "provides Julian with the companionship of playmates."

Estée huffed her disbelief. "My dear, when he is old enough to appreciate the distinction, he will choose with whom he spends his time, and believe me, it will not be with the sons of wetnurses!"

Antonia tilted her head and pretended a moment of dullness. "Distinction?"

"La, my darling girl," Estée said with a tinkle of incredulous laughter. "I do not need to remind you that our children are singular, and as such they must grow up amongst their own kind. That requires he be taught the difference between those who are served, and those who serve us. In this way all children, low and highborn, learn their place in this world."

Antonia clenched her hands in her lap. "Madame, Julian is an infant. His needs are simple: To be well-fed, to be kept warm and dry, and most of all to be loved. Everything else, it is unimportant."

"Who can blame you for such naïve pronouncements, *ma très chère belle-sœur,*" Estée replied on a condescending sigh. "Your unusual upbringing lends itself to extraordinary ideas. I do not mean to criticize—and no doubt you are very aware—as the son and heir of M'sieur le Duc d'Roxton, Julian's upbringing must and will be vastly different from your own."

"I am not only aware of it, but I am also determined he will remain protected from this awareness while in the nursery. Here he is an infant, no different from any other infant and small child." Antonia smiled knowingly, the dimple in her cheek showing. "But you are wrong if you think his upbringing will be so very different from my own. Just as my father showered me with love and understanding, Monseigneur and I, we will do the same with Julian—"

"Of course you will but—"

"Madame," Antonia continued, cutting off her sister-in-law because she needed to get across her point for the last time. "I am well aware that once Julian he leaves the nursery, he will spend his entire life being reminded, not only of his nobility, but that he is the son of M'sieur le Duc d'Roxton. He will live in his father's shadow, and that cannot be helped. I want him to be proud of his blood and who he is, but he must also be content, and have a life knowing that he is loved for being our son first. Only in this way will he ever find the courage to step out into the light and be who he is truly meant to be, yes? *C'est tout ce qu'il y a à faire!*"

"Of course, my love," Estée agreed without fully understanding, and thus she could not resist voicing a niggling incomprehension. "Which is why I wonder if it might not be for the best to begin those lessons and that awareness from the cradle, to surround him with those who understand the shadow his father casts, rather than those who might hinder its progress. He will then be better prepared for his future. One day he will be M'sieur le Duc d'Roxton and inherit vast wealth and power, and everyone will bow down to him. Such a future is immutable."

"One day. But not today, and not tomorrow," Antonia stated firmly. And frustrated at not being able to make her sister-in-law understand that love and being loved mattered most to her, emotion got the better of her and she blurted out, tears welling up, "But me, I mean to do my best not to think of the far-flung future, to the time when Julian he is addressed as M'sieur le Duc! Because that future is one without Monseigneur, and I will not allow myself to contemplate that eventuality—*ever*."

Estée reached across and gently squeezed Antonia's clenched hands. "There is no need for you to think of it today. Please. Do not distress yourself. But one day you will have to do so, for the sake of your children. Because if something were to happen to Roxton and you were left—"

"No!" Antonia shot up off her chair. "No! I am sorry, Madame. But no! We will never speak of such an eventuality again. I understand why you have such maudlin thoughts because of what happened to your own father. That was a tragedy. Your mother she lived the rest of her days in sadness with eyes that had wept so many tears she could weep no more. But Monseigneur he will not fall from his horse. And his children will know their father, and if I ever weep, it will only be from joy. Now let us have our coffee. But in the breakfast room, I have something to show you there which I think will please you."

Estée caught at Antonia's wrist before she could turn away. She remained seated, and looking up at the Duchess with a sad smile, said with contrition, "Forgive me for spoiling your morning revelries—"

"You did not do—"

"I did. And you are right. I do dwell too often on the unhappy past. More so, if that were possible, now this new life is growing within me. That is odd, do you not think—with my thoughts occupied with what has been rather than what will be?"

"It is only natural. The future, it is the unknown. Every female, from the time she discovers she is to become a mother, worries about every little thing to do with the baby. But most of all we worry about the birth. My mother she died in childbed. So my thoughts while pregnant would often wander to that unhappy circumstance." Antonia squeezed Estée's fingers and smiled. "But everything will be well, with you, and with your little one. I know it."

Estée nodded and kissed the back of Antonia's hand. And once on her feet, she linked arms with her and they strolled a little way up the room toward the cots and cribs, which were once again hidden behind tapestry screens. From behind one of these screens stepped Martin Ellicott carrying his godson. The baby was nestled into his neck and sound asleep. He waited for them to join him.

Seeing him with her nephew, Estée's sour expression returned. She stopped in the middle of the room and said under her breath, "He is rather assiduous in his duties as *le parrain*."

"As Vallentine will be, too, when Julian he is old enough to be taught how to use *son épée*."

"Sword play is not conducted in a nursery, my dear, which is no place for a man. And Lucian is a nobleman and a master swordsman, *and* my brother's oldest friend. Whereas this man is—"

"—also Monseigneur's great friend, and he, too, is Julian's godfather," Antonia interrupted firmly but gently. "Those two facts are—what was the word you used that I liked very much—Ah! I remember!—*immutable*. Come!" she continued with a bright smile, "Coffee and cake await us." And she bustled off to join Martin.

Estée followed, mouth firmly shut on any further advice, knowing it was futile to continue. Her sister-in-law was too kind, too benevolent, too keen to have a happy household at any price, and her youth was against her. The Duchess had no idea when she was being taken advantage of, particularly by the Duke's former valet.

When she had voiced her apprehension to her brother regarding the running of her nephew's nursery, and her grave misgivings about Antonia's familiarity with well-meaning servants and toadying former lackeys, he had dismissed her concerns as inconsequential. But now, being here at the villa and seeing how things stood with her own eyes, she was determined the Duke be brought to his senses and see that, under the Duchess's lax control his household was becoming ungovernable.

She would take matters in hand, curb the excesses and familiarity within this household, and return it to its natural state, how it had been run under her guidance. And she would start with the one person she was convinced had undue influence over the Duchess. If anyone was casting a shadow over her nephew's nursery and manipulating her sister-in-law, it was her brother's former valet. And she intended to see that the impudent wheedler was put back in his place, and there remained.

HALF AN HOUR before she was called to join the family for dinner, one of her ladies-in-waiting admitted a visitor to her small sitting room off the boudoir. Seated in the center of a silk striped chaise— the only chair in the room—with her quilted petticoats carefully arranged, and fluttering a gouache fan, Estée beckoned the visitor forward with a lift of her chin.

Martin Ellicott stepped into the room, and the lady-in-waiting disappeared behind a tapestry *portière*, within earshot so she could instantly respond if called.

Alone with the Duke's sister, Martin could not imagine what she wished to speak to him about. Yet, knowing her well, he mentally prepared himself for any and all accusations she might care to throw at him.

THREE

WHENEVER THE rare circumstance occurred that he was summoned into the presence of the Duke's sister, Martin made sure to keep his feelings and thoughts to himself. He maintained a neutral expression and forced back down deep within him the assault to his senses.

First to be assailed was his sense of smell. The air was pungent with her sickly-sweet perfume which was too liberally splashed about her person. His eyes blinked dry from the sight of her heavy cosmetics that, had they been lightly applied, would have better suited her complexion, and complemented rather than detracted from her beauty. The metallic taste on his tongue developed from his need to keep his mouth shut to whatever abuse she meted out. As for touch, well he was spared that because he never sat in her presence, and kept his hands clasped in front of him. And finally, his ears were assaulted, ringing with her petulant homilies, scathing verbal attacks and threats. And when she could not get her own way, there were screaming tears of frustration, directed at the Duke but taken out on him as her brother's messenger.

He did not know what to expect with the change to his position within the Duke's household. But he suspected she would not have taken the news well, and that he would always remain a servant in her eyes. After all, she had no experience of the world beyond the perfumed boudoirs of her aristocratic friends and relations; even the bourgeoisie were considered another country to French nobles. Thus her views were constricted by her prejudices. To her kind, no bridge existed which could span the enormous void between those who ruled and those who were ruled.

And as he approached the chaise, bowed, and waited to be addressed—which was her due—he wished with all his heart, for the sake of the Duke and Duchess and the domestic harmony of their household, she would surprise him, and prove him wrong.

ESTÉE LOOKED him up and down, shut her fan with a flourish and tossed it aside on the upholstered cushion. When it slid off onto the carpet, Martin scooped it up and held it out to her. But she did not take it, merely jerked her head for him to place it back on the cushion. He did so, slowly and deliberately, then stepped back to stand before her. And while his expression did not betray his thoughts, the fact he did not respectfully lower his gaze but stared straight into her eyes was indication enough of his lack of subservience—that he no longer considered himself a servant.

"Do you know who is with M'sieur le Duc?" she asked at her most condescending.

"I do, Madame." When she made an impatient gesture he added, "M'sieur le Comte d'Hozier, *Sa Majesté's* genealogist."

"Genealogist and keeper of *L'Armorial général de France*. Do you know what *that* is?"

"I do, Madame."

When she made another show of exasperation, he remained silent, forcing her to spit out, "Well!? Tell me what it is!"

"A register created by Louis XIV that has recorded within its pages the names and coat of arms of every French noble family dating back to the reign of, I believe, King Charles the Sixth."

She had no idea whether he had named the correct king or not, because she did not know herself, but she believed him. Besides, all that mattered to her was that he knew the particular register so she could make her point and put him in his place.

"The Salvans are inked in *L'Armorial général de France*, and M'sieur le Duc and I, we are the grandchildren of the Comte de Salvan. Our mother was a Salvan…"

When there was an extended silence, Martin wondered if he were to respond. He was too slow for her, again forcing her to state the obvious.

"Did you know that?"

"I am well aware of those facts, Madame."

"Good. Just as you must be aware that—" She could not suppress a smile of superiority. "—none of your ancestors are found within the pages of that register."

"Yes, Madame," he stated, gaze on hers. "That too is known to me."

She dared to stare back, and if she was unsettled, she tried to hide it. Yet Martin knew that whenever she was flustered, she plucked at her clothing. She was doing that now to one of the silk bows on the *échelle* of her bodice. Five seconds of silence passed between them and then she rolled her eyes and threw up a hand.

"And yet here you are! Living amongst us, no longer a servant but as if you belong here. As if you are one of *us*."

"Pardon, Madame, but I would never presume to be one of *you*, which I take you to mean, of noble birth."

"Of course that is what I mean! What else would I mean?"

"Then I do indeed know what you mean."

"Why are you not a valet still?"

"Surely M'sieur le Duc informed you of my change of circumstance—"

"Naturally! I am his sister. But that does not mean I understand why *you* accepted M'sieur le Duc's most extraordinary offer. Indeed, I am shocked that you did."

"To be candid, I am still in a state of disbelief myself."

"Then you acknowledge that you have no right to live as one of us?"

"Madame, I acknowledge that just as the majority of the populace know for a certainty that they will live, work, and die in the place of their birth, I will always be the son of a butler and a housekeeper; that my ancestors, as far back as we have any record of them, spent their lives in service to their masters."

"Then you should have refused my brother's offer and remained where you are most comfortable and useful, what you were born to do, and what you should still be doing."

"If life were that simple, Madame. I may have been a valet most of my life, but my vocation tells you very little about me."

"About you?" Estée blinked at him uncomprehending. "What is there to know?"

Martin involuntarily twitched a smile, not at all surprised she would not understand. He tried to explain.

"It is the same with those fortunate to be inked in *L'Armorial général de France*. It lists all the names of the French noble houses, to be sure, but that tells us nothing about each individual born to a particular great house—whether he be a good man or bad; whether he be a man of honor or a liar; a spendthrift or a miser—"

"*L'Armorial général de France* has nothing to do with you abandoning your post to masquerade as a gentleman of means!"

Martin wanted to sigh his frustration; instead he said calmly, "Madame, I merely wished to point out that a man's circumstance —where he was born and into what family—does not give you an indication of his character and whether he is good or evil. A chandler can live an honorable life, and a nobleman can be a scoundrel. It is only the luck of birth that allows one to claim dominion over the other—"

"Luck? You believe it is luck and not the will of God that determines into what family we are born? Are we not taught that He ordains all things? Do you believe in God?"

"Yes, Madame, of course I do. Perhaps a better choice of words would be *good fortune* rather than *luck*—"

"Luck or good fortune, it is the same. Chance has no place in the teachings of the Church. A candlemaker is a candlemaker because God has willed it. And by your own admission, your lineage is one of serving, so that is what you should be doing —serving."

"That is what I intend to continue to do, Madame, but in a different way."

Estée sat back, nonplussed. She made a gesture for him to explain himself.

"If, as you say, such a thing as luck does not exist, and all things are determined through His will, then my good fortune at being elevated out of servitude must also have been ordained by Him—"

"Do not twist my words!"

"—through the love and generosity of M'sieur le Duc and Mme la Duchesse."

"Prettily said. But whatever your elevation or ambition, you are not, and never will be, one of us, because you were not born to it. Which is why I do not understand why you would even attempt to be anything else!"

"I sympathize, Madame. And I understand that it must be truly difficult for one of your birth to comprehend what your brother has done for me. But I assure you, my only ambition is to be of service to M'sieur le Duc and Mme la Duchesse, in whatever capacity they care to have me." He made her a bow, and with his hand on his heart said gently, "I am and always will be a most faithful and devoted servant to your brother's ducal house and family."

His words and manner appeased her somewhat. She stirred on the chaise, and swiping up her fan, flicked it open and fluttered it. Pouting, her gaze met his, and when he stared back at her openly and with a small smile, she could not help herself but put him back in his rightful place.

"You always were possessed of a silver tongue," she sulked. "My brother taught you well. I only hope you know how to keep it firmly behind your teeth, now you are no longer M'sieur le Duc's valet, because he is no longer responsible for your conduct—you are. Which means you are no longer under his protection. Do you understand what that means for you?"

"Yes, Madame. You can be assured of my circumspection at all times. I am not one to put myself forward—"

"A little too late for that! Your elevation is already the subject of gossip amongst our relatives and friends. Take heed. If you wish to be of service to my brother and his wife, you would do well not to be seen in their company when they are away from the house. And when we have guests, you should retire from the public rooms and remain out of sight. Your presence will only make everyone uncomfortable. How will any of our friends or family know how to address you, to treat you, or what to say to you? Such unpleasantness must be avoided for their sakes. I am certain you wish to set my mind at ease on this matter, and so will agree to undertake—"

"Madame, I understand you have reservations," Martin interrupted. "My elevation is a most unusual circumstance. And I apologize if my presence in any way offends you, but to be truthful, how I conduct myself and how I spend my time and with whom is none of your concern." He bowed. "Now you must excuse me. I do not want to be late joining the family for dinner."

"No! Stop! How dare you!" she demanded, when he turned on a heel without being dismissed. "I did not give permission for you to leave, and I have not finished—"

Martin bowed again and looked at her with an expression that was all too familiar—her brother had that same unpleasant stare when he was irritated. It caused tears of frustration to well up in her blue eyes.

"Madame, it is only the respect I have for you as M'sieur le

Duc's sister that made me turn. Let me be politely blunt: I am not beholden to you, nor do I require your permission for how I conduct my life." He bowed his head. "I wish you well, and sincerely hope we can be on amicable terms for the sake of family harmony."

Estée blushed scarlet, and despite her pregnancy was quickly up off the chaise just as the passageway door was flung open. In strode her husband. Instantly, she burst into tears.

"Hey lovedy, I'm happy to see you too!" Vallentine declared, unperturbed by her tears. Gathering her in an embrace, he was forced to kiss the top of her coil of braids because her face was buried in his chest. "You've every right to be annoyed by my tardiness. I'd hoped to be here when you arrived, but somethin' came up, and who says *no* to your brother, eh?" He tried to step back so he could lift her chin to better see her, but she clung to him. "I'll have to change this frock if you water it much longer! Come, let's sit for a moment. I want to know how you and the little one are keeping—hey! Why are you still standin' there gawping at us?" he growled over his shoulder when he sensed a presence. "Take yourself off and be useful!"

"I beg your pardon, my lord. I was just taking my leave—"

"Wh-what?" Vallentine swirled about in shock, taking Estée with him. "Egad! It's you!" He went red in the face. "I thought you were a lackey."

"It is of no importance, my lord. Servants all look alike."

"No. No! That's not what I meant! Apologies. I just didn't expect to find you here—"

"Why are you apologizing to *him*?" Estée demanded, incensed. She broke from her husband's embrace to flounce to the chaise. "It is your pregnant wife who is owed the apology! Not this barbarian—"

Vallentine strode after her. "Now hold on a minute, Estée! You can't go callin' Ellicott names. He's not a lackey anymore."

"Ha! My absent husband he returns to this-this—*hovel*, and his principal concern is a lackey, not his pregnant wife. I truly am abused!"

"Steady on! Play fair," His Lordship whined, throwing himself on the chaise beside her. He snatched up her hand and proceeded to kiss each of her fingers, saying in a soothing voice between kisses, "You are my only concern—you and the babe. Truly."

Somewhat mollified, Estée turned to look at him. "Truly?"

"Aye. But don't let your brother hear you call this pretty little villa a hovel. It may be cramped and raucous, but we must make do, because Antonia has created a home here, and—"

"I wondered how long it would be before you took *her* side—"

"Now, Estée. Don't start—"

Martin ducked out into the passageway and closed the door on the arguing couple.

It was no surprise to him when they arrived late to dinner. Sliding on to their respective chairs, Vallentine was uncharacteristically grim, while Madame's blotchy face was carefully concealed under a layer of cosmetics. However, any lingering resentments were suppressed, and put aside altogether when, with the serving of coffee, the Duke and Duchess made a surprising announcement.

FOUR

I F THE DINERS were aware of the tension between the Vallentines, they did not show it, and continued on with their conversation as if nothing were amiss. Time, the consumption of several courses of meats, fish, and vegetables smothered in a variety of delicate sauces, and table talk on the most general of topics, soothed the way for a pleasant repast. Finally the Vallentines were joining in the discussion as if nothing untoward had occurred between them, and normality was restored—the Duchess animated and bantering with His Lordship, Martin Ellicott politely contributing, Estée acting as referee, and the Duke his customary taciturn self.

It was only after the remnants of the sweet pastries, tarts, and baked custards had been removed, and the diners settled in the snug drawing room with coffee, various liqueurs, and sweetmeats, that the Duke finally took control of the conversation.

Antonia snuggled into him on one chaise, while the Vallentines sat opposite. Estée had a cushion at her back to make her pregnancy more comfortable, her stockinged feet upon a padded footstool. And settled in a wingchair, between both chaises and facing the fireplace, was Martin Ellicott. All were sipping coffee and partaking of the liqueurs, attended to by the butler and several of the footmen.

Before telling them the reason for the visit by the King's genealogist, the Duke enquired of Vallentine as to the success of the venture he had sent him on at first light.

"It's all arranged," His Lordship confirmed confidently. "The ceremony is set for the end of the week, contingent on the timely arrival of Touraine's consent in writing. But you don't foresee any objection to the match from him, do you?"

"Once he has read my letter and M'sieur Haudry's offer, I am confident Alphonse will send his approval by his swiftest courier."

Estée's ears pricked up at the mention of their cousin the Duc du Touraine, and at the words 'ceremony' and 'match' she could but draw one conclusion. She gasped and smiled, eyes bright.

"Do not tell me! Cousin Alphonse has finally decided to remarry!"

The Duke lifted his gaze from swirling the brandy in his crystal tumbler. "What a fanciful notion. No. His youngest daughter is to marry."

"About time!" Estée exclaimed. "Elisabeth-Louise must be twenty if she is a day."

"Such a great age," Antonia muttered, a sidelong smile at Vallentine and Martin.

"I dare say twenty is not so old to a widower," Madame countered. "Maurice de Chesnay is fortunate Touraine accepted his offer."

Lord Vallentine gave a snort of disgust at his wife's suggestion. "No offence, Roxton. I know de Chesnay is a close friend, but that girl can thank the alignment of the heavenly stars she isn't being forced into a match with the likes of him!"

"Why would you say that?" his wife demanded. "De Chesnay will make her a marquise and she will have a place at court."

"There's another reason not to marry him!"

"Touraine's youngest is marrying the Chevalier Montbelliard," stuck in the Duke, before his sister could formulate an argument against her husband's continued objection to the Marquis de Chesnay. "A match approved, not only by her father, but by her grandmother."

"Indeed? Now there is a surprise," said Estée. "*Tante Philippe* certainly kept her cards close to her chest. She gave no hint that she was considering marrying her granddaughter to the Chevalier."

"They fell in love, Madame," Antonia told her. "And so they will be infinitely happier than if either had been forced into an arranged marriage."

Vallentine raised his brandy glass. "I'll drink to that! Imagine a girl of twenty bein' married off to a bloated toad twice her age!"

"What are you implying, Lucian?" Estée demanded. "De Chesnay may be a barrel, and I concede he has the lips of a fat frog, but any girl of twenty left to rot in a convent would gladly accept him. The worried whisper in the family was if Elisabeth-Louise would ever find a husband—that there was something wrong with her. Never mind a fat frog, had an octogenarian duke offered for her, *Tante Philippe* would have accepted him without a blink!"

The Duke looked sideways at Antonia and threw back the last drops of his brandy. "Thank the heavenly stars I am neither bloated nor a fat frog," he added with a smirk, "nor an—er—octogenarian. Though I am most definitely a duke."

Vallentine never failed to react to the hook the Duke dangled before him.

"Hey!" His Lordship exclaimed, blushing. "We didn't mean— you can't think we were referrin' to-to *you*?"

"Why would Roxton think that?" Estée replied hotly. "De Chesnay and my brother may be close in age, but they are nothing alike. You might as well compare a toad with a Roman statue!"

Vallentine appealed to his neighbor. "Help me out here, Ellicott. You know what I meant, don't you?"

Martin Ellicott was saved from responding because he was in

the middle of swallowing a sip of coffee, and because the Duchess intervened.

She said with a twinkle, her dimple showing, "Do not coerce Martin to rescue you, Lucian. Besides," she added, addressing the Duke in Italian, "you do not need to thank the heavenly stars. But I thank you for sharing them with me."

Roxton smiled into her upturned face and lifted an eyebrow in enquiry. "Do you indeed?" he murmured, following her lead. "*Perché?*"

She smiled cheekily, whispering, "Every time."

Roxton stared at her. "*E' così?*"

Antonia giggled at his puzzlement and nodded, saying archly, "The third heaven is said to exist amongst the stars, *sì?*"

Knowing that the third heaven was another name for Paradise, he suddenly realised her mention of the heavenly stars was an oblique reference to their mutual enjoyment of making love. He chuckled, and pinching her chin, gently kissed her. This took everyone by surprise, not because they understood what the ducal couple was talking about but purely because the Duke rarely allowed himself to be unconstrained in company, even with family. Antonia, who was well-pleased with his response, returned to sipping her coffee.

"I will have to send to Paris for another of my gowns," Estée announced with a sigh, returning the conversation to matters she understood, and which were of interest to her. "What I brought with me is simply unsuitable for a Salvan wedding."

"There is no need—"

"But—Roxton! You do not understand. My court gown took up most of the space in my trunks. Anything else my women managed to pack is house wear, as I did not foresee the need or that we would be here for more than a few days."

"You packed correctly. There is no need."

"How can you say that, when now I learn my cousin is being

married at the end of the week, and I have nothing to wear to the ceremony!"

"You won't be attendin', lovedy," Vallentine stated quietly.

Estée was incredulous. "Do not be absurd, Lucian! Of course I must be at the wedding of our cousin. The marriage of *Tante Philippe*'s granddaughter—the daughter of the Duc du Touraine—to the Comte de Salvan's heir, is a celebration all the family must attend. And it is such an important union, I expect the Court to be in attendance, too. The pews will be squashed with our friends and relations!"

"The ceremony is to be a small one," stated the Duke, handing off his tumbler to a hovering footman. "In fact it will be so small and private that the couple will be off to start their new life before word gets out to the wider world."

"But—! Elizabeth-Louise cannot possibly be wed so shabbily. She has Salvan blood and is marrying Salvan's heir—"

"I'd have thought those reasons enough for our absence," the Duke stated, in a tone that said there was nothing further to discuss.

"If it makes you less disappointed, Madame, the guest list I can count off on the fingers of one hand," Antonia said soothingly.

Estée looked from her brother to her husband and then at her sister-in-law, still mystified. "How small? Who will be there?"

Antonia told her. "Elisabeth-Louise's sister Michelle Haudry as her attendant, Mme Haudry's father-in-law M'sieur Haudry is to give away the bride, and Martin. He will attend as Monseigneur's observer."

"Montbelliard has leaned on me to be his best man," Vallentine confessed to the Duke with a blush of embarrassment. "But if you'd rather I not—"

"You may do him that honor with my blessing, Lucian," the Duke replied. "A second pair of—er—eyes will not go astray." He glanced at Martin Ellicott. "And you can prop each other up. A papal wedding mass requires stamina."

"You give permission for my husband to attend, and for-for —*him* to go in your stead," Estée jerked her head in Martin Ellicott's direction. "But you refuse me—*your sister*—who is not only the girl's cousin by blood, but also a Papist! I should be the family's representative. I should—"

"No," the Duke stated. He took a breath and said with forbearance, "Allow me to spell it out before the wound to your pride deepens further. Unlike us, Vallentine and Ellicott do not have a drop of Salvan blood between them. I will not, and never will, acknowledge the Comte de Salvan, or that he has an heir, and neither will you. And if you wish company for your misery, then know that none of our aunts will be attending either."

"Only because you forbid them, too!" Estée threw at him sullenly and sniffed. "I feel for Elisabeth-Louise. To have such a paltry wedding!"

"I do not think she will mind in the least, Madame," Antonia assured her. "All she cares about is marrying the Chevalier. Not even the thought of him one day inheriting a title is of great importance to her at this moment."

Estée had a sudden thought and threw it at her brother. "They may be forced to have a quiet wedding at your instigation, but how do you propose to stop Society making a fuss once it becomes known the Duc du Touraine's daughter and the Comte de Salvan's heir are married? Everyone at Court will want to visit them with their good wishes."

"They are welcome to do so, should they exert themselves to travel to Arles, where the couple are to settle for the foreseeable future."

"*Arles*! But—"

"They will take up residence in a not-insubstantial estate," continued the Duke. "Their chateau overlooks the Rhône and was built at the beginning of this century for the archbishop of Arles. The acquisition of the property for the newly married couple will, I am told, ease the financial burden on the priest's family. So everyone is satisfied."

"Arles was once part of the Roman province of *Gallia Narbonensis*," Antonia told them. "M'sieur le Duc has promised to take me there one day, so that we can explore the remains of the Roman town together. Is that not so, Monseigneur?"

"Just so, *ma fée*."

Estée looked from her brother to her sister-in-law, baffled. "What will the newly married couple care for a pile of ruins when they are thousands of miles from their family!"

"Surely not—er—thousands," muttered the Duke.

"Madame, it is not respectful to call the remains of the greatest empire a pile of ruins, just as it is not respectful when Vallentine he calls M'sieur le Duc's Parisian home a heap of old bricks."

"I wondered when you'd find the opportunity to revisit that," Vallentine quipped without rancor.

"Not everyone has your inordinate interest in ancient wreckage, dearest," Estée stated primly. "In fact I do not know any other female who does. You are very singular. Which is not a bad thing, but it is something to remember when talking with others. They are not like you—"

"An unnecessary observation and one that does not bear repeating," the Duke stated flatly.

"—and so I doubt very much that Elisabeth-Louise or Montbelliard, like the vast majority of Society, care or know the first thing about the Roman Empire," Estée continued, hardly drawing breath.

"That is a great shame, Madame," Antonia said with a huge sigh, a glance first at the Duke and then at Martin, before adding with a cheeky smile, "To be surrounded by so much history, and not know it must be akin to sitting at a banquet and eating without tasting, yes?"

"Perhaps, Mme la Duchesse, the young couple will develop a—um—*taste* for history once they settle?" Martin Ellicott offered.

"Haha! Taste! Clever! I see what you did there!" Vallentine announced with a crooked, knowing smile, wagging a finger at Martin Ellicott. "And if they don't take to the history, I guess they can always cultivate a taste for the wine and lavender."

"Wine? Lavender? *Ruins*? What does *any* of that matter?" Estée threw up her hands in frustration. "*Écoutez-moi*! I tell you what will be in ruins—their marriage, if they are not able to live near their families. By my reckoning, Arles must be at least a hundred and thirty leagues or more from Paris. It might as well be in Sweden!"

"One hundred and forty to be precise," drawled the Duke. "Once again, your aptitude for mathematics never fails to impress me, though your geography leaves much to be desired. But do not distress yourself further. They will indeed be near family. Montbelliard's sister and her husband reside on the outskirts of Arles. Ah!" he added, mentally sighing with relief as he turned to the door at a familiar sound which never failed to lift the corners of his mouth. "Here is my heir, ready for bed, and with plenty to say to his mother."

FIVE

A NTONIA WAS UP off the chaise and had swept to the door as soon as the head nurserymaid entered the room with his little lordship in her arms, two attendants following behind. He was dressed for bed and wrapped in a soft woolen shawl, wide-eyed and alert. He looked anything but sleepy. Seeing his mother, his face split into a gummy grin and he squealed his delight. The joyous sound had everyone instantly uplifted and smiling. Antonia scooped him up, welcoming him with kisses and non-stop chatter, and resumed her seat on the chaise, Julian on her lap. She smiled up at the Duke, and asked excitedly,

"Now we have all the family gathered, shall we tell them our news?"

"*Mon Dieu!*" Estée blurted out, aghast. "You're pregnant again!"

"No, Madame. At least, I do not believe so. Why would you think that?" Antonia asked, puzzled.

There followed an awkward silence, until Estée replied in a small voice, "It was the first thing I thought of which would require all the family to be together. Forgive me." She waved her hand in embarrassed dismissal. "Take no notice of anything I say. I have *bébés* on the brain. Lucian will tell you so."

"It's true," His Lordship agreed. He gave his wife's hand an affectionate squeeze, leaning into her and saying reassuringly, "But nothin' for you to be worried about, lovely. All perfectly reasonable in your condition. And there's already a little one amongst us, ain't there. Ha!" He pointed his empty glass at the Duke. "Your finger must be mighty tasty, eh, Roxton!"

The baby had tipped forward in his mother's arms when the Duke gently stroked his rosy cheek, grabbed onto his father's finger, and promptly latched his mouth to his knuckle.

"Cecile says Julian he is already *toothing*," Antonia revealed proudly.

"I expect nothing less of my heir," Roxton replied, gently disengaging his knuckle. He dried his son's chin of drool with his lace-bordered handkerchief and looked across at his sister. "I had a vivid flash of memory just now, of you doing the same to me when you were on our mother's lap. I—er—poked you, and you grabbed my finger and wouldn't let go."

Antonia glanced up from searching amongst the folds of the baby shawl for her son's coral teething ring, attached by a small gold chain, and said with a chuckle, "I imagine you were not at all happy to have drool on you *then*."

"I was not," admitted the Duke, as he stood and shook out the skirts of his black silk frock coat. "I complained bitterly to our mother. Her response was to laugh… Excuse me while I fetch the documents…"

Antonia found the coral teether, and with a smile and wide eyes, she put it into her son's fist and up to his mouth, telling him what it was for.

"D'you think he understands what you're sayin'?" Vallentine asked seriously.

"Naturally all babies understand their mothers," Antonia replied loftily, adding with a twinkle, "And being so very clever,

Julian he understands what his Papa tells him in the English tongue also." She turned to Martin with a bright smile. "Please hold your godson so that I may help Monseigneur with our announcement."

"With great pleasure, Mme la Duchesse," Martin replied, settling a cushion on his lap to receive his godson.

With her son secure in Martin's arms, and the coral teething ring returned to his fist, Antonia went over to Vallentine, whereupon she kicked off her mules and put out her hand, "I wish you to help me stand upon the footstool."

His Lordship did not hesitate to comply. Yet, unconvinced she would remain steady on her feet, despite the footstool being less than six inches off the carpet, he remained by her side until the Duke returned from his desk, then resumed his seat and waited like the others, expectantly and without any idea what the announcement could be about. Not even the rolled-up parchment the Duke brought back with him, with its broken but unmistakable *le sceau du roi*, provided any clues.

But before addressing the family, the Duke turned to Antonia with an involuntary smile—despite gaining in height by standing in her stockinged feet on the footstool, she was still a good head shorter than he. "You wish our announcement to be made from an —er—elevation, *ma vie*?"

"It is only fitting, Monseigneur, that I honor *la mère de mon père* in this way. It is because of my grandmother that I am now elevated in every sense, yes?"

"She would approve—and of you."

Antonia plucked at one of the silver buttons of his silver-threaded embroidered waistcoat, and confessed with uncharacteristic solemnity, "Renard, I truly hope I will do justice to her memory tomorrow."

"Of that I have no doubt," the Duke assured her, bowing over her fingers. Still holding her hand, he turned to address the family, all of whom were trying to contain their curiosity, and their impatience. "As you are all no doubt aware, this morning I was visited by the King's genealogist. What you do not know, and what we can now reveal, is that M'sieur Hozier brought with him the news that this document—" He held up the parchment. "—confirms Mme la Duchesse's French nobility stretching back the requisite number of generations, so that she may be formally introduced to Their Majesties. I am certain you have been wondering how an English Duchess could be officially presented at the French Court without a diplomatic delegation from the Court of St. James's—"

"The thought never crossed our minds!" Vallentine interrupted. "Did it, Estée?" When his wife rolled her eyes, he quickly admitted, muttering, "Well, not to this mind…"

"That is because you never make the effort to learn what I have tried to explain to you a hundred times about court etiquette," Estée retorted with a huff of laughter. "Your eyes they always glaze, and then you yawn. But who can blame you?" she added with a shrug of resignation. "You were not born to it. Those of us who are, we all know almost from the cradle what is required of us."

Vallentine sat up and lifted his chin. "I'll have you know that I've learned more than I ever wanted to about it since comin' here. Ellicott and me were pressed into service to play our parts, all so Mme la Duchesse could practice her introductions."

"It is true, Madame," Antonia assured her. "They helped me greatly, taking turns at being Their Majesties. Both were superb as Louis—"

"What did I tell you!" Vallentine interrupted with a firm nod.

"—but I have yet to decide who was the better Queen of France."

"Mme la Duchesse, I yield to His Lordship's superior curtsy," Martin announced.

"Thank you, Ellicott," His Lordship replied, chin a little higher.

Estée dug an elbow in her husband's ribs and hissed, "Lucian! Are you deaf? He is saying you were the better Queen!"

"I know! I know!" Vallentine hissed back. Despite his blush, which belied his awareness, he added audibly, "I may have the superior curtsy, but Ellicott here has the finer wrist work. He knows how to work a fan!"

"Thank you, my lord."

"I am pleased you are both in agreement," muttered the Duke with restraint. "Or we may have required a demonstration of your —er—considerable skills to settle the matter."

Antonia giggled. "There would be no contest, M'sieur le Duc! Martin he would win—"

"Hey! That's unfair!" His Lordship complained hotly. "I'll take on Ellicott's superior wrist work with my expert knee bendin' any day!" When everyone chuckled, he grumbled, "I don't find anythin' amusin' in that…"

"I despair of your competitive nature, dearest husband," said his wife on an annoyed sigh. "Now do be silent to allow my brother to make his announcement with the dignity that is required of Antonia standing on a footstool."

"Monseigneur, Vallentine he will not to interrupt again—"

"Hey!" Instantly realizing his mistake in a further interruption, His Lordship quickly offered an apology before mimicking buttoning his lips together.

"I will do my best to give the occasion the gravitas it deserves," said the Duke. "But as our son has begun to fuss—possibly because he is as impatient as his father to make his mother known to her relatives by her French title—I will—er—hurry along." Still holding Antonia's hand he stepped a little away from her so that she had sufficient space to make her curtsy, which she did with his next words. "I have great pleasure in introducing to you the Comtesse de Roucy, who has this day received official recognition of her elevation by *Sa Majesté*, with M'sieur Hozier adding her name to *L'Armorial général de France*—"

"*Oh là là! Incroyable!* What wonderful news!" Estée exclaimed excitedly, clapping.

"Mme la Comtesse inherits her title in her own right through her paternal grandmother *Adélaïde-Mathilde*, Comtesse de Roucy," the Duke explained, as if he had not had further interruption. "And like her grandmother before her, has been officially acknowledged as a direct descendant of *Aelis de Roucy* wife of Renaud de Vermandois, Comte de Roucy, a lineage which stretches back before the Battle of Hastings—"

"1066?" Vallentine blurted out, and blew out his cheeks. "Egad! That's a mightily impressive pedigree!"

"I wish I could jump up and hug you, and curtsy to your elevation!" added Estée, blowing several kisses Antonia's way before asking her brother with bright eyes, "You intend for Antonia to be introduced at court not as Mme la Duchesse d'Roxton, but as Mme la Comtesse de Roucy?" When the Duke inclined his head with a knowing smile, she waggled a finger at him. "*Oh là là*! You are very clever, brother dear."

"But of course, Madame," Antonia agreed with pride. "And I wish to assure you all—though I know you know this—I will always be Mme la Duchesse d'Roxton first and foremost."

"Good! Glad to hear it," Vallentine announced. "As much as a French title ain't somethin' to be sneezed at, and it honors your grandmother, no one should ever forget that you're Roxton's duchess. And a duchess takes precedence over a countess any day of the week."

"I would agree with you, Lucian, were we on English soil. But here in France and most particularly at court, a comtesse *always* outranks an English duchess *every* day of the week," Estée stated with a click of her tongue. "Which is why my brother, he has gone to great lengths to ensure Antonia's ancient French lineage and her title were officially recognized *before* her appearance at court, so that when she is presented to the King and Queen, it will be in her own right. No one can dare to question her position. Is that not so, Roxton?" When her brother again inclined his head, she blew another kiss at the ducal couple. "Bravo, Roxton! Bravo, my love!"

"Thank you, Madame. It pleases us for me to be able to honor my grandmother and my family in this way."

"But did I hear you correctly, Roxton—that Antonia inherits the de Roucy title through her grandmother?" Estée asked with a frown. "If so, that truly is the surprise."

"It is certainly unusual," replied the Duke. "But inheritable titles through the maternal line are not—er—*uncommon*."

"How fitting Mme la Duchesse should inherit her grandmother's title in this way," added Martin Ellicott, venturing to contribute to the conversation, and inclining his head to Antonia with a soft smile. "For she, too, is uncommon."

"What is *common* are unnecessary interruptions!" Estée snapped, fan fluttering in agitation.

"*Merci*, Martin. Monseigneur he says so, too," Antonia responded with a kind smile, ignoring her sister-in-law's terse aside. Adding with breathless excitement, addressing the room, "But that is not the most surprising thing of all about being a French comtesse. Your jaws they are certain to fall open!"

SIX

THE VALLENTINES unconsciously leaned forward in anticipation of Antonia's announcement, and she did not disappoint from atop her footstool pedestal.

"The title of Comtesse de Roucy has attached to it a court-appointed position. It is true. M'sieur Hozier, he confirmed it to Monseigneur."

"*Mon Dieu! C'est incroyable*!" Estée blurted out. And while she instantly comprehended the full extent of this revelation, she did not quite believe it so again sought confirmation from her brother. "Roxton? The Comtesse de Roucy has an official place at court?"

"That was what I was about to tell you, yes."

"Ah! I am sorry, M'sieur le Duc," Antonia apologized with a sigh of disappointment, realizing what she had unwittingly done. She kissed the back of his hand. "You were to make the announcement and instead I have and spoiled our oh-so-big surprise."

"Not at all, *ma vie*. But perhaps you would like me to explain the full extent of your inheritance to the family as confirmed by M'sieur Hozier?"

"*Merci*, M'sieur le Duc," Antonia said and confided in the

others, "M'sieur Hozier he insisted on meeting with Monseigneur without me because he does not believe females capable of comprehension beyond the trivialities. *Y croyez-vous!*"

"He obviously ain't met you," Vallentine said in all seriousness. "One look over your shoulder at the text you've got your nose stuck in would convince him otherwise."

"That is what I think too," Antonia replied with the same solemnity. "M'sieur le Duc was prepared to insist on my presence, but I told him there was no need as I had an important appointment to keep in the nursery, and did not want to disappoint—"

"Important? La! *Voilà qui est absurde!*" Estée interrupted with a snort of derision, adding, tongue-in-cheek, "M'sieur Hozier would agree that racing sedan chairs for the amusement of servants is *far* more important than an audience with *Sa Majesté's* genealogist!"

"Yes, Madame, it is," Antonia stated, affronted. "They were not only for amusement, as I told you. Julian he was afraid of riding in my sedan chair. And now, after the races, with the encouragement of his maman and yes, our servants, he is afraid no more. The problem it is solved, and now he will ride with me in my birthday sedan chair without complaint. *Voilà.*"

"Egad! I wish I'd been there to join in the merriment!" Vallentine said with relish, oblivious to the tension that now surrounded him. He looked at Martin Ellicott. "I'll wager you were in on this sedan chair caper!"

"I was, my lord. I—"

"But of course!" Estée huffed. "*He* encourages *her* waywardness at every turn! You *all* do!"

"Hey! Now you can't—" His Lordship began and, to his great relief, was cut off.

"I may now be a French comtesse as well as an English duchess," Antonia announced with dignity, ignoring her sister-in-law's derision, "but there is one to whom I will only ever be *la mère*, and that pleases me most of all. Excuse me."

Hands to her waist, the Duke lifted her up and off the footstool and down to firm ground so she could attend to their infant.

The baby was grizzling and squirming on the cushion on his godfather's lap, so much so that the head nursery maid had come out of the shadows and was hovering behind Martin Ellicott's chair. Scooping up her son with a bright smile, Antonia turned him to face the family and wished everyone a goodnight on his behalf. She then disappeared into the shadows to hand him off to his nurses for the night.

Roxton remained by the footstool, pensively staring after her, his son's complaining having transformed into lusty cries in the shadows in what seemed the blink of an eye.

"M'sieur le Duc, his little lordship must feel keenly the separation from his mother when he is in pain from toothing," Martin reassured him. "And no doubt that adds to Mme la Duchesse's difficulty in getting him to settle—"

"Difficulty? If it is not one difficulty, it will be another," Estée commented flippantly. "No small wonder he screams as he does, when she chose to suckle him, so that he now demands none but her breast, which has led to an unwanted and unnatural attachment—"

"And you would know this *how*?" was the Duke's caustic response, turning on a heel to face his sister. "When you have birthed you may expound on the care and nourishment of infants, not before. Martin! My son is without his shawl. Be so good as to return it to his mother…"

Teeth set, he waited for Martin to scoop up the shawl and vanish into the darkness, before resuming his seat on the chaise longue. Alone with his sister and brother-in-law, and confident he would not be overheard, he made Estée uncomfortably aware of his thoughts.

"You accused Antonia of waywardness—she is nothing of the sort. She is steadfast. Learn the difference. As for your snide asides flung at Martin—it is beneath your breeding to deride one who only ever offers Mme la Duchesse encouragement, and does so with kindness and intelligence." He dropped his gaze to his knee, to brush away an imaginary piece of lint; all to give his sister a moment to compose herself, for her bottom lip had begun to quiver. Raising his dark eyes to hers again, he said less harshly, but no less forcefully, "My son's needs and wants will always take precedence—regardless of who is demanding of our time and attention, M'sieur Hozier, and *Sa Majesté*, notwithstanding. Oh! And the next occasion—though I have every confidence there won't be one—you needlessly upbraid Mme la Duchesse, or throw a pettish remark at Martin, I will not hesitate to publicly put you in your place. And not only will I do so in front of your husband, as I am doing now, but I will also ensure that the occasion warrants an audience of our relatives and servants as happen to be within earshot. I gave you fair warning in Paris, Estée. This is your last. No! Do not apologize to me. But I do expect you to apologize to Antonia, and to Martin." He smiled crookedly. "Not tonight. By the end of the week—Ah! I do not hear him, *mignonne*," he said in an altogether different tone, as Antonia reappeared from the shadows. "Did he finally settle?"

She sighed heavily and spread out her quilted petticoats to resume her place beside him on the chaise. When he put out his hand, she placed hers within his warm clasp, and felt better for his touch.

"Renard, it is very difficult. He never likes to be separated from me at night. He thinks he is coming to our room, and when he realizes he is not, he becomes very disagreeable. My heart it breaks when his little chin it quivers, and I must turn away before my eyes, too, they fill with tears." She sighed again. "But I know it must be done, and so I do it. But I tell you, it does not get any easier!"

"That is understandable," the Duke responded, giving her fingers a gentle squeeze. "Why would he want to leave you? But if you wish a peaceful night's rest then we must persist with our regimen. If you do not…"

"You are right of course, and we will." She rallied, adding cheerfully, bringing the others into their conversation, "Besides, I know that not a minute after he leaves me, he is a happy *bébé* once again, and it is me, his poor maman, who is the one fretting. And so it is not as bad as I imagine."

Curious, Estée asked meekly, "How do you know this, *ma chérie?*"

"I send Gabrielle to the nursery after he leaves me," Antonia confessed. Her eyes went wide, and she leaned forward, confiding, "And do you know what Gabrielle she tells me? Julian's crying it stops *immédiatement* the moment I am out of his sight! With the maids he is again content. *Incroyable.*"

"What a little charmer! I predict he will break many a girl's heart when he is older."

"But of course, Madame," Antonia stated matter-of-factly. "He is M'sieur le Duc's son."

Vallentine coughed into his fist. "As much as I would like nothin' better than to expound upon my nephew's abilities to charm the ladies—even at his tender age—the hour is late, and this charmer has a question about tomorrow's presentation—"

Antonia giggled and Estée snorted behind her fan.

"We do love you, Lucian," declared his wife, her husband's naïve presumption making her feel so much more herself after her brother's scolding that she could barely contain her laughter. "Charmer? Please do not make such ludicrous assertions! Besides, there is an unwritten rule amongst relatives that there can be only one charmer per family, and that title has been claimed by my nephew—for life."

"Mme la Comtesse and Mme la Duchesse both wholeheartedly agree with you, Madame," Antonia said with a significant cheeky look at His Lordship that had everyone else chuckling.

"Oi! Now don't you make a habit of throwin' *both* your titles at me, or you'll breach all m' defenses!"

"Your question, Lucian?" enquired the Duke, with a thin smile and a raise of an eyebrow, grateful his best friend had deliberately set about to lighten the mood with his hollow boast.

"Ah! Yes! M' question… None of us would've predicted a twelvemonth ago, when you rescued Mme la Duchesse from the palace, we'd be back there tomorrow watchin' her make her curtsy to Louis as the Comtesse de Roucy," said His Lordship with a shake of his head. "But what has me stumped—and if I'm honest, makes m' head pound to think about it—is that you've always said Versailles is a nest of vipers. You never permitted Estée to go near the place. Yet—and I take nothin' away from your new title, chit —" he said as an aside to Antonia, before again addressing the Duke. "—tomorrow we're off to watch Antonia enter that very viper pit, and well—Damme! You tell me!"

"Tell you what, Lucian?" Roxton drawled, teasing his best friend. "That was not a question, but a speech with a demand attached." When Vallentine threw up his hands in frustration and fell back against the cushions he relented. "I have no wish for your brain to be—er—pounding any more than it already does. But as Martin has joined us again just as the fresh coffee pot has arrived, I intend to do the honors, and so you may ask your question of one who is just as capable as I of giving you the answer you seek. In fact, you will possibly receive a more satisfactory response." He looked to Antonia. "With Mme la Duchesse's permission."

Despite the cryptic nature of his reply, the Duke did not need to explain himself to her. Antonia understood at once. They both looked across to the coffee trolley where Martin was politely waiting for a pause in the conversation to resume his seat. He stared back at the ducal couple and hard swallowed. He, too, understood. Lord and Lady Vallentine remained befuddled. They were soon enlightened.

SEVEN

"My lord, may I first provide you with an explanation as to the need for tomorrow's ceremony," Martin Ellicott said, in the quiet aftermath that follows the pouring, stirring, and savoring of freshly brewed coffee. "Which I hope will negate the necessity for you to ask your question."

"Sounds fair," replied Vallentine, chomping on a whole macaron. "Questions give me an infernal headache. I like answers much better."

With everyone's coffee needs accommodated, and the plate of macarons and small delicate pastries passed around a second time, there were no further excuses for Martin to delay. He took another sip to clear his throat then set his dish aside. Elbows to the padded arms of the wingchair, fingers interlaced, and with back straight, he appeared as composed as always.

In truth his stomach felt full of fluttering moths, such was his anxiety. He, who was always in the background, always out of sight, was being pushed front and center. But he knew why the Duke had singled him out in this way. It was in an effort to cement his place within the family fold, and most importantly, so he would gain Estée Vallentine's grudging acceptance. And while grateful for the opportunity and not wishing to disappoint the ducal couple, he was philosophical about his chances of being accepted by the Duke's sister, even grudgingly. But if the prophet Jeremiah believed a leopard capable of changing its spots, perhaps there was hope for her yet…

He chanced to glance across at the Duchess then, and found her smiling at him over the gold rim of her dish. Instead of increasing his nervousness, he was surprised to discover that with her silent encouragement, the moths stopped fluttering. Not in a thousand lifetimes would he ever disappoint her. He took a deep silent breath and prayed he could live up to expectations.

"Pardon me for stating the obvious, but everyone knows one must be formally presented at court to be invited to *Sa Majesté's* little intimate suppers," Martin stated after quietly clearing his throat into his fist. "Yet supping with the King is not M'sieur le Duc's primary motivation. Having Mme le Duchesse presented in front of the entire world by her French title will be the final chapter and close the book on the Comte de Salvan and those of his closest relatives who conspired to force Mme la Duchesse into an unwanted union with him—"

"There is no need to be reticent," the Duke interjected quietly. "The relatives Martin is referring to are our ancient aunts," he told the Vallentines. "Specifically *Tante Philippe*. Pray continue. I will not interrupt again."

Martin inclined his head. "The long-held belief is that by marrying Mme la Duchesse, the Comte would gain access to the considerable dowry left to her by her grandfather. This would then alleviate the Salvan family's most pressing pecuniary troubles. There is no doubt that this was one of their objectives, but what they were in fact eyeing was a much more dazzling prize. There is something the Salvans crave more than money, something they lost when they were stripped of their court positions in punishment for M'sieur le Duc's mother eloping with Lord Alston—and that is the prestige that comes with power. The only way to gain that is to occupy an official position at court—"

"He knew!" Vallentine blurted out, looking from Martin to the Duke, and then at Antonia. It was not a question, but a statement. Furious, he stabbed a finger in the air in Martin's direction to make his point. "That damned worm Salvan! He knew Mme la Duchesse was set to inherit not only her grandfather's coin but her grandmother's title, and he knew that it came with a position at court! Of all the nerve!"

"Yes, my lord. That does seem to be the case," Martin replied evenly. "M'sieur le Duc postulates that the Chevalier Moran confided about his mother's title to the Earl of Strathsay, who in turn told the Comte de Salvan. That revelation decided the Comte to substitute himself for his son in the marriage bargain struck with Mme la Duchess's grandfather—"

"The Chevalier Moran being Mme la Duchesse's father," Estée stated unnecessarily.

"I'll wager Salvan weaseled that interestin' tidbit out of the old man on his death bed," stuck in His Lordship on a growl. "Damned—damned—*weasel*."

"You should have run him through when you had the chance, Roxton," Estée threw at the Duke, dabbing at her moist eyes and sniffing. "When I think back to that horrid time, it makes me ill. I do not know why we must relive—"

"Please do not upset yourself, Madame," Antonia interrupted. "We will never have to talk about that time ever again after tonight. But we—M'sieur le Duc and I—we think it important our family is aware of the reasoning behind why I am being presented to *Sa Majesté*."

"Antonia's in the right, lovedy. No need to upset yourself," Vallentine added soothingly. "Let Ellicott get on with the tellin', and then we can get you to bed, eh?"

Martin hesitated, disconcerted by this interruption, and wondered if it was a deliberate bid by the Duke's sister to make him lose his train of thought. Not once had she looked his way while he was speaking, but down at her fluttering fan or out across the room giving him a view of her lovely profile. But he did not have time to concern himself with her prejudices, he needed to get on with the telling; M'sieur le Duc was relying on him. Yet, just as he managed to regather his thoughts, the miraculous happened—or so it was to him, because it was a novel experience.

Madame turned her head to openly meet his gaze, and without her usual theatricality or hint of ridicule. "We interrupted you, M'sieur—El—*Ellicott*," she said punctiliously. "In fact, I do believe I have done so several times this evening; for which I—I —*apologize*. Pray continue. Your précis of my cousin's vile machinations is most—is most—*illuminating*."

If there was not an audible sigh of relief at this apology, there was most certainly a mental one, and the tension eased in everyone's shoulders.

"Thank you, Madame," Martin replied respectfully, biting back the smile that wished to break out over his face. He coughed again into his fist and continued as if he had never been interrupted. "The court-appointed position which comes with the title of Comtesse de Roucy is in the Queen's household. And had the Comte married Mlle Moran, as she was then, the Salvans would have achieved their object and been returned to the royal inner circle. This would have allowed them to further their ambitions and strengthen their influence by whispering in the ear of the Queen and her advisors, to find places for their offspring within the court administration, and line their pockets with bribes—"

"Pardon another interruption," said Madame, "but what you describe is nothing out of the ordinary. That is what all good courtiers do in such positions—find posts for their family and friends, and it is not considered a bribe, but acceptable payment, when one exerts oneself on behalf of others."

"That is true, Madame," Martin agreed. "But what is also true is that a husband not only has jurisdiction over his wife's dowry, but her entire life, including her court position. M'sieur le Duc has intelligence suggesting that once the Comte de Salvan married, he intended to exile his wife to Limoges. Mme la Marquise du Touraine-Brissac would then take on the duties of the post belonging to the Comtesse de Roucy—"

"Outrageous!" Vallentine declared. "I take back what I said. Salvan ain't a weasel—he's a worm!"

"Just so, Lucian," said the Duke, and with a nod to Martin, let it be known he would now take up the rest of the telling. When Martin briefly closed his eyes and slumped against the upholstered wingchair with relief, he smiled to himself before saying to the Vallentines, Antonia's hand firmly in his grasp on his crossed knee. "Suffice that tomorrow's presentation will serve to drive the final nail into the Salvan ambition. With the Comtesse de Roucy receiving the royal approval in front of the entire court, all Society will know to whom she owes her loyalty—"

"You!" Vallentine declared with a firm nod.

"Yes—er—to me. It is important that the court, but most particularly our Salvan relatives, are made aware that they cannot outwit me, nor force my hand, or conspire against me, or there will be consequences. And it will also serve as a reminder to those who think they can manipulate my wife, that they cannot. They—" He stopped, blinked, and looked at Antonia as if a thought had just occurred to him. He was self-effacing. "And here am I putting words in your mouth, *ma belle*. Excuse me. It is for you to say."

Antonia shrugged. "But I do not mind in the least that *you* do so. Your words are my words, Monseigneur. I know this because you always talk to me about matters first before we speak to others." She smiled shrewdly and leaned into him. "And do not worry. If I did not agree with you, I would tell you so *immédi-atement*."

Roxton chuckled and leaned into her. "That," he said on a murmur, gaze raking over her beautiful face, "is very true."

"I'm loath to interrupt once again," declared Vallentine with a deliberate cough into his fist to break the ducal couple from their preoccupation with each other. "But I've got a dozen more questions about Mme la Comtesse's new court position. Does it have an official title? How close is it to the Queen? Will she be expected to wait on her like a lackey—"

"Lackey?" Estée immediately riled. "Those who wait upon *Leurs Majestés* are not lackeys, Lucian. They are nobles who are honored to—"

"Honor? Ha! Bein' subservient ain't an honor! It's—" Vallentine began and was cut off.

"That is enough for tonight," the Duke ordered. "Estée needs rest. We all do. Tomorrow is a momentous day. Lucian, you may have the answers to your questions upon our return from court. No doubt by then, you'll have compiled a list."

"Capital idea!" His Lordship declared, unfolding his long legs, and easing himself off the chaise longue as everyone made motions to rise. Martin Ellicott's next words had him staggering back, and he had to put out a hand to stop himself falling. "Eh? What? What d'you mean?" he demanded loudly, as if he were deaf. "Say that again!"

"I beg your pardon, my lord. I said that I look forward to your unique perspective on the day's events upon your return home."

"But you'll be gettin' your own unique—*whatsit*, because you'll be there," Vallentine replied. He looked to the ducal couple, baffled, and thumbed a fist in Martin's direction. "He's comin' with us tomorrow, ain't he?"

Antonia put her fingertips to Martin's sleeve and looked up at him. "*Je ne comprends pas?* You must be there tomorrow. I cannot do this without you, too."

Martin was suddenly dry in the throat. "Mme la Duchesse, I thought—I thought perhaps it would be for the best if I remain here." He smiled. "I can spend time with his little lordship and—"

"Have you had one too many guzzles tonight, Ellicott, 'cause you're not makin' sense,' Vallentine demanded. He squinted at

Martin. "You and I—we didn't spend all those hours play-actin' at being King and Queen of France for you to not be part of this theatrical spectacle we're all bein' dragged along to—No offence," he apologized to the Duke. "But spendin' the day kickin' m' heels about the gilded halls of Versailles has as much appeal as havin' a tooth drawn—"

"Lucian!" His wife was affronted. "You are Antonia's brother-in-law and my husband. So you must attend." She shrugged a shoulder and tried to appear disinterested. "But I do not see why Ellicott he is required to be there. If he chooses to remain behind that is his affair. Besides," she added airily, "all of our ladies and some of the household attendants are required to assist Antonia and me with our court gowns, that I do not know where they are all to fit in the carriages—"

"Blast it! One more pair of buttocks crammed on a bench hardly matters!" interrupted His Lordship hotly. "Tell him, Roxton! Tell Ellicott he must be there too!"

"I am flattered by your support, my lord," Martin replied, a flush to his cheeks. "But Madame is in the right. I should give up my seat to accommodate—"

"Nope! You're not gettin' out of it that easily." His Lordship was stubborn. "If you ain't bein' dragged along, then neither am I! It's that simple."

"You are being ridiculous!" Estée complained.

"No, Madame. Lucian is being a loyal friend. And Martin, he is being foolishly noble." Antonia was emphatic. "I do not care in the least if we fill a hundred carriages with our retinue. But those who are important to me, whom I care most about, whom I want at my presentation, they are here in this room. And all of you must be there with me."

"Mme la Duchesse speaks for both of us. And so there is your answer, Martin," stated the Duke. "One of the many—er—joys of being part of my family is fronting up at functions I deem important for all members to be present, whether you wish to be there or not. However, I have some sympathy for your reticence. No doubt it stems from stepping out from the shadows of personal servitude and into the light of family service."

He let his gaze wander and hold on his sister for a moment, before meeting Martin's gaze openly, and with the hint of a smile.

"Strive to suppress your natural reticence in the future; it will only upset Vallentine. And there is no need for concern about family arrangements and carriages. Our Salvan relatives will greet us *en force* at the palace." He smiled crookedly. "It will be a—er—spectacle to be sure." He put out his hand to his wife, and said to his family, "*Fais de beaux rêves, ma famille.*"

EIGHT

T HE DUKE'S light-hearted remark about making a list may
have been a throwaway comment on his part, but this was
precisely what the Vallentines did when in the privacy of their own
rooms. Estée, in frilly nightcap, and black curls in one long plait,
was propped in bed with a mountain of pillows at her back to make
her comfortable. While Vallentine, a colorful silk banyan thrown
negligently over his nightshirt and a matching tasseled cap at a
jaunty angle crammed on his close-cropped fair hair, sat hunched at
the spindle-legged escritoire by the curtained window, knees about
his ears, and with quill and ink and a sheet of crisp paper found in
one of the drawers.

List completed, His Lordship scrambled up into bed and read it
aloud to his wife, in the hopes it would help her fall asleep. It did
not. It was not only the excitement of attending court the following
day, but her baby—moving about and making her uncomfortable
—which were keeping her awake. To distract her further, Vallentine
suggested she tell him all about her plans for the redecoration of
the rooms in their apartment at the Hôtel Roxton.

It was the last thing he wished to hear about, but if it lulled his darling wife to slumber, then he was happy to oblige. To his great surprise it reinvigorated her. He was the one who nodded off. His head was rolling back on the pillows, and he was snoring when jolted awake by a poke in the ribs.

"Persian Earth! It's purple!" he bellowed. Half-asleep, he gave a series of snorts before sitting bolt upright, nightcap falling over one eye. He bellowed some more. "Ghastly! She hates it!"

Estée squealed, half in fright but mostly with delight, then fell into a fit of the giggles.

One of her ladies pulled aside the tapestry *portière* in alarm and popped her head into the room, thinking something the matter.

The couple was sitting up in bed, her mistress giggling into a hand pressed to her mouth, while her husband, dazed and blinking from the one eye that was visible, looked the startled pheasant. The maid's eyes widened, and she quickly disappeared again before they saw her, the tapestry *portière* dropping back into place.

"What—why would you think I-I don't l-l-like P-P-Persian Earth?" Estée stammered between gasps and giggles. "I l-like the c-color p-p-*purple*."

"Eh? What are you talkin' about? Why are you laughin'? Persian *what*? What time is it? Where's m'mornin' chocolate?"

"It will be here when it is morning—"

"Ain't it mornin' now?"

"You've been asleep for five minutes, not five hours, foolish man!"

"Asleep? I wasn't asleep! I only nodded off for a second—"

Estée's eyes narrowed to slits. "If you were not asleep, then why did you think it morning, *hein*?" When Vallentine waved a hand in dismissal, as if her logic were inconsequential, she stuck out her bottom lip, adding sulkily, "A man who is awake does not snore!"

"Snore? I don't snore! And I wasn't asleep," he stated, sliding his silk cap back off his eye and setting it to rights. "You were tellin' me what fascinatin' colors you'd chosen for your boudoir—"

"Put yourself out of your misery, Lucian," she said, with an exaggerated sigh. "Admit you fell asleep! But it is of no matter," she added in an about-face. "What does matter is—have you chosen the colors for *your* rooms?"

"I have!" Vallentine replied proudly. "Let me show you." He scrambled off the bed and had taken a few steps across the room in his stockinged feet when he had a revelation. "Damme! I've left m' selections on Roxton's desk."

"Then let us fetch them."

"I'll send a lackey—"

"No. Do not wake them."

"What?" His Lordship was in shock. He had never known his wife to show undue consideration for servants. "Are you well, *ma chérie*?"

"As well as to be expected with this baby of yours performing somersaults!" She waved him over to her side of the bed. "Help me to the carpet."

"Let the night footmen fetch those samples. That's what they're there for—to be awake when we need 'em. And we need 'em now." But his actions were in direct contrast to his advice, for while he was offering it, he was gently lifting her down off the bed to her stockinged feet. He kept an arm across her back. "You can't be traipsing about darkened corridors in your condition. Sit here and I'll fetch—"

"No. I need to walk so the baby it will go back to sleep, and then I can sleep too." She looked up with a smile from slipping on her mules. "We will go down to the library together."

"Very well. But you wait in the corridor while I pop in and fetch 'em. That way you don't see my choices until we're back here and snug in bed. No argument!"

"None from me! The anticipation makes it even more exciting."

Vallentine smiled down at her in surprise. "It does, doesn't it? Never thought I'd say this about bits of fabric, but I'm just as eager to show you!"

THE COUPLE ARRIVED at the library double doors to discover two attendant footmen huddled close together, an ear turned to the sliver of a gap created where one of the doors had been clicked open and left slightly ajar. They were listening intently for sounds within, while communicating their shared enjoyment of what they heard with exaggerated eye rolling.

Vallentine shoved a candlestick at them. "Hey! What's goin' on here?"

Neither servant moved a muscle despite now being bathed in light.

"Shhhhh!" one of the footmen demanded, while the other flapped a hand in His Lordship's direction, at the unwelcome intrusion.

Lord and Lady Vallentine blinked at each other, stunned to receive such a response. But before Estée could take matters in hand and express her displeasure, there was a rumble of unintelligible repartee from inside the room followed by laughing, squealing, and a series of thuds, as if furniture was being knocked about in a pursuit about the room.

Intrigued, His Lordship moved closer to hear better.

Affronted, Her Ladyship fell back, incensed.

The two footmen continued to strain an ear, so caught up in the moment they were oblivious that their transgression had been discovered, and not only by the noble couple.

The night porter appeared out of the darkness and sidled between the couple and the footmen. With one hissed sentence over his shoulder, and the blink of an eye, the eavesdropping footmen found themselves relegated, replaced by two of their fellows—footmen who immediately stood to attention, backs up against the double doors and eyes straight. The porter also managed to secure the doors without so much as the sound of the latch clicking into place. And while this deadened the sounds within the library, it did not erase from memory the laughing and squealing and running about, or the fact two footmen had been caught out spying on whoever it was and whatever was going on in the library. Which is why Estée stepped up to the porter and demanded an explanation.

"I hear nothing, Madame," was the porter's even reply.

"Oi!" Vallentine hissed hotly, poking a finger in the servant's direction. "You may not have heard anythin' but Her Ladyship and I, we ain't deaf, and neither were those two eavesdroppin' whifflers you just dismissed!"

Estée's eyes had narrowed to slits and she stared steadily at the porter.

He dared to stare past her without blinking.

She turned to her husband and said in a fierce whisper, "This is what happens when servants are given a long leash! They become arrogant, and discipline, it is tossed out with the bathwater! I warned this would happen, and it has! She is too young to control my brother's household—"

"No she ain't. She'll do it her way, with Roxton's help, and this lot will toe the line or else. You'll see, lovedy."

Estée huffed her incredulity. "We are seeing just how obedient they are, are we not, with them listening at door cracks and pretending to be deaf—" She waved a hand of dismissal at the porter."—just as this fellow's counterpart was deaf when I arrived at the villa to the thuds of sedan chairs being raced up and down the nursery! And now they are playing at being deaf *and* mute to what is going on in there!"

Vallentine regarded the two footmen and the porter, who remained to attention in front of the library doors staring off into the black void of the passageway. He drew but one conclusion.

"You're not goin' to let us in there, are you?" he stated, squinting hard at the porter.

"M'sieur, the hour is late—" the porter began.

"Ha!" hissed Madame. "Late enough that you all thought we were abed and would not catch you running riot!"

The porter showed the first signs of affront, taking a deep breath through his wide nostrils. "Madame, I assure you, M'sieur le Duc's household does not run riot at any time, day or night."

"Then you can tell us what is going on in there!" Estée demanded.

"Estée, I think you'll find the reason we are being barred from enterin'—" His Lordship began, and he too, was cut off.

"You do not have to tell me," Estée continued, hardly drawing breath. "The reason it is obvious! They are shielding their fellows, who are up to no good with one of the kitchen wenches!"

Vallentine was aghast. "Steady on! You can't toss such accusations at your brother's servants—"

Estée turned on her husband and looked up at him archly. "You think me foolishly naïve to the ways of the world that I do not understand what is meant by all that laughter and squealing and running about! *No*, I say! I know precisely what is going on in there!"

Vallentine drew his wife a little away from the door and lowered his voice.

"The reason the porter is barring the door ain't because some of his fellows are actin' up in there, lovedy. It's your brother—"

"What? My *brother*?" Estée blinked up at her husband. "How do you know this?"

Vallentine was coy. His face burned. He shrugged a shoulder. "Ain't it obvious? He's—he's bein' playful—"

"*Playful?*" Estée snorted her skepticism. "Do not be absurd, Lucian! Roxton has never been playful a day in his life."

Vallentine controlled the urge to roll his eyes, but he did raise an eyebrow.

"He's not alone, is he?"

Estée continued to stare up at him, confused. Then it dawned on her. She drew in a sharp breath, squeezing her husband's silken forearm. "My brother, he is the one pleasuring a-a kitchen wench. My poor sweet Antonia—"

"For God's sake, Estée! Don't be witless!" Vallentine growled, face hotter than ever, all reticence for his wife's sensibilities abandoned. "Of course he ain't! Damme! He's bein' playful with his *wife*!"

"Oh? Oh! Oh! I *am* witless! Of course! Forgive me. How could I have such wretched thoughts—"

"No doubt your priest will forgive you, even if Roxton don't," her husband muttered. "Now let's go back to bed." He offered her the crook of his arm. "Tomorrow is goin' to be the longest and most tedious day of m' life!"

"Why could they not be playful in their rooms," she grumbled mournfully. "It is most inconvenient!"

"'Cause now you have to wait until mornin' to see my color choices?"

"Yes. Lucian—" she confided, a glance over a silken shoulder at the library doors as she was being led back to the staircase. "I think we should keep to ourselves that my brother he makes love to his wife in the library—"

"You won't get any argument from me!"

"—because it would not serve his reputation."

"Eh? How so?"

"Think! The great noble satyr making love to *his wife* and not some pretty whore? *Pfah*! Society, it would be scandalized."

Vallentine gave a start, hardly believing his own ears at his wife's skewed sensibilities, then broke into such raucous laughter it reverberated up the staircase and woke half the villa.

NINE

T HE LIBRARY shelves were in deep shadow. Candles flickered in sconces on either side of the portrait above the mantel where a new log placed upon the hearth cast a golden glow on the couple in silhouette before the fireplace.

She knelt on the chaise facing him. He knelt on the carpet before her. She was kissing him—light, barely-there brushes across his face from forehead to bare throat. Teasingly she avoided his mouth.

It was a game they played often.

She kept herself steady with arms stretched out behind her and hands clasped as a counterweight. He kept his arms by his sides, body as still as cold marble. It was the clenching and unclenching of his fingers that gave him away. He was using every drop of willpower to stop himself from touching her. But he was struggling. She meant for him to struggle, and continued on with her delicious torture.

Then she stopped and sat back on her haunches. Slowly she removed the last of her hairpins. The few remaining braids coiled about her head bounced to her shoulders and unraveled down her back. Still kneeling, she bunched up her white cotton nightgown, pulled it up over her head and dropped it to the floor, leaving her naked but for her white silk stockings, tied at the knee with fat silk ribbons.

Not once did he allow his eyes to stray from her face. Not even when she combed her hair with splayed fingers, raking the long golden curls down over her breasts to her thighs. Resolute, his gaze remained fixed on her slightly almond-shaped eyes, chin straight and mouth set.

And so the game continued, but with every passing second his self-control slid closer to the abyss.

Who would win?

Upping her game, and with a deceptively sweet smile, she took his fingers and placed a hand either side of her hips. He did not flinch. His fingers settled there on her warm flesh without a blink. And all the while she kept her eyes locked to his. And still his gaze did not stray. But when he swallowed, and she caught the movement of his Adam's apple, she knew he was fast losing his resolve.

She kissed him again, this time on the mouth, but ever so lightly that he wondered if she had kissed him at all. Yet, this did not break him either. What finally did was breathing in the delicious flowery scent of her soft warm skin as she leaned into him. He could take no more. He was undone. He capitulated—utterly.

Pulling her hard up against his naked torso, he pressed his mouth to hers. Triumphant at his ardent surrender, she threw her arms about his neck and eagerly returned his fervent kiss. His guttural chuckle and her giggles fell away as they sank as one amongst the cushions before the fire, neither aware of the shout of laughter which pierced the still night beyond the double doors.

THE COUPLE WAS WOKEN at dawn, the velvet curtains drawn back and tied on the view of the royal parkland, blanketed in heavy mist.

And while Antonia splashed water on her face from the porcelain bowl at the washstand, Roxton took the silver breakfast tray from a footman and padded back to their bed.

He placed the tray holding a plate of warm croissants, silver chocolatier, whisk, and porcelain mugs on the crumpled coverlet, and set about preparing their hot chocolates. When Antonia joined him, climbing back up into bed, she noticed that on the tray was also a long flat parcel, wrapped in black velvet and tied up with a wide silk ribbon. This the Duke handed to her.

"A little something to remember the day of your presentation to *Leurs Majestés.*"

"You give me too many gifts, but I thank you, *mon homme adoré.*" She turned the parcel over. "I cannot guess what this could be!"

The Duke tapped the whisk and set it aside, closed the lid of the chocolatier, and slowly poured forth the frothy beverage into the two mugs.

"Good. Then it truly will be a surprise."

Without further ado, she untied the ribbon and unwrapped the gift. What lay before her was a black velvet pouch. From inside she extracted a slim, three-sided baton of highly polished oak. All three sides were inlaid with tiny ivory figurines—cupids with bows and couples embracing—and there were hearts and flowers tangled in scrolls of acanthus leaves. Carved at its point were two small hearts intertwined; one contained the initial A, the other an R.

From its shape Antonia knew instantly what it was—a busk, that most intimate article of a female's undergarments which when slipped into the front center pocket of a pair of stays kept the garment's correct shape, and her bosom in place. She also knew from common report that a busk given by a lover to his sweetheart was considered the most personal and sensual of souvenirs, for it symbolically positioned him between her breasts.

"Lest you wonder, I have never gifted one of these to another—"

"Ah, Renard, you need not have offered such a reassurance. But it does make it that much more special to me. It is very beautiful and perfect, because when I wear it you will be closest to my heart."

He leaned down and kissed her forehead. "As was my intent, *mignonne*," he murmured, and winked. He handed her a mug of chocolate, adding with a smile, "I hope this busk will serve to make today less fraught for you, knowing that while I cannot be by your side as you make your curtsy to *Leurs Majestés,* but must remain watching on with everyone else, I am in fact, right there with you."

Antonia sipped at her chocolate, gaze on the busk and a finger tracing the ivory inlaid figures of a couple embracing. "You are always so thoughtful and are the most romantic of husbands—"

He lifted an eyebrow. "You have more than one?"

"Silly!" She set aside her mug and snatched up the busk, kissed it, then pressed it to the front of her cotton night chemise, and smiled up at him pertly. "And while I am making my curtsy and showing the proper respect for *Leurs Majestés*, you can think of this busk and have improper thoughts of where you would rather be!"

"Never *improper*, surely."

"Oh?" She frowned. "But I have improper thoughts about you all the time—and at the most inconvenient moments."

He laughed out loud.

This pleased her and she feigned surprise, giving a start as if she had just thought of something, and gasped. "What if—what if I have one of these shameful thoughts while I am making my curtsy?

"Then I suggest you store it up for when you can share it with me, and then I can act upon it."

She leaned back against the pillows and stretched like a cat, drawing up one stockinged knee to say archly, "And what if I were having an improper thought at this very moment?"

He took the busk from between her fingers and used it to gently caress and then tilt her chin up to him.

"It will come as no surprise that I would rather stay here in bed with you all day, satisfying your improper thoughts—but—" He leaned and kissed her, this time on the mouth, then let the busk drop amongst the rumpled bedsheets. "—we cannot disappoint Lucian, who is eagerly looking forward to kicking his heels before royalty."

Antonia giggled and returned his kiss. "So eager I predict he will be the last to come downstairs, and the carriages will all be awaiting his pleasure so we can leave!" She sighed, feigning disappointment. "I shall do my best to—what do you tell me? *behave*—until this evening—For Lucian's sake, of course…" She hopped off the bed and threw on her silk banyan before scooping up the busk and pointing it at the Duke. "But I give you fair warning, Renard, I intend to steal a kiss in the carriage. Dressed in your black and jet —" She gave a little shudder of delight. "—you are *plus qu'irré-sistible,* so the kiss it cannot be helped!"

He made her a sweeping bow. "Thank you for the warning, *ma petite*. I will try and bear it as best I can."

She came around to his side of the bed and fell into his arms. Looking up she said sweetly, "You told me being dressed for this grand occasion will take longer than does the ceremony, so Mme la Duchesse she will use the time to continue with her study of Livy's *Histories*. But she still very much hopes M'sieur le Duc he will visit her boudoir, to assure himself she has not wilted from fatigue!"

"I will, and bring our son to see his maman and how goes the tiresome business of donning your court wardrobe."

"That pleases me very much and is something to look forward to." She took a step away as if she meant to leave, then truly surprised him by asking, all banter aside, "Renard? You write to Lady Paget every week, yes?"

"I do," he said evenly, wondering if the gift of the busk was why she had chosen that moment to broach the subject of his regular exchange of letters with an ex-mistress, one with whom he remained on excellent terms.

Antonia knew this, and about their correspondence, and that he considered Kate Paget a close friend. He even read out particularly amusing parts of Kate's letters to her. And so he waited for further explanation, hands in the pockets of his silk banyan, face betraying nothing of his thoughts. But he could not hide from Antonia. She saw the frown of puzzlement in his dark eyes, and it made her smile.

"It is not because of your gift, *mon homme chéri*," she gently reassured him. "I wanted to ask you this question yesterday, but with Madame's arrival I did not find the appropriate moment. Of course I know you write to Lady Paget—Kate—and that was not my question. What I want to know is whether Kate would wish to receive a letter from me?"

"She will be elated."

"Truly? I like Kate very much, and it made me sad when we parted on ill terms. That was my fault. At that time I was still unsure of-of—*us*."

"She does not blame you." He was sheepish. "She blames me— for not declaring my intentions and marrying you sooner. And I know that she would much prefer to hear from you about our son. She bemoans my lack of—er—depth where Julian is concerned. She tells me in her candid turn of phrase—that is strikingly like yours—I am devoid of a mother's vast vocabulary where the raising of infants is concerned."

Antonia chuckled. "You write that our son is well and thriving and that is that! Which must be very dissatisfying to your female correspondents."

"What else is there of importance?" he asked rhetorically, and pulled a face when she rolled her eyes at him, adding gently, "But thank you for relieving me of a task that was becoming burdensome. Kate will be over the moon to hear all about our son from your quill."

"It is my pleasure, Monseigneur." She laid a hand on his silken chest and looked up at him. "Something, it is bothering you… It has to do with you being woken at first light, yes?"

He did not hide his surprise at her perspicacity. "I had hoped not to disturb you."

She smiled gently. "I always wake when you leave me." She tried to sound disinterested. "Is everything as it should be…?"

"It will be. A courier from England with a letter from Shrewsbury—"

"*Monsieur Spymaster-Général?*"

"Yes. I have read it, but nothing that cannot wait until after your presentation."

As he offered no further explanation and she too wanted nothing to spoil this day, she did not press him. She just wished to get through the ceremony with minimal fuss. However, this did not stop her wondering why and what had bestirred England's Spymaster-General to send a courier across the Channel to Versailles to wake her husband at dawn.

It was as well then that from the moment she entered her boudoir to be pounced on by her maids, her hairdresser, and her ladies-in-waiting, she had not a single second to ruminate. And when later that afternoon she emerged transformed, hardly recognizing herself, she was not at all surprised when Lord Vallentine blurted out in a hushed foyer,

"Well! Well! Who is this beauteous Pandora come amongst us then, eh?"

TEN

Contrary to what his family privately assumed about His Lordship's hostility to being part of the audience for a French court presentation, Lord Vallentine was the second, not the last, to arrive in the entrance foyer as the carriages began lining up under the *porte cochère* for the short drive to the palace. Martin Ellicott was the first downstairs, which was of no surprise to His Lordship, who joined him under the chandelier.

"The porter tells me people have started gathering in the streets along the route," Martin told him. "All for a glimpse of Mme la Duchesse—or should I say—*today*—Mme la Comtesse de Roucy."

"That's understandable," His Lordship replied with a knowing smile. "Not every day any of us get to witness such a spectacle, is it? But with us all—includin' the carriage horses—in black, we're more likely to be mistaken for a funeral procession!" He leaned into Martin. "But don't tell Their Graces I said that. Got to keep it merry for her sake, and his, even if we're feelin' anythin' but enraptured at the prospect of bein' gawked at all the way to Louis's drawin' room and back again."

Martin took a sidelong look at His Lordship's upswept

powdered hair—two large curls above each ear, and an enormous black satin bow at his nape that was so starched it stuck out halfway across his shoulders—and the phrase "gawked at" was apt. He suppressed a smile.

"You're right of course, my lord—"

"Vallentine," His Lordship hissed with a wink.

"I beg your pardon, my lor—"

"No! None of that when we're *at home*. And no need to look the startled pheasant about it!"

"I am not entirely sure I understand you, my—"

Vallentine grabbed Martin by the sleeve and hauled him out of earshot of the always-deaf porter and footmen, and over to the long, gilt-framed looking-glass. Here he pretended to regard his reflection. He put up his square chin and plucked at the froth of white lace tumbling forth from the opening of his embroidered wool waistcoat, all the while speaking to Martin in a low voice.

"Listen, Ellicott. I did some hard thinkin' about all this *my lord* business this mornin' while m' valet was fussin' at me," he confessed. "And I've decided that you can't go on callin' me *your lordship this* and *my lord that* when you're now part of the family —*particularly* not when it's just us. Bein' family comes with certain privileges, as you know. And one of those is callin' a fellow by his name.

"You don't hear me callin' Roxton *His Grace*, do you? A'course not! Never have! Well, not since Eton, when we wrestled, and he put me in a Cornish Hug and demanded I call him *M'sieur le Duc*. And he wasn't even duke *then*." He snorted and turned away from his reflection to face Martin. "I called him a damned French frog, and we had an almighty tumble about in the mud with fists flyin' every which way. But never a bad word since—"

"—because he beat you to a—um—pulp…?"

"Well—um—yes! But that's neither here nor there! I don't call him *Your Grace*, and you don't call me *my lord*—not when it's just family present. It's Vallentine—"

"But as you say so yourself, you've known His Grace since you were at Eton, and I-I—No! I couldn't! No, my lord!"

"What's it goin' to take? Me puttin' *you* in a Cornish Hug?"

Martin smiled in spite of himself, saying on a more conciliatory note, "It wouldn't be correct form for me to address you in any other way than is proper for one of my station." He gulped. "And what would Madame say—?"

"*Station*? What are you blatherin' about? Got too much pomade in your locks and it's seeped into y' brain! I'll say this—and it stays between you and me—it's none of the wife's business how we fellows address one another; it's men's business. Understood? So you just do as I tell you, and no argument!"

"Or it will be a Cornish Hug for me…?"

He patted Martin's sleeve, "Glad we've come to an understandin'!" and stepped past him to join the small crowd milling about at the foot of the stairs. His wife was there, being fussed over by her ladies-in-waiting, and so too were a handful of the Duke and Duchess's entourage. All were facing the staircase and looking up at the procession slowly making its way down to the foyer.

FIRST CAME THE Duke in all his black velvet magnificence, from polished leather shoes with black velvet-covered buckles, and matching silk stockings, on up to a pair of thigh-tight velvet breeches. Both waistcoat and frock coat were cut from the same luxuriously soft cloth, with ebony buttons, and the front panels of both—and the enormous, upturned cuffs of the frock coat— smothered in tiny beads of jet. A froth of fine white Brussels lace at throat and wrists where it cascaded over the backs of his hands, and a large black silk bow at his nape completed his ensemble. Adding to this perfection were a pair of black velvet gloves, a velvet tricorne carried under his arm, and his sword in its ornate silver sheath.

Descending the final step, he turned and joined everyone else in admiring his Duchess in her *deuil de la cour* gown, the black velvet threaded with thousands of tiny jet beads worked into embroidery of swirling scrolls and flowers. With tight half-sleeves covered in layers of the finest and frothiest lace, and extra-wide petticoats spread over silk-wrapped wire-cage panniers, Antonia made slow progress down each step to make certain she did not pitch headfirst down the staircase.

But she need not have worried unnecessarily, for not only did she have her women front and back, but they were also either side of her. Two maids had lifted and concertinaed the panniers up against her flanks, carefully bunching the layers of delicate fabric, a quantity of the gown draped over an arm.

Keeping her chin parallel to her feet, Antonia wondered if she would ever breathe normally again. But it was not the stiffness of her heavily boned bodice that made her short of breath, but anxiousness. It was the enormity of the task before her—which until this moment had remained in the future—and the fact she would be the center of attention for the hundreds who crammed the corridors of the palace, from curious tourist on up to Their Majesties.

She was now a figure of curiosity, even to herself. For she had become someone else entirely in her appearance, from the moment her hairdresser had drenched her coiffure of coiled braids in powder, and the bright-red rouge required of court ladies was applied to her cheeks and lips, the powder and cosmetics even more vibrant and garish with her dressed in black.

And as if the heavy application of makeup were not enough to make her self-conscious, there was the wide oval neckline of the embroidered bodice, cut so low across her full breasts that it bordered on the indecent. But the Duke had assured her that this too was a requirement of court attire, and she must try to disregard it for once at the palace, she would be surrounded by women dressed similarly and would be more comfortable.

She did not mention that having lived for a time at the palace with her grandfather, she was well aware of how the ladies dressed and behaved, but that she, who had always been on the periphery of life and events at court, had never had all eyes turned in her direction—until today. Nor had she ever worn court dress before.

But something else had bothered her about the low cut to the décolletage, and the Duke knew what it was. Smiling in understanding, he kissed the tip of one long finger before lightly placing it above the puckered scar below her collarbone, careful to leave undisturbed the dusting of powder that covered it. Despite the application of this cosmetic dust, there was no hiding the disfigurement to her porcelain skin.

"Never let this concern you, *ma fée*. To be sure, it is a stark *aide-mémoire* of Salvan treachery, but to me it is much more than that. It is a reminder of what I almost lost, and what is most important in my life—you."

Now safely down the stairs and standing in the foyer, the panniers of Antonia's gown were eased back in place and the petticoats of the wide gown shaken out and arranged to everyone's satisfaction. The ladies-in-waiting accompanying their mistress to the palace, and the maids who had assisted in dressing her, then stepped aside to allow the Duke to greet his wife.

But before he took her hand, Roxton bowed his head then made her a sweeping bow with tricorne in hand, one so low that the lace at his wrists brushed the black-and-white marble tiles. And as he sank down before her, so too did everyone in the foyer, from the porter to the Duke's sister. The only one left standing tall in a sea of black was Antonia. Overcome with emotion at such veneration, her hands shook, and her bosom heaved. All she could do to stop herself bursting into tears was to press her painted lips together and hold tight to the closed sticks of her folding fan.

It was left to Lord Vallentine to lighten the mood.

"Well! Well! Who is this beauteous Pandora come amongst us then, eh?" announced His Lordship as he straightened out of a deep bow. He had a sudden thought and elbowed Martin in the ribs, adding audibly, "That's what a fashion doll is called, ain't it? A Pandora?"

"Yes, my l—Vallentine," Martin replied in a whisper. "It is."

His Lordship's eyes went to the plaster ceiling, and he heaved a sigh of relief so loud it reverberated around the foyer. He then gave Martin another friendly shove with his elbow, adding with a wink, "That wasn't too hard to say, now was it?"

"No, Vallentine. It was not," Martin quipped, smiling despite himself. "Though I fear you may have cracked my rib!"

"Eh?"

Madame bustled up to her husband then, not at all pleased to see him heads-together with Martin Ellicott, and tapped him with her fan.

"Lucian! Is that the best you can offer, comparing Antonia to a Pandora!? Fie! Nonsense!" And swirling about in her wide court petticoats—sending several footmen scuttling to get out of her way —she said to the Duchess, blowing her a kiss, "You look *magnifique*, my love! You will be the envy of every lady at court. And I cannot wait to see *Sa Majesté*'s face when you curtsy before him. *Tu es si belle!*"

The Duke stepped aside to allow Antonia to come closer, and with her breathing more regular and composure returned, she replied brightly,

"Thank you, Madame. But Vallentine he is right to call me a Pandora because I am as painted and as stiff as a doll! And Monseigneur, he was not at all pleased to see the powder in my braids and the rouge to my cheeks. But he said it is a necessary evil. And so, I do not complain as much as I would like to, because today it is exciting for all of us!"

"Just so, *ma belle*," the Duke agreed, and signaled for the double doors to the *porte cochère* to be thrown wide. "You will soon forget all about the paint and powder, and even the weight of your gown, once we arrive at court and join the rest of the—er —Pandoras."

She beamed, and confided to her family, "And to think the last time I departed Versailles I was just as painted—but in a different way entirely!" She smiled cheekily up at the Duke—who was exchanging a knowing glance with Martin Ellicott, adding, "And now I make a return as a Comtesse—*comme si de rien n'était*. M'sieur le Duc de Richelieu, he will have the surprise of his life today!"

"And he, not the only one," muttered Roxton, escorting her out to the line of waiting carriages, the rest of their family and entourage falling in behind, eager to finally be off to the palace. He was thinking of his Salvan relatives, and upon arriving at the stairs, he was not disappointed by their reception or their reactions.

ELEVEN

"THERE IS NO NEED to acknowledge everyone we pass, *ma petite chérie*."

Antonia continued to wave her lace-bordered handkerchief from the carriage window at the people, old and young, who had stopped along the route, eyes wide and mouths agape as the Duke's convoy of carriages in stately procession slowly rumbled along the *Avenue de Paris*, led by an escort of liveried postilions mounted on impressive high-stepping steeds in polished tac and white-plumed headdress.

Pedestrians halted their daily routines the moment the postilions had appeared outside the villa's walls and headed down the *rue des Reservoirs*. And by the time the last of the carriages entered the broad *avenue de Paris*, even those in a hurry minding their own business, were congregating with the wide-eyed tourists and women with small children to speculate on the identity of the illustrious occupants in the line of carriages.

All were in agreement that it had to be a foreign dignitary—an ambassador prince at the very least—come to pay homage to *Sa Majesté*, newly returned to the palace for the upcoming

Christmas festivities. Who else would have the audacity to hold up the flow of traffic? Those on horseback were compelled to look for an alternate route to their destinations, while carriages, sedan chairs, and travelers crammed into a carabas, were forced to the side of the avenue to allow the procession to pass unhindered.

"As they have done us the courtesy to stop in the cold, I must respond," Antonia replied mildly. "Particularly when the children they wave with such enthusiasm. It is good manners to do so, yes?"

"Courtesy? Or is it curiosity? No matter. We will believe the former." Roxton smiled crookedly at some private thought. "What a pity it is winter, or I would have had flower petals strewn along the way to elevate our procession—"

"—to a Roman triumph?!" Antonia exclaimed, green eyes bright at the thought, a smile over her shoulder at the Duke. "*Ce serait époustouflant!*"

"Breathtaking? Yes. Very fitting."

She put her shoulders back against the soft velvet upholstery.

"I think you are not disappointed it is winter for its own sake," she said sweetly, adding with that streak of perceptiveness which never failed to surprise him, "But you are disappointed we lack rose petals. Had our carriages arrived covered in flowers it would have added to the discomfort your Salvan relatives are already feeling at *ce geste grandiose* we are making. Which is to put them—how did you describe it to me earlier?—ah yes!—*back in their box.*"

He caught up her gloved hand and said with a forced lightness that belied the hard glitter in his black eyes, "They will wish they had a warm box to hide in after today's events. And I have ordered we travel as slowly as is possible for the wheels to turn so when we do finally arrive at the gates and my Salvan aunts and cousins are there to greet us in the winter air, so too will a crowd, cheering our approach."

"Cheering?"

"Just so. I would have rose petals for you, *ma belle*, but for the people, I have thought of something more practical and welcoming."

"Coin would be more practical."

"It would if we wish to start a riot. But I anticipated your wishes. And thus in honor of your presentation, I have gifted our curious onlookers with something more sustaining. Men were sent early to the taverns along our route, with coin enough to provide all and—er—sundry with ale, compliments of the Comtesse de Roucy. The townspeople will toast your health and be singing your praises for days to come."

"Oh! Monseigneur! Thank you! You are too generous!"

"I am not generous at all. You are. I do this for you, and you alone." He let go of her fingers and crossed his gloved hands over one velvet knee and raised an eyebrow, "I am," he drawled, "what will soon be whispered behind my back, if it is not already—no matter, it is true—an *indulgent* husband."

Antonia leaned toward him as best she could in her concertinaed panniers, surrounded by layers of embroidered black velvet petticoats. "Do such whispers bother you?"

He tried to appear grave, though his mouth twitched with a smile he could not suppress.

"I have had much worse whispered about me—and all of that was true." He had a sudden thought. "Does it bother you—?"

"The whispers? Or that you are an indulgent husband? Not at all. If the former be true and are not falsehoods, and they do not bother you, then why should I be bothered? As for the latter?" She smiled, her dimple showing. "It makes me happy that you indulge me."

The Duke's close-shaven cheeks diffused with color. "Your happiness is all that matters."

"As yours does to me. And I love you even more if that is possible, for saying so, *mon mari bien-aimé*."

"Whisperers be damned," he murmured as he leaned in to kiss her.

Their kiss was feathery-light, eyes half-shuttered as they drank in the moment. They may have stayed that way a little longer if not for the loud sniff, followed by several snuffles, which caused them to fall back in their seats and turn their attention to the only other occupant of the large carriage, who sat opposite—Antonia's maid, Gabrielle. The Duchess asked her if she were unwell.

Gabrielle sniffed again and quickly dabbed at her eyes and pinched her nose with her handkerchief. She shook her head and did not lift her chin, eyes on her handkerchief.

"No, Mme la Duchesse! I apologize if I disturbed you," she muttered. "I am very well indeed. In fact, I am *so* well, I am crying happy tears. Please disregard me!"

When the Duke pulled a face, not at all convinced, Antonia giggled behind her hand, and said in English—a language her maid had yet to master, "It is true. She is overcome by Your Grace's generosity."

"Let us hope my French aunts are equally—er—*afflicted*."

Antonia's head tilted in enquiry. "How could they not be, when you have paid their debts?"

Roxton held Antonia's gaze, saying flatly, "You know as well as I, my love, that everyone at Versailles has a price, most particularly those to whom one is related. The expectation always was that, in exchange for being your sponsor for this presentation, I would discharge Aunt Victoire's most pressing debts. Generosity and obligation are interchangeable."

"Not to me, Your Grace," Antonia stated emphatically. "Or to Madame, or Vallentine, or Martin. I do not wish you ever to think you need do something for me out of a sense of obligation. That would be burdensome."

"It is. But you are not, and never will be." He needlessly adjusted the large, upturned cuff of his frock coat, saying with a sigh, "Family obligation for its own sake is a tedious business. A drop of blood is all that is required for a connection to be exploited, and I do not refer only to coin." When Antonia leaned closer, intrigued, he added gently, "Loyalty, feelings, even love, are often used as weapons of manipulation to press for a desired result."

Antonia thought about this for a moment, then said with a soft understanding smile, "*Monsieur Spymaster-Général* he has joined us in the carriage, yes?"

The Duke lost his frown and sat back with a huff of laughter.

"Yes! I suppose he has. You are quite right. Shrewsbury's letter is indeed weighing on my mind," he confessed, then rallied to say on lighter note, "But my old school friend has no place here. My apologies for distracting you from this momentous occasion."

"There is no need, Your Grace. The distraction has stopped me worrying so much about what is to come."

"You need not worry, my love," the Duke assured her gently, continuing in the English tongue. "Louis's court is a stage, and its courtiers, actors upon it. Success depends on how well one plays to the audience. I have every confidence in you playing your part well. That you are an exceptional mimic and can slip into the cadence peculiar to the court will be applauded and appreciated—it is a skill, one Louis's mistress has yet to perfect. You are to enjoy yourself. I know I will, watching you." He indicated the window with a languid hand and reverted to her native tongue. "Please. Do not allow M'sieur le Duc to take up any more of Mme la Comtesse's time. The curious and the courteous are demanding of her attention."

They exchanged a loving smile, and then Antonia returned to waving out the window while the Duke sat back and closed his eyes to appreciate the last remaining moments of tranquility before they were to be thrust front and center into the intrigue and formality of the French court.

TWELVE

Peering out the window as the carriage slowed, Lord Vallentine was surprised to discover a large crowd congregated at the *Place d'Armes*. And then he was taken aback when the ornate central gates to the palace were swung wide, allowing the Duke's company of postillions to lead their winding convoy of carriages into the enclosure and across the snow-covered cobbles, straight up to the wide stairs of the Royal courtyard.

"Hey! They've let us pass through the main gates!" he announced, throwing his wife a look of amazement.

"What? The center ones?" Madame responded, just as wide-eyed. She craned to see out the window. Frustrated she could not move in her wide panniers, she shooed a hand at him. "Look again! Look! Are you certain? Surely you are mistaken, and it is the *side* gate that was opened to us."

Vallentine did as he was ordered though there was no need.

"No. Not the side gate. And yes, a' course I'm sure! Roxton's postillions rode straight up to the golden gates smack in the middle, as if they were expectin' 'em to be thrown open. And the guards did just that. I thought only Louis and his blood relatives got a special pass to access the Royal courtyard through those gates?"

"This pass, it has a name, Lucian. *Les honneurs du Louvre,*" Estée explained, her chin a little higher, realizing that through her brother, she was now one of the privileged few to receive such a high honor. "It is used only by the King and his family. Rarely, under special circumstances, and then only to very important visitors, the central gate is opened to others." She shrugged, as if unconcerned. "I have only ever heard of Princes of the Blood and ambassadors receiving such a privilege. But we should not be surprised. With my brother, anything is possible. And so when we leave this carriage, we will take this honor as we do everything else —as if it were a commonplace occurrence. Roxton would expect nothing less of us."

Vallentine snorted his skepticism of his wife's insouciance. He knew she was mentally jumping for joy that her peers would be envious of this singular honor done her family. But he was conciliatory. "Aye. Don't you worry. I'll be on m' best behavior."

"Thank you," she replied with a smile that almost immediately dropped into a frown. She gave a sigh of resignation. "I did not think my Salvan cousins could fall any further in *Sa Majesté*'s estimation, but with Roxton granted *les honneurs du Louvre* and Antonia's presentation as Comtesse… I do not see them ever making a recovery—*C'est trop tard*. My brother has seen to that."

"Ha! You got that right!" Vallentine replied with a laugh, only half listening.

He'd been staring out the window again, distracted by the traffic of carriages and sedan chairs, mounted postillions, and liveried servants ducking and weaving amongst carriage wheels and horseflesh, when something caught all his attention. Which is why he had only one ear open to his wife's conversation.

He had picked up on the word *fall,* and replied with a laugh,

"Your Salvan cousins are not only fallin' but trippin' over one another! They can't get to the stairs quick enough to greet us! Roxton either didn't tell 'em we were comin' through the gates, or they were arrogant enough to ignore the directive to be at the stairs and not the gates, because they knew better! Ha!" He had a sudden thought and glanced over his shoulder at his wife. "To be fair, I'd have not believed Louis would grant Roxton *les honneurs du Louvre*—"

"Tell me what you see! You know I cannot get to the window!"

"Eh? Ah! Sorry, lovedy! Happy to oblige." He turned to the window again and resisted the urge to pull down the sash and stick out his head because of the bitter cold. "Most of the Salvan miscellany were waitin' for us to alight at the gates. And now that we've come through them, they've had to up petticoats and hold on to their tricornes to scramble as fast as they can to get to the stairs. They're providin' the crowd with the day's entertainment, I can tell you!"

"Entertainment?" Estée asked in alarm.

"Aye! In their rush to get here, they forgot the cobbles are icy. Some of your cousins have had their pattens slip out from under 'em and are now buttocks down in the filth!"

"Oh dear! Oh dear!"

"Lackeys are doin' their best to pick 'em up out of the slush. But it don't help that it's just as slippery for them to attempt the rescue—"

"*Mon Dieu*, my poor tantes," Estée muttered.

"No need to waste y' worry on them, lovedy. All your tantes are still upright. None of 'em were capable of rushin' anywhere in their wide hoops, nor would they! And *Tante Victoire* heeded your brother's directive 'cause she's waitin' at the top of the stairs with her cabal of ladies. If you can believe me, her face is split in two, such is her smile!"

"She has every reason to beam. *Tante Philippe* tells me my brother settled *Tante Victoire*'s enormous debts in payment for her being Antonia's sponsor for today's presentation. And I believe *Tante Philippe*, because it would take just such an incentive for *Tante Victoire* to visit court again. She vowed never to do so while the Pompadour was *Sa Majesté's maîtresse-en-titre*."

"A bitter pill—or should that be big fish given Pompadour's name was Poisson—for her to swallow then, eh?" remarked His Lordship with tongue in cheek, before turning to the open carriage door where a footman waited to help him alight.

Safely on solid ground, sword and sash adjusted, and with his tricorne secured under his arm, he left his wife to her women and joined the Duke.

QUIZZING GLASS held to one eye, Roxton surveyed the frenetic activity that accompanies the arrival of honored guests to the palace. To the casual observer, this ocular affectation gave him an unruffled and unhurried air. Yet one look at the firm set to his mouth and the intensity of purpose was evident. He was determined nothing and no one would ruin his wife's official introduction to the French court, and was on the alert for just such an eventuality.

Martin Ellicott was at the Duke's shoulder. But his gaze was not on the passengers alighting from the dozen carriages. It was on the Duke's majordomo, admiring the man's skill in coordinating events with all the aplomb of a circus ringmaster. Every servant from postillion to maid was aware of their role in ensuring the success of this most important royal presentation.

Lackeys ran about strewing straw across the icy cobbles and up the steps, while others unfurled Turkey rugs and followed behind their fellows to lay these rugs over the straw. In this way the hems of the ladies' gowns remained dry, and they were able to ascend the steps in comfort and without trepidation of a fall.

Six of the postillions had dismounted and stood between the

Duke's entourage and the curious crowd, keeping everyone at arm's length. Antonia's ladies-in-waiting and several maids were gathered at her carriage door, to help the Duchess alight, and make last minute adjustments to her grand habit and coiffure, before falling in behind to form part of the entourage accompanying their mistress indoors.

Satisfied the Duchess was ready to ascend the steps, Gabrielle gave a nod of dismissal to the maids, then took her place behind those relatives honored to play the role of lady-in-waiting to their cousin's wife. Once indoors she would remove and take charge of Antonia's fur-lined cape, finally revealing to the world for the first time the magnificent splendor of the Duchess's court gown.

Watching these preparations from the top step were the Duke's Salvan relatives, who formed a dour-faced and imperious welcoming party. Some were disheveled and breathing heavily from their exertions of scuttling from the other side of the gates, while those who had followed Roxton's directive to meet at the inner courtyard were smug. All shared a resentful commonality: While waiting on their English relative's pleasure, they were careful to hide a seething resentment under a veneer of filial obedience. Reason for the Duke's brief smile of satisfaction, for he perfectly understood their private feelings, and he rejoiced in their discomfort.

With a final sweep of his quizzing glass across this sour group, he let drop the accoutrement on its black ribbon and turned to speak with Martin and Vallentine, who had just joined them, saying in English,

"Martin, stay with her, in case she has need of you."

"Of course, Your Grace."

"Eh? Aren't you escortin' her indoors?" asked Vallentine.

"No. Here is where *Tante Victoire* and our Salvan relatives play their part. We go on ahead to sweep any obstacles from her path."

Vallentine gave a start, instantly on the alert, a hand to the ornate hilt of his silver smallsword. He let his gaze dart about, out across the noisy, congested courtyard where carriages were coming and going. "You expectin' trouble—*here?*"

"I always expect it. In that way I am always prepared."

"But—surely not with Louis at home to visitors?"

"You may rest easy, Lucian, and release your grip. If there is—er—trouble it won't come from the point of a rapier but the tip of a tongue."

Vallentine let his hand drop and rolled his eyes. "Ugh. I should've guessed. A woman! You think Duras-Valfons is out to cause trouble?"

"A display at the very least, yes." The Duke smiled crookedly. "That is what her husband warns—"

"Eh? Her-her—husband?" Vallentine blustered. "Rick—Ricky told you? Hahaha! Well a' course he would! He knows where his loyalty lies! Good for him!"

The Duke bowed his head in acknowledgement of this, adding with an eye to his Salvan relatives,

"Before visiting Louis's study we make a short stop at the *Galerie des Glaces*. There the captain of the *Gardes de la Porte* will make himself known to you. I want you to enjoy the grand prospect from the windows, where you will keep an eye on proceedings. Should there be an attempt to intervene, you have my permission to give whoever it is a little—er—prick. The captain's men have been ordered to prevent the general rabble from entering the gallery, while keeping their noble masters at a welcome distance until I give the signal."

"You want an audience?"

"I do. The right audience."

"So you *are* expectin' trouble from that harpy!"

"Not if I can clip her wings first. I mean for this nonsense to end today, and before Antonia's presentation to *Sa Majesté*."

The Duke went to ascend the stairs when he was forced to pause at the imperious call of his name. It was his sister, wide panniers rocking widely from side to side as she bustled up to him, knocking lackeys left and right, determined to avert what she considered a social catastrophe. She caught at the velvet skirts of his frock coat, hissing lest she be overheard,

"Roxton! Do you see who is a lady-in-waiting to your wife? Madame Haudry! Yes. Our disgraced cousin! You must do something before our *tantes* make a mockery of this day before it has begun!"

THIRTEEN

THE DUKE took a frowning glance over his sister's coiffure to where the entourage of females was fussing about the Duchess. Michelle Haudry was indeed one of their number. He met Estée's blue eyes, which were wide with indignation, giving away nothing of his thoughts. But his response startled her.

"She is here at my behest, not theirs."

"Yours? Why? How? But—but I do not understand—"

"There is nothing for you to understand—yet."

Estée was incredulous. "She was banished from the family and forbidden the court for marrying a lowly bourgeois. That is what I do understand. She has no more right to be here than Jean-Honoré!"

"Now, lovedy," Vallentine cautioned. "Let's not bring that weasel's name up on this of all days—"

"Be quiet, Lucian! You have no notion of what I speak! It is the height of court heresy for a banished commoner to show her face before *Sa Majesté*!" She fixed on her brother and pouted. "You have invited her as part of some devious scheme to further embarrass our Salvan cousins, but I want no part of—"

"You have no part. It is none of your concern," the Duke interrupted flatly.

"Good," Estée replied, and somewhat appeased added in an about-face, "Cousin Michelle may have married the son of a tax-collector, but no one can deny her birthright as daughter of a duke. Unlike the King's latest whore, who is not only common but from a family of *fish*—fishmongers."

The Duke smiled, which always unsettled her.

"Thank you. Your acerbic and inane observation vindicates my —er—what did you call it—Ah yes!—*devious scheme* for Michelle Haudry to be one of my wife's ladies-in-waiting." He lost his smile. "But let that be the last time you utter such comments about la Pompadour, lest they find themselves whispered into her little ear."

Estée sniffed and shrugged a shoulder. "What do I care if she hears what I say. It is the truth."

"You should. And I do. So you will do as I say. Be warned, Estée. This mistress isn't going anywhere." He made her a courteous bow. "As my sister, allow me to provide you with a choice. Take your place beside Madame Haudry as a lady-in-waiting and remain mute, or you may return to the villa. It is of supreme indifference to me. Come, my dear," he ordered his best friend, and went lightly up the steps.

Vallentine watched him go, and only looked at his wife when she spoke his name. Her moist eyes made him instantly uncomfortable, and he blushed. But he did not offer her any words of comfort. With a shrug of inevitability, he obediently followed the Duke.

THE PALACE WAS PREDICTABLY CROWDED and noisy. From the booths lining the courtyard where shopkeepers sold overpriced souvenirs, and guidebooks, hired out tricornes, and offered sustenance at exorbitant prices with all the enthusiasm of a fair day, to the scriveners busy in murky corridor corners with quill and ink, writing up petitions for the illiterate and the desperate. Lackeys, footmen, and servants darted amongst the faceless crowd, fetching and carrying for their masters all the accoutrements necessary to make their visit as pleasant as possible, be it a footstool to sit upon or a chamber pot to pee in.

At every turn and in every alcove, a Swiss guard. A patrol took turns about the grounds and larger rooms, all with an eye to trouble. They were also on the lookout for any inappropriately dressed visitor who tried to gain entry to the King's palace. A hat and sword were obligatory for gentlemen, no matter the state of their clothing, how many darns to a worn sleeve or a stocking.

All manner of persons from every social class were permitted the King's house for a glimpse of the royal family going about the ritual of their daily lives. With everything and everyone draped in mourning, poverty and affluence were disguised alike. Those who could not afford the costly trimmings, expensive fabrics, and jewelry on any normal day were relieved by this, while those with unlimited means or who were obligated by social position and pedigree found ingenious ways to advertise their status through the expense, cut, and yardage of their somber outer garments.

French subjects and foreign visitors moved shoulder to shoulder through the crowded corridors and stairways of the public apartments, while those nobles in the service of their royal masters went out of their way to avoid these areas, using hidden passageways or staying away from the palace altogether until next required to perform their ceremonial duties.

But today was different. Today the nobility had gathered in the Galerie de Glaces in small whispering groups awaiting a grand spectacle said to involve none other than the Duke of Roxton. The delicious rumor came from the painted lips of the Marquis de Chesnay. Always up on the latest gossip, de Chesnay had murmured a story about his good friend the English duke, in the ear of none other than the First Gentleman of the Bedchamber, the Duc de Richelieu.

M'sieur le Duc had always deluded himself that he was Roxton's equal when competing for the sexual favors of beautiful women, and the affections of *Sa Majesté*. Unequal to the task on both counts, Richelieu could barely contain his bitterness. Thus what de Chesnay breathlessly told him left him seething. Yet he was incredulous. He could not help himself and spread the story everywhere, exclaiming there could be no validity to it. Roxton would have to be mad to attempt such a thing, for it would surely ruin him.

This was all that was needed for every noble in the palace to scamper to the Galerie de Glaces in anticipation of something monumentally scandalous about to take place. They turned up in droves. Just as Roxton knew they would.

WITH HIS LIVERIED footmen before him and his best friend at his shoulder, the Duke processed through the congested palace corridors, handkerchief and snuffbox held aloft, black lace cascading from his wrists, jet-bead embroidery glinting in the winter sun streaming in from the full-length windows. He looked neither left nor right, and to the tourists his entire being and singular demeanor marked him out as a courtier, while his height and width proclaimed a man more than capable of clearing his own path through the rabble, should the need arise. It did not. Unhurried and unworried, and seemingly unaware of the stares of those who flattened themselves against the walls to get out of the way, his entourage sliced a path for him like a battleship through rough seas.

It was only when the Duke stopped under one of the brilliantly lit chandeliers in the center of the Galerie des Glaces that Vallentine became aware it had been emptied of tourists, just as his best friend had predicted. Swiss Guards were at either end at the ornate double doors, while several of their fellows sauntered in pairs the length of the hall in the sunshine streaming through the floor-to-ceiling windows. Opposite, against the full-length mirrors, clusters of perfumed and pomaded nobles were talking amongst themselves, seemingly uninterested in events unfolding in the center of the room. Yet Vallentine was certain that while they might appear unconcerned, all had one eye on proceedings.

He might not have any idea as to the Duke's intentions, but he had every confidence his best friend would achieve his object. He could not wait to see what played out in this stage-managed scene and sauntered across to the windows to take up his position as he had been directed.

The captain of the *Gardes de la Porte* came up to His Lordship at once. His vacant expression told Vallentine that he also had no idea of what was about to transpire, and reinforced when this head of the King's internal security confided that should the Swiss need to draw their swords, he would be honored to have such a great swordsman as M'sieur Vallentine to fight by his side. Vallentine did not have the heart to tell him that should a fight break out in this glorified setting, it would be of the feminine variety only—either weeping and wallowing or kicking and screaming.

WHILE VALLENTINE and the captain of the Swiss Guard were in brief conversation, the Duke's footmen set to work in the center of the hall. A Turkey rug was unfurled and laid across the parquetry, just large enough for three silk-upholstered, gilt walnut tabourets set in proximity. Upon the middle tabouret was placed a silver tray that held a brandy decanter and four crystal glasses. These came from a *nécessaire de voyage* that was then taken away by a servant. Having arranged everything to their master's satisfaction, the footmen bowed and disappeared amongst the pockets of nobles.

The Duke of Roxton was now alone in the center of the room being stared at by an astonished and slack-jawed nobility. No one could believe his audacity. No one had ever thought to do what he was doing. No one would dare to flout the rules. Everyone waited to see what would happen next. At the very least it was expected the Swiss would step in to put a stop to this monumental societal transgression. But no one wanted to be first to speak out or move. It was all too tantalizing. What would the English duke do next, and on this of all days—his duchess's presentation, no less!

A frisson of fearful expectation rippled around the hall. What followed was the stuff of societal self-annihilation. The entire fraternity of French nobles could not have been more thrilled.

FOURTEEN

UNRUFFLED, and with his satisfaction concealed under a habitual inscrutability, the Duke gave an outward flick of his stiff frock coat skirts and sat upon one of the upholstered stools —all the while ignoring the collective gasps of his audience.

Here he remained in the center of the hall of mirrors, back ramrod straight, and with one leg forward, the low-heeled black kid shoe slightly turned out, all to show to best advantage his well-developed calf muscle. He then unfobbed his small gold-and-enamel snuffbox and took a leisurely pinch of powder.

And then he waited.

THE COMTESSE DURAS-VALFONS was not long in coming. She sailed into the hall with a smug smile, two female friends in tow. Tall and willowy, her upswept blonde coiffure of intricate braids heightened the length of her swan-like neck and bare alabaster shoulders. Wearing the obligatory grand habit of black velvet with capped sleeves of gathered silk, the bodice was cut so indecently low across her flat chest that had the sticklers for correct form been able to drop their already slack jaws further, they would have.

She was halfway up the room, nodding here and there to friends and family clustered about in small groups opposite the long windows, when she chanced to glimpse her own reflection in the full-length mirrors. Her conceit heightened, if that were possible. She had never looked more beautiful or in better health.

But when she finally turned her gaze to the length of the long room, an unwelcome crease appeared on her usually smooth brow. Yet she forced herself to continue smiling.

She was confronted with the astonishing sight of a solitary figure seated upon a tabouret under one of the magnificent chandeliers, conduct so shocking that it was at first disbelieved. She blinked. He was still there! And then she realized just who it was— her former ducal lover. It set her heart racing and her breathing became short and quick.

A glance about and she realized everyone else was in a state of disbelief, too. No one sat in the King's home except members of the royal family and duchesses given permission to do so. No one had ever dared such a blatant display and in such a public space as the *Galerie de Glaces*. And yet not one guard, not even the captain of the Swiss who was in conversation with Roxton's best friend Lord Vallentine, or any of the wide-eyed courtiers, dared to chastise the English duke.

She wondered what Roxton was playing at. And as he had requested she meet him here, she realized she was now part of a scheme of his devising. Her instinct was to flee but she knew there was no backing out. Not unless she wanted to face the social ridicule of her peers. Her step slowed but she continued on to meet him, chin a little higher than before. Her two companions quietly and quickly abandoned her, melting into the crowd to watch proceedings from the anonymity of the crowd.

WHEN THE COMTESSE was within a few feet of him, the Duke rose to sweep her an elegant bow of welcome. She replied with a respectful curtsy and a smile that held a hint of surprise. He returned her smile, quickening her pulse and heating her heavily rouged cheeks. Whatever her trepidation, just the sight of him—all six feet, two inches of handsome self-assured male arrogance—made her want to swoon. And with his smile she forgot her surroundings and closed the gap between them so that they were in intimate whispering proximity.

Their audience instinctively leaned forward, eyes bright and ears wide open in anticipation, confident that what they were about to witness between these ex-lovers would be talked about for days, if not weeks, to come.

"M'SIEUR LE DUC."

"Mme la Comtesse."

"This is—this is indeed a-a surprise!"

"Surely not," he drawled. "I asked that you meet me here. And here you are."

"I was most disconsolate when you did not take up my invitation to join me at Fontainebleau," she replied sulkily, before adding at her most coquettish, "Can I presume you've had a change of heart and now wish to resume our agreeable liaison?"

"You know as well as I that our—er—agreeable liaison was never about the heart—yours or mine." His lips twitched. "And I am reluctant to disappoint you, but the truth is I would not be here if not at the urging of my wife."

That broke the spell.

The Comtesse fell back a step, mouth screwed up as if she had tasted something sour. "Your-your—*wife*? What has she got to do with this?"

The Duke blinked at her, feigning surprise.

"Why, everything."

It was a simple enough statement quietly spoken, and it cut the Comtesse to the quick, because she knew he was speaking the truth, and from the heart.

Society might snigger behind his ducal back that he had made a love match, but secretly they all craved the very thing they derided, she included. And she had deluded herself with the wishful thinking that with the birth of a son and heir he would come to his senses and resume his previous lascivious lifestyle. Regarding him now, she knew this was never going to happen. He was not only deeply in love with his wife, no doubt he would remain so for the rest of his life. Vigorous lotharios, when they fell, fell hard and forever after.

With this wretched knowledge came the realization that she had no idea as to the purpose of this meeting with her ex-lover. That she was standing before him, not because he wished to see her, but at the behest of his duchess brought her to a sense of her surroundings.

"Then I do not understand at all why I am here, and this of all places," she pouted, "except because your wife she wishes to humiliate me!"

"Mme la Duchesse does not possess a vindictive hair on her head. The meeting may have been her idea, but its location and execution are mine."

"Indeed! I do not know her but—"

"You do not. But I know you."

"Then you know I would not wish for us to meet like this!"

"No?" The Duke pulled a face. "But all the court is here, as it was at Fontainebleau. So I have given you your wish of a very public spectacle. Only the setting has changed."

The Comtesse glanced across at her friends and relatives gathered along the wall of floor-to-ceiling mirrors, all staring at her in solemn but expectant silence. She quickly looked away, gaze falling on the arrangement of tabourets, and the silver tray holding crystal decanter and glasses. She put up her chin.

"You are sadly mistaken if you think I will flout the court and sit and sip with you!"

"I am not sad or mistaken. The stool and brandy are not for you." Roxton slipped his snuffbox into a large frock coat pocket and came to the point. "Our meeting is not about you or—er—*us*, but about your son—"

"*Our* son."

"Come, Thérèse. That is a lie. You know it. I know it. The Duchess knows it. And so do my Salvan cousins, with whom you conspired to foist the infant's paternity onto me."

The Comtesse gave a non-committal shrug. "I had always planned for you to give me a son. And so to my mind, he is yours."

The Duke's gaze shot to the painted ceiling and down again.

"That is absurd in the extreme."

"How so? With your satyr's reputation you have no doubt fathered any number of infants over the years, so why not mine, too?"

"If I were not a gentleman, I would point out that your reputation is no less sullied, and thus your son's questionable paternity will come as a surprise to nobody." He smiled coolly. "But as I am a gentleman, I will make no such riposte. But there is one matter of which I am supremely confident: I am not your infant's sire." The corners of his mouth lifted. "And there's the rub, is it not?"

The Comtesse pouted, the deepening color to her throat indication his barb had found its mark. To her great bitterness he spoke the truth, but as her pride had been irreparably damaged when he forsook her, she was never going to concede.

"If you are not prepared to own him, I do not understand at all your interest. This meeting between us it is meaningless. But it does hold significance for those watching, does it not?" she added slyly. "This is the court, and we of the nobility. The more a thing is denied, the more the opposite is believed. So I beg you, M'sieur le Duc, to continue to deny you are my son's sire—for his sake. You may have truth on your side, but what of that when I will continue to perpetuate my lie in whispers while publicly denying you are his father? A hundred—no a thousand—others will then believe me. Truth is inconsequential. My son is your son by public opinion. *Voilà*!"

The Duke countered to five. He couldn't care any less for this woman or her son. And he had always shrugged off the gutter gossip spread about himself and his affairs. If it were up to him, he would not be here. But Antonia did care about the infant. Was it the infant's fault he had a calculating and uncaring mother? she argued. No! He was the innocent in this melodrama of his mother's making and deserved a future in spite of her.

And as Roxton would do anything to save Antonia distress, he was determined she would have the outcome she desired—the Comtesse's neglected son would have a future. They could then put this distasteful (for him) and distressing (for her) episode behind them. But he intended to achieve the desired outcome his way, the consequences for the Comtesse Duras-Valfons be damned. He quelled his internal fury and replied with a studied indifference, saying smoothly,

"By all means continue the lie if it gives you a hollow satisfaction. But you are doing your son a grave disservice by denying him legitimacy—"

"I am reminded of the time we were strolling the Tuileries," she interrupted, as if he had not spoken at all. She laughed behind her hand at some private fancy, gazing over his shoulder into the distance as she recounted chattily, "Maurice my brother started waxing lyrical about his recent journey into the provinces to visit his youngest son. Do you remember? He was as proud as a peacock that the boy had a second tooth! You could not have been more bored. Your look of pained disgust was worthy of oils! We females fell into such a fit of the giggles that everyone around us thought us addle-brained." She lost her smile, saying silkily, "Who could have predicted M'sieur le Duc d'Roxton would go on to marry, least of all profess concern for the welfare of an infant for whom he denies any connection whatsoever."

"No one, I suspect."

"Everyone says marriage has softened your brain."

"Everyone does not know me."

"Do you know what is being whispered behind your back—"

"Are there enough hours in the day?"

She laughed, as if told a good joke. It was brittle and unconvincing and made several in the crowd shuffle forward, straining to hear their conversation.

"Droll! I am sure you can guess at least one of the whispers!"

"I do not have the patience or the inclination, so I beg you to enlighten me."

"That you've been struck down in your prime with a contagion usually confined to green youths and convent maidens." When the Duke put up his brows and waited further explanation, she said with relish, "You are infected with *la maladie de l'amour*!"

"Love sickness? How trite. I was expecting any number of maladies, and far more odious."

"But, Roxton! To be ridiculed for—"

"—being in love with one's wife is a mortal sin to those of the court? Yes. But no matter. I do not recoil. And I have no wish to be —er—cured. It is in the blood, for my father suffered with it too. But we digress, and time is moving on, and no one, least of all me, wishes to be late for my wife's presentation. Which leads me to return to the object of this meeting, and the reason for the brandy —I am waiting to toast your son's health and prospects."

"Ha! Are you not a little premature?" the Comtesse scoffed. "Perhaps when he has been breeched, then he is more likely to have prospects and a future, then you can make your toast. Do not waste your brandy on an infant!"

"I should agree with you," confessed the Duke, all arrogance aside. "Most noble infants are fortunate if they survive long enough to celebrate their fifth birthday. It is the way of the world. But it is not a view Mme la Duchesse subscribes to." He smiled softly, a hint of color ripening his thin close-shaven cheeks. "She sees the world differently. She believes that if an infant receives an inordinate amount of care and every attention from birth, he has the best chance of surviving—"

"Whether a child lives or is taken early is at God's mercy." She frowned. "I do not understand why you permit her such absurd notions about the world."

"I like her world. It is a—er—joyous place in which to live."

"Good God! Such an absurdity proves you do indeed have *la maladie de l'amour*. You deny my claim that you are my son's sire and yet you permit your wife to have dominion over his future? *Balivernes*! No! He is mine, to do with as I please—"

"It pleased you to abandon him to starve in the care of a wine-soaked nurse…?"

"That was not my doing! I had to return to my court duties. Cousin Philippe she offered to find suitable rustics to take on the care of him. And I—"

"If a blind man leads a blind man, both will fall into a pit," muttered the Duke, quoting the disciple Matthew. He gave a sympathetic huff. "I am sure *Tante Philippe*'s offer coincided with your lie that I was the infant's sire. No matter. She was a poor choice. She may have birthed five children but that was the sum of her exertions on their behalf. Her ignorance of the needs of infants matches yours—hardly your fault, given those attached to the court are woefully neglectful and uninterested in their progeny."

"And yet here we are—you and I—discussing that very thing!"

"Thankfully, not for very much longer," he quipped and stepped past her. "M'sieur le Marquis! M'sieur le Baron!" he announced loudly, with a sweeping bow of welcome. "Mme la Comtesse and I are all smiles to have you finally join us."

The Comtesse swirled about. Her eyes widened and her mouth fell open. Confronting her, and with all the fanfare of a circus performance, was the arrival of her estranged husband, and with him was that inveterate scandalmonger and her eldest brother, Maurice de Chesnay. She staggered back and collapsed onto one of the upholstered tabourets the Duke had thoughtfully placed there for just such an eventuality.

FIFTEEN

THOSE IN THE *Galerie de Glaces* thought they had seen it all when the English duke broke every protocol by sitting on a tabouret in the middle of the vast hall. And then they were treated to a delicious meeting between ex-lovers when the Comtesse Duras-Valfons joined him. In close conversation, their audience had to rely on the couple's every expression and gesture to gauge the mood. But as the Duke was predictably urbane and enigmatic, they had to look to her, and were gratified when she appeared on the verge of histrionics. But no one could have foreseen she would so far forget herself as to commit the cardinal transgression of sitting on a tabouret, a stool reserved—no exceptions—for Royalty and duchesses.

There was a collective gasp as everyone went into shock, and minds raced to the speculated outcome for the Comtesse when this break with rigid protocol, put in place by none other than the Sun King himself, came to the ears of the Marquis de Dreux-Brézé, *Grand maître des cérémonies de France*. Banishment to the provinces was not out of the question—at the very least she would be punished with an enforced leave of absence from her duties. For a courtier whose societal and familial survival hinged on being near *Sa Majesté*, banishment was tantamount to be sent to wandering a desert.

And just as the courtiers were mentally dining on the delectable banquet of the Comtesse receiving a *lettre de cachet* (all stares and slackened jaws fixed on her), the Duke stepped past his forsaken mistress to make a sweeping bow of welcome to newcomers to the deathly silent hall. This snapped heads around and to an astonishing sight. There was no doubt that the gluttony of scandal to follow would be ruminated on for months to come.

Trotting alongside a vinaigrette—the two-wheeled sedan chair pulled by a robust but red-faced liveried servant—was the Marquis de Chesnay, sweaty and breathing heavily from such unfamiliar exertion. The nobleman had never done anything more strenuous in his entire life. Yet here he was trotting at pace beside his brother-in-law's preferred mode of transportation when visiting the palace. Everyone was aware that the Jacobite Baron Thesiger was incapable of moving from room to room in any other way; he was grossly fat.

Their haste was because they were late for this prearranged rendezvous, and thus were in a panic. No one kept M'sieur le Duc d'Roxton waiting, not unless they had an exceptional excuse, such as bleeding out from a sword point jab. Only then might the Duke forgive the crime of unpunctuality.

Coming to a standstill before the Duke and Comtesse, the contingent of servants surrounding De Chesnay and the vinaigrette dispersed. A few came to attention behind the vehicle, while several of the more muscular servants went about separating master and vinaigrette. This required that they grab the Baron above the elbows, and with a heave-ho, yank him as forcefully as possible from his seat. When he was freed and swaying upright, another couple of servants put their shoulders into their master's back to ensure he did not topple, and once he was steady they retreated to catch their breath.

At any other time, the surprise arrival of these two noblemen would have been met with sniggers, but the audience was still reeling in shock from the Comtesse collapsing on the tabouret, so they remained paralyzed and mute. As for the Comtesse, all she could do to stop herself from vocalizing her fury at being tricked into the company of her craven husband—whom she had publicly ignored and privately belittled for years—was to bite down on her lower lip and dig the nails of her left hand into the palm of her right. She had no idea how Roxton had brought about this public reunion, but she was certain of one thing—the Duke was the puppet master, and they, his marionettes.

When Lord Vallentine and the captain of the *Gardes de la Porte* crossed to join the Duke, Roxton said to his best friend, "Be good enough to pour us all out a measure of brandy. There is to be a toast."

"Forgive our lateness, *mon cher ami*," De Chesnay heaved, still out of breath and partially bent over, hands on his splayed knees. He sidled crab-like up to the Duke and murmured, "There was a difficulty with the first vinaigrette. One of the wheels it cracked, and so another had to be found—"

"While he was in it?" the Duke interrupted, with a raise of an eyebrow and an eye on the Baron, who was preoccupied with tugging his waistcoat over his paunch. "No matter. You are both here now."

The Marquis was about to comment when he chanced to glance over at his sister. Seeing her as if for the first time, his face drained of color. "What-what—*Mon Dieu*," he blustered., "she is *seated*!"

"Yes," was the Duke's drawled reply. It held a note of satisfaction which lifted the corners of his mouth when he added, "But save outrage so we can get through this theatrical performance as swiftly as possible." He swirled about and with the smile still lingering offered his gloved hand to the Comtesse, "Madame, if you remain seated much longer your brother will not be the only one to think you have been made a duchesse. Do please join us in a toast."

Mechanically, the Comtesse rested her fingers in the Duke's palm and rose. "A toast?" she asked curiously, distracted by his touch. She looked at the others standing about the tabouret that had upon it the silver tray with a crystal decanter and glasses. It was only when Lord Vallentine offered her a brandy that she reluctantly removed her fingers from the Duke's to take it. "What is the occasion?"

"Why, the birth of M'sieur le Baron's son and heir," Roxton replied dispassionately. And as de Chesnay, Vallentine, and Thesiger also now held glasses, he raised his to the Baron, saying in a strong clear voice that was sure to carry across to his audience, "M'sieur le Baron, we congratulate you on the birth of your heir. May he have a long, healthy life."

"Hear! Hear!" announced Lord Vallentine, and threw back his brandy with relish.

"To my nephew!" added the Marquis De Chesnay and drained the entire contents of the small glass before sticking it out at His Lordship to have it refilled. "I am honored to not only be his uncle but his godfather."

"Thank you, M'sieur le Duc," the Baron Thesiger replied diffidently, cheeks rosy, and eyes averted from his wife. "Thank you all. His—my son—his arrival has been a long time coming—"

"And now that he has finally arrived," the Duke interrupted in a flat menacing tone, handing off his empty glass to Vallentine and turning an eye on the Baron, "you will leave your wife alone."

"I gave you my word, M'sieur le Duc."

"There, Thérèse!" said the Marquis, pursing his painted lips with satisfaction. "You have finally secured your wish. You are to be separated from your husband—"

"In exchange for my son, I no longer have to share his couch?" the Comtesse asked breathlessly.

"It is for the best," De Chesnay reassured her, misconstruing her concern. "You could not have owned him. This way, he gets a father, and you have your freedom. It is a most generous offer. M'sieur le Baron need not have acknowledged him—"

"Yes! Yes! Yes," the Comtesse interrupted dismissively, eyes bright. She turned to the Duke. "This is your doing?"

"I cannot take all the credit," Roxton confessed, understanding her mood better than her brother. With her, self-preservation was paramount. He knew the infant's welfare was the last thing on her mind. "It was Mme la Duchesse's wish for your son to have a future—"

"Oh, not about that!" she said dismissively. "Freeing me from my wifely obligations to that toad!"

"It will be a comfort to Mme la Duchesse to know separation from your son never aroused any—er—motherly instincts," drawled the Duke with amusement. "I doubt you are aware whether your son breathes or not. Rest assured, M'sieur le Baron," he added, turning to make his fellow Etonian a sweeping bow. "Your son is in excellent health and being cared for in the provinces by an experienced *nourrice*—"

"Another *wish* of your silly little wife, M'sieur le Duc?" the Comtesse scoffed with a trill of bitter laughter.

Roxton's smile was dazzling. "While she is delightfully petite, she is most definitely not silly."

"Come, Thérèse!" the Marquis announced throwing up his lace covered wrist in a dramatic gesture of impatience. "You owe M'sieur le Duc your gratitude for this most agreeable resolution, for you, and for your child—"

"No, Maurice," corrected the Duke. "I am interested in neither. If not for Mme la Duchesse, I would not have bestirred myself to get involved." He made the Comtesse and the gentlemen a short bow of farewell. "Excuse me. I am expected elsewhere."

"'Bout time!" Vallentine muttered with annoyance, falling in step behind his best friend as he turned and strolled the length of the Galerie des Glaces, the Captain of the *Gardes de la Porte* ushering forward the Duke's servants to remove tabourets, rug, and laden tray. "Antonia'll be wonderin' where we are, and never forgive us if we're late."

"We won't fail her," the Duke assured him in English. "She knew to hang back and slow her progress through the state apartments to Louis's council chamber. Not difficult, given the ancient aunts will be—er—shuffling along in burdensome court attire they have not worn in years. Not to mention the hordes trying to catch a glimpse of Antonia in hers—"

He paused and stopped, distracted by muffled sounds behind him that were becoming louder. They had arrived at the double doors leading out of the *Galerie de Glaces*, where stood two guards to attention. Beyond the doors were more Swiss, keeping the curious from entering the hall. Here the Duke turned to face back into the long room, Vallentine by his side. What confronted them startled His Lordship, though the Duke was not so surprised.

Scurrying up the hall in the sliding gait peculiar to the court, was a wall of courtiers stretching out across the width of the hall from mirrors to windows, the very noblemen and women who were sent into shock by the Duke's theater piece with his ex-mistress, her husband, and her brother. No sooner had the Duke sauntered away, than they picked their metaphorical jaws up off the floor, and rallied themselves, intent on following the Duke to his wife's presentation with their king.

Vallentine's immediate reaction was to presume they were hostile—after all, his best friend had just broken almost every rule of the court these sticklers lived to perform. So he was all for stepping forward and warning them directly he would brook no retaliation or insult towards his best friend, that they were to behave themselves at the presentation; he wasn't above calling any one of them out. He'd had enough of preening, pea-brained peacocks for one day, and the day just begun. But when he took a step forward, to shield the Duke, with this speech on the tip of his tongue, Roxton gently squeezed his arm.

"Allow me, my dear."

Vallentine's impassioned warning fragmented before he had uttered a word. He acquiesced, leaving the Duke to confront the crowd which had come to a silent standstill before him.

Scanning the powdered and rouged faces of these nobles in their drab mourning garments, Roxton remained defiant, jaw locked and eyes unblinking. He waited for one or more of their number to denounce him for his shocking breaches of court etiquette, to threaten a *lettre de cachet* at the very least. None of that bothered him. He had achieved his object, and Antonia would be happy with the outcome, and her happiness was all that mattered. Thus when no immediate rebukes were forthcoming, he lost patience. His only pressing concern was being on time for Antonia's presentation, so he brought this unwanted continuation of the theatrical moment to an abrupt end with a suitably grand gesture.

He made a low sweeping bow to this silent crowd, the cascade of fine black lace of one wrist brushing lightly along the polished parquetry. He did not expect a response, but no sooner had he straightened out of his bow than one of his noble audience, none other than the Duc de Bouillon, the *Grand Chambellan de France* stepped out from his fellows to return the gesture. Before de Bouillon had straightened, one of his peers followed suit, to also acknowledge M'sieur le Duc d'Roxton. And then another. And then a lady-in-waiting to the Queen pushed forward and dropped a curtsy. Not to be outdone, two more ladies did the same. And soon every noble was bowing or curtsying in unanimity with the English Duke.

Without another word or gesture, Roxton turned on a heel and left the hall of mirrors, Vallentine following on his skirts. The crowd surged forward, jostling one another to pass through the double doors in pursuit, just as eager to bear witness to Mme la Duchesse d'Roxton's presentation as the Comtesse de Roucy.

SIXTEEN

"THERE SHE IS!" Vallentine hissed with satisfaction, and so loudly that several present in the packed council chamber snapped their heads about to glare at him. But as he was deaf and blind to the affected nuances of the courtiers, he ignored the visual reprimand, adding in the same loud voice in English, "Makes me jittery bein' here. But she'll do you proud, I guarantee it!"

"Thank you, Lucian. Having your guarantee, I may now rest easy," Roxton quipped, raising his quizzing glass. He turned a magnified eye on his former valet, who had slipped away from Antonia and the Salvan women, to join him. "I presume your procession through the state rooms was without incident?"

"Yes, Your Grace," Martin assured him, replying in English. "It was slow progress through the lanes of tourists, but she was protected on all sides, and anyone who looked remotely unsavory was swiftly dealt with by your men." He dared to smile. "And may I presume your own venture was successful…?"

"Successful?" His Lordship snorted. "With a hall full of toad-yin' courtiers makin' their bow to Roxton? I'd say it was an absolute bloody triumph, damme!"

"Mme la Duchesse will be pleased."

"She will indeed, Martin," stated the Duke, a slight flush to his cheeks. "Now do let us give her our full attention."

ANTONIA WAS HALFWAY across the room, wedged between Roxton's ancient aunt *Tante Victoire*—her sponsor, and Estée Vallentine, who was directly behind her. Following up this procession were Michelle Haudry and several of the Salvan female relatives. The male Salvans were grouped just inside the door, talking quietly amongst themselves, while the rest of those present mingled and chatted and feigned disinterest, when in truth all eyes were upon the Comtesse de Roucy.

Louis was by the fireplace, imperturbable, yet unable to conceal his weariness at having to participate in this mundane but obligatory royal undertaking. Those being presented were inching forward in small sliding footsteps as they had been instructed, fighting nervousness and nausea, and praying not to make a mistake that would guarantee scorn and mimicry amongst their fellow courtiers.

A chamberlain "named" a gentleman or lady who then glided into the royal presence with their sponsor, to be acknowledged with an innocuous comment from their monarch, to which they answered with a similarly bland response. And if it were a lady being presented, she then departed, making three curtsies as she walked backwards out of the royal presence. If all went well and there were no slip-ups or stumbles in word or deed, the courtier was now "known" to *Sa Majesté*, and secured the enviable privilege of supping with Louis and his favorites in his private dining room, if Louis felt so inclined to offer the invitation. Retreating from the royal presence brought instant relief and all persons involved in that noble's presentation could breathe easy, duty done.

When the Comtesse de Roucy was named, a hush went round

the room; heads turned to level their gaze upon Antonia. Those who were unaware of her French title looked about at their fellows in slight confusion. But not wanting to appear ignorant, they masked their surprise with indifference.

Taking a deep breath and showing no emotion, Antonia went forward, her ladies-in-waiting keeping a respectful distance as she made her deep curtsy before the King. Everyone from the King to the lowliest courtier, was aware that this presentation held a special significance. Antonia might be acknowledged as a comtesse in her own right, but as the wife of M'sieur le Duc de Roxton, any social solecism on her part would reflect keenly upon him, and his friend-ship with Louis.

When Antonia dipped into her low curtsy—performing the action with a natural elegance no one could fault—there came a collective sigh of relief from most, and a sniff of disappointment from a few that the Comtesse de Roucy was as elegant as she was beautiful.

All eyes transferred to the Duke to catch his response to his wife's curtsy. His Lordship said it best, when he nudged Martin and leaned into him to whisper, "Look at him! He's as proud as punch with her, ain't he? And before you say it! I know! So he should be! And we can thank ourselves for the part we played in her success, can't we, eh?"

"We can, my lord," Martin agreed, smiling gaze upon Antonia as she rose up out of her curtsy, adding with tongue firmly in cheek, "Without our expert tutelage, who knows how this may have played out."

"Precisely!"

Martin was about to comment further when he was startled into losing his train of thought. He was not the only one to inhale sharply in surprise. He heard Vallentine do the same, and all because the King took it upon himself to deviate from what was customary.

"You are indeed a fairy, Mme la Comtesse," commented Louis of France.

As she straightened out of her curtsy, Antonia's gaze flickered up at the King with surprise. His handsome features might remain static, but she caught the glint of humor in his blue eyes. She dimpled.

"And you are every inch a King, Your Majesty," she said evenly. "That pleases us both—that we are not disappointed in the other, yes?"

No one was close enough to hear this exchange, but everyone saw the King's reaction to her quip. He blushed, blinked, and shot a hand up to his mouth—Martin was very sure—to stifle a laugh.

However, the King's chamberlain and aides were so bewildered by their royal master's behavior and this deviation from protocol that they had no idea what to do next. By the time they came out of their stupor, Antonia was backing out of the royal presence with the requisite three curtsies, and the King had regained his composure. But he stopped his chamberlain before he could name the next noble to come forward and finding who he was looking for on the edge of the crowd he made a slight gesture for Roxton to join him.

As the Duke and Duchess passed each other on the deep carpet, he winked at her, and she smiled up at him. And when Louis greeted Roxton with an easy-going familiarity he rarely displayed, and then only with a true intimate, it was apparent that whatever the exchange between His Majesty and the Duke's wife, Louis approved. The ducal couple had joined that rare breed of courtier—favored by Louis, and thus could do no wrong in his eyes, which meant they were the envy of all. It remained to see how they would be received by Louis's new *maîtresse-en-titre*—Madame de Pompadour. The Court did not have long to wait.

As Roxton joined Louis by the fireplace, Antonia turned away, having completed the last curtsy without incident. Her duty done and presentation to the King over with, she was eager to join her ladies-in-waiting, sister-in-law, and Salvan relatives assembled on the other side of the crowded council chamber. Vallentine and Martin Ellicott were there, too. All were looking as relieved as she felt, ready to accompany her back across the *Salon de l'Oeil-de-Boeuf* to the Queen's room, where she would be presented to Her Majesty.

But as Antonia went to join them, several ladies stood in her way. Thinking she had accidently crossed into their path, she politely excused herself and moved aside. But they moved with her, and then one of their number came straight up to her, forcing Antonia to take a step back so she could look up to see who it was. Recognizing the woman, her instinct was to recoil but she did not, steeling herself for what was to come. Blocking her path with two female friends at her back, and standing between her and her family and in full view of Louis and Roxton, was the beautiful and statuesque Comtesse Duras-Valfons.

SEVENTEEN

"YOU HAVE SOMETHING to say to me, Madame?" Antonia asked the Comtesse Duras-Valfons quietly but firmly.

"La! How direct you are! No polite conversation whatsoever. *He* probably finds that delightful. *I* think you naïve and crude."

"What you think of me is unimportant."

"Not a truer word spoken!" the Comtesse replied with a wide smile. "But I could not pass up the opportunity of telling you how chivalrous M'sieur le Duc your husband was to me in the hall of mirrors in front of everyone who matters," she gloated. "He has freed me from my husband, which just shows how much he still cares for me—"

"No, Madame," Antonia stated without rancor. "M'sieur le Duc would not have exerted himself on your behalf had I not asked it of him. And that was so your son he would have a father."

The Comtesse stiffened but her smile remained fixed. She managed to put a purr in her tone. "My son has a father—M'sieur le Duc d'Roxton."

If she hoped to intimidate Antonia by this boast, she was to be disappointed. Antonia sighed her annoyance and was unsurprisingly candid.

"You forget you are speaking to a female who is also a mother. Courtiers may be ignorant about infants, regardless if they are mothers, but me I spend every day with my son. And so I know the difference between an infant who is a few weeks in this world and one who is many months old. Your son cannot be the son of M'sieur le Duc, however much you wish it. You have lied to everyone, which is shocking and unforgiveable. But your son is still an infant, and so there is still time for him to have an unblemished future. So I tell you, Madame—"

"T-*tell* me?" blustered the Comtesse.

"—for the sake of your son, put aside your bitterness—"

"Bitterness? *Mon Dieu.*"

"—at no longer being M'sieur le Duc's mistress—"

"As if I care for—"

"You care, Madame, or you would not be spinning fantasies."

"You—you—presumptuous *morveux*," Duras-Valfons spat out, shaken.

She had never been spoken to so bluntly, and by a girl who had been at court for all of half a day. It sent her into a white-hot rage, which manifested itself in the strangest of titters. She tried to control her fury, acutely aware of where she was and that the King, who was notoriously shy, would not appreciate her drawing attention to herself which would disrupt his daily routine. Forcing down her seething resentment, she leaned into Antonia with a wide smile, itching to slap her face. Instead she hoped to goad her into causing herself embarrassment. Her smile twisted and she put up her chin, a sidelong glance across to the fireplace.

"I'll wager you are ignorant as to the true nature of the nobleman you married. Everyone says he fell under the spell of your—" She paused, gaze dropping to run an exaggerated sweep over Antonia's sizeable breasts. "—*beauty*. But now having met you, it is apparent he wanted a wife who was as feeble-minded as she was young—"

"Think of me what you will, Madame. You do not know me. But you are wrong if you think I do not know everything there is to know about M'sieur le Duc's past."

"Then it will be no surprise to you that he is, and always will be —*an unfaithful lascivious goat*—"

"Now it is you who are being crude," Antonia admonished, cheeks aflame under the heavy application of rouge. She cocked her head. "Perhaps I am stupid because I do not understand at all your great resentment of him. What is his crime? Was not M'sieur le Duc most generous to you while you were his mistress? Did he not satisfy your pleasure—?"

"*What*? I won't—you can't—" the Comtesse blustered, losing her train of thought at having her vitriol met with unapologetic forthrightness.

"It is true I am young and inexperienced, but me I do know a little about the court and its ways, having lived here for a time with my grandfather. It would suit you if I were stupid, but me I am not. It would also help you recover the great loss of your most experienced lover, if M'sieur le Duc had married me for any reason but the one that makes you most uncomfortable—he fell in love with me." Antonia dimpled, adding simply, "I have my husband's love and devotion, as he has mine. That is all that truly matters to either of us."

"Now who is spinning fantasies!" the Comtesse scoffed. But the deep crimson on her throat disproved her indifference. She shrugged her dismissal, smile firmly back in place, thinking she held the trump card when she said, "You can believe fairytales about your husband—what do I care? What you will never rid yourself of is my son, tangible proof of Roxton's libidinous nature—"

"Madame, I beg you to not be so cruel as to use your son, an innocent, as a weapon of revenge," Antonia countered, looking up at the Comtesse with green eyes damp with sadness. "If you choose to corrupt him with lies and false expectation—that M'sieur le Duc d'Roxton is his father—his life it will be made miserable. He does not deserve that—no infant does, whatever the circumstances of his birth. Robert has his whole life ahead of him, and Baron Thesiger has owned him. Regardless of how unhappy you are in your marriage, are you not thankful your son has been given a secure future? As his mother, is that not what you wish for him most of all?"

The Comtesse was rendered speechless by Antonia's emotional candor. She could not quite believe the Duke's wife was championing an infant who was not her blood relation and whom half the courtiers present believed was the Duke's bastard son. It took the Comtesse several seconds to collect her thoughts, forcing a smile and pretending to be amused.

She glanced over at the fireplace. The King and Roxton continued in easy conversation, and she being statuesque, and Roxton being a good head taller than the rest of the assembled courtiers, she caught him looking past the King's shoulder in her direction. He had done so several times during her exchange with his wife. It gave her the confidence to delude herself that perhaps the King had sought him out to ask his advice on her suitability as the next royal mistress. After all, the First Gentleman of the Bedchamber, the Duc de Richelieu, had confided he had put her forward as his replacement for Mme de Pompadour, whom he loathed with every fiber of his being as unworthy of holding the title of King's chief mistress. He was intent on ousting the commoner as soon as possible.

Eager to make herself available should the King request her to join him and the Duke, she was impatient to terminate her conversation with Antonia—a conversation she had initiated, yet one where the Duchess was making her increasingly uncomfortable, and thus irritable.

"My son is not your concern," the Comtesse replied impatiently, distracted gaze still on the King. "Nor do I have the slightest interest in your opinion on how he should be raised. You, on the other hand, would do well to take my advice and stop suckling your son. It is vulgar for one of noble blood to function as a cow, and best left to feeble-minded peasants—"

"*Eh bien*," Antonia sighed, exasperated. "I have never questioned or insulted you about what it is you do with your body or with whom, so do not be so discourteous as to question what it is I do with mine! And now, me I have wasted enough time trying to make you see reason, so, Madame, you will excuse me. I am late to Her Majesty—"

"Do you know why His Majesty is conferring with M'sieur le Duc?" the Comtesse interrupted as if Antonia had not spoken, and with a superior smile and jerk of her powdered coiffure in the direction of the King. "Of course you do not! Let me tell you. I have every expectation of being installed as His Majesty's next mistress. And when I am, one of my first decrees will be to sweep the palace free of barnyard animals." She tittered at her own lame humor, and to ensure Antonia understood, added unnecessarily, "You the cow and your husband the goat will no longer be welcome. So yes, I agree with you that you have wasted your time today being presented."

"Now who is feeble-brained," Antonia muttered, before saying audibly, and with fervor, "Madame, you are bound for disappointment. His Majesty is in love with Madame la Marquise de Pompadour, and she with him. They are so in love that they *see* only each other. Please believe me when I tell you I know how that is."

The Comtesse giggled like a girl, incredulous. "*Love? See?* La! You are truly artless! That *trollop* will be gone before the new year. Mark my words!"

"I assure you, Mme la Comtesse, I am not going anywhere," stated a sweet firm voice. It was the Marquise de Pompadour. "Oh, unless it is in the company of His Majesty. Mark those words. And now you are excused, Madame. Her Majesty must be wondering why you are not at your duties. Ah! Mme la Comtesse de Roucy!" she exclaimed in the same breath, a dazzling smile at Antonia. "What a delight to finally make your acquaintance. M'sieur le Duc your husband has told me so much about you…"

THE TWO WOMEN greeted one another with the obligatory polite curtsy then a light kiss near each cheek, before Madame de Pompadour suggested they move off to an alcove to become better acquainted, eager not to draw attention away from the King. Several courtiers had already turned from the royal presence, and more would follow once they were aware to whom she was speaking. But Antonia made a gesture for the Marquise to await her pleasure for one moment, causing the breath to catch in the throats of the Marquise's ladies-in-waiting and those courtiers in closest proximity.

But the Marquise showed no annoyance and acquiesced by taking a step away, as did her ladies-in-waiting and those standing closest to them. It gave Antonia the space to turn half-circle in her wide panniers to the direction of the King and her husband. As providence would have it, the little groups of courtiers gathered closest to their monarch had dispersed, allowing Antonia, who was the shortest in the room even in her two-inch heels, a clear line of sight to the fireplace.

She did not even glance at Louis, so intent was she on reassuring the Duke, knowing he was anxious on her behalf from the moment the Comtesse Duras-Valfons waylaid her. To this end, she lightly placed a hand to the front of her beaded bodice—at the low neckline where the busk he had gifted her was sheathed and nestled between her breasts—and smiled into his eyes, dark eyes that locked onto hers with an intensity that proved her assumption about his apprehension.

Though he openly exhibited a courtly ease of manner, her intimate gesture instantly eased the tension in his limbs, and he released his fingers from the fist in his pocket. He returned her private smile with one of his own, one that he reserved for her alone, expressed with his eyes and the barest lift of the corners of his mouth. It was all that was required to convey meaning.

The Duke's equilibrium restored, he resumed giving Louis all his attention, while Antonia completed her circle to again join Madame de Pompadour. The intimate exchange between the couple lasted nothing more than a few moments. And while the entire room was watching on, none would have caught the subtle exchange, except perhaps Martin Ellicott, who was well-placed to witness it, standing as he was at the Marquise's shoulder with Michelle Haudry by his side.

"M'sieur le Duc he says it is rare to come across a female whose great beauty is matched by the intelligence in her eyes," Antonia said conversationally to the Marquise with a frankness that was typical of her, "but that you are such a one, Madame."

"M'sieur le Duc is too kind—"

"Oh no, Madame. He would not say it if he did not believe it to be true. I believed him when he told me but now that you and I we have finally met I agree with him." She dimpled and her green eyes sparkled. "There is a difference, yes?"

The Marquise gave an involuntary laugh, instantly captivated by this petite, lively beauty whose openness was a refreshing change from the scheming mendacity of the courtiers who surrounded the King, and the undercurrent of hostility that swirled about her in her position as *maîtresse-en-titre*. She decided there and then she and Antonia would be fast friends. Heedful that her every word was scrutinized, she was measured in her response.

"As much as I am eager for us to become better acquainted, I know Her Majesty is waiting to meet you. We will have the opportunity to know one another better at His Majesty's supper table, and perhaps a little before that in my apartment, if you would care to join me for coffee?"

"I would like that very much, Madame," Antonia replied with genuine warmth. "M'sieur le Duc he very much enjoys *Sa Majesté's* suppers, so I cannot wait to join him. Though it is not usual for wives to accompany their husbands, so I am doubly honored *Sa Majesté* has made an exception."

"It is not usual, that is true. But," the Marquise added, leaning into Antonia, to say at her ear so she would not be overheard, "M'sieur le Duc your husband he apologized to the King—in the politest way possible of course—that regrettably he would be unable to attend future suppers if you were not with him."

Far from being surprised, Antonia sighed resignedly. "It is true, Madame. We do not like to be apart, for any reason." She frowned and said in all seriousness, "I do not know how we managed before we met, or how we would manage again without each other. It is as if we have always been together. It is how we both feel. I have always believed in fate."

"Fate?" Madame de Pompadour repeated with a smile, a glance across to the fireplace at the King. "Oh yes! I am a great believer in fate. And I cannot wait to continue our conversation, but for now we must part, as your family they are waiting to take you to Her Majesty—"

"*Oh là là*! I am running on at the mouth! Forgive me. Ah! And here are Martin and Mme Haudry come to fetch me," she announced with a smile, noticing Martin and Michelle Haudry for the first time, hovering behind the Marquise. And with them were two of the female Salvan cousins acting as her ladies-in-waiting. "Before I depart, allow me to introduce you…"

"*Mon Dieu*! I cannot believe that even she would do something so outrageous," Estée fumed. "Introducing the King's *maîtresse-en-titre* to Roxton's valet. *Incroyable*. The shame of it!"

"*Former* valet, lovedy," Vallentine corrected. "Besides, no one here knows Ellicott from a copper kettle, so where's the shame? And as only Mme la Duchesse could get away with introducin' a copper kettle to la Pompadour, where's the harm?"

"I agree with you, Vallentine," stuck in *Tante Victoire*, making motions to leave, a nod to the Salvan clan to fall-in to depart with her. "She is sunshine to Roxton's nightfall. As for la Pompadour she derives a false satisfaction from her newly acquired status that if she were introduced to the chimneysweep, it would be a high honor for *him*! I said it before—malodorous lot, the bourgeoisie. Now do move your feet! Philippe is waiting—"

"Surely you mean Her Majesty, *Tante*?" Estée corrected.

The old lady snorted her contempt. "Don't be foolish, Niece! The Queen is pious and forgiving, and indescribably dull. Philippe is none of those things. And when you are on the wrong side of my sister, she is terrifyingly vindictive. Nothing and no one frightens her, not even her son, and he is a General! Ah! Except of course my nephew your brother. Which is why, if I were not sponsoring his wife, I would have abandoned her for Philippe and been in the Queen's apartment half an hour ago."

His Lordship misread her observation completely and flared up. "Hey! Mme la Duchesse doesn't possess an ounce of vindictiveness in her pinky, and she certainly ain't frightenin'—"

"Lucian!" His wife sighed her exasperation. "Not Antonia. *Roxton*." She gave a little shudder. "I am glad I am his sister. And you should be thankful you are his brother-in-law. I hate to think what he would be like if we were on his wrong side and *not* related to him. He is frightening enough as it is!"

"Touché!" agreed Vallentine with a sigh.

Yet, His Lordship was to discover, to his surprise and discomfort, just how redoubtable his best friend could be, upon the Duke and Duchess's return to the villa after supper with Louis, King of France.

NINETEEN

T HE CLOCK in the library chimed the half-hour past one o'clock in the morning as two carriages pulled up in procession under the villa's *porte-cochère*. The Duke and Duchess alighted from the first of these to be welcomed into the warmth and light of the vestibule by the butler and several sleepy-eyed footmen. The second carriage followed the first on through to the inner courtyard where it was met under torchlight by several of the household, to help offload the clothing trunks and paraphernalia their masters had required for their visit to the palace.

And while their exhausted and sleepy personal servants could not wait to tumble out of this second carriage and into their beds after a day that had begun at first light the day before, the ducal couple was wide-awake and animated. Divested of velvet cloaks, fur muffs, and kid gloves, Antonia waited while the Duke had his sword and sash removed and taken away, then fell into his arms. She looked up at him feigning apology.

"Gabrielle I have sent to bed, so, M'sieur le Duc, I am sorry, but I will need your assistance to undress."

He chuckled. "I can see how disappointed you are to have me as your attendant."

"I assure you I am all devastation to put you to the trouble."

"And why is that, *ma vie*, when I am expert in divesting you of your garments…"

"You are, but I do not wish to ruin your ensemble." She smiled sweetly. "I am very sure there is enough flour spilled down my bodice from playing at bullet pudding to cover us both!"

"Thank you for the warning." With a crooked finger under her chin, he lowered his mouth to hover as close to hers as was possible without kissing her. "Then perhaps it would be best if I undress first before offering you my assistance."

Unable to resist, she kissed him. "Oh, I like this idea much better! But I think I should help you before you help me."

He seemed to give the notion some thought as he straightened, then shook his head.

"No, *ma chérie*."

"No? But why? I—"

"It would be a torment."

"Oh? Because you think me incapable of undressing you?" she enquired, pretending offense.

"Because, *petite malheureuse*, you know very well *I* am incapable of resisting *you*. Two buttons unfastened, perhaps three, of my waistcoat and I would be completely undone. I could not get out of these clothes quick enough, and this waistcoat would be ruined."

She put her hands flat to the front of the black silk beaded waistcoat and looked up at him from under lashes. "I will be very careful and promise to take my time—"

He gave a huff of laughter. "*Mon Dieu* you *do* wish to torture me!"

"—so your waistcoat it is not ruined."

"Thank you for your consideration, but—"

"I am considerate am I not?" she replied buoyantly, fiddling with a silk-covered button of his waistcoat. "Shall we begin?"

"Here?" He raised an eyebrow, and when she continued to unfasten the button, added with a glance toward the library, "Or in there?"

"There," she agreed, and lead him across the black-and-white marble tiles to the library where two blank-faced footmen opened the doors, waited for them to pass through, then closed them without a blink at their noble masters. "Behind closed doors is best because Estée she says as your duchess, I need to exhibit more decorum and restraint—"

"God forbid!" the Duke drawled.

Antonia giggled and threw her arms about his neck, "That is what I think too!" She pressed herself against him. "I confess I did not want to wait until we were in our bedchamber. Since first seeing you this morning dressed all in your black, I have wanted to strip you out of it!"

"My poor darling," he murmured without sympathy, and scooping her up, carried her across the darkened room towards the fireplace. "That is indeed a torment which I will take great pleasure in relieving—"

"There you both are!" announced a friendly voice. It was Lord Vallentine. He had been sprawled out on the sofa, dozing on and off, but at the sound of voices, sat bolt upright. His nightcap was askew, and his silk banyan rumpled. He yawned. "Excellent timin'. Supper's on its way. And I don't mind tellin' you I'm famished. We almost gave up on you gettin' home before the cock crows!"

NOT A MINUTE after His Lordship's pronouncement, a contingent of footmen arrived with the tea trolley and silver trays laden with sliced meats, fruits in season, and an assortment of pies and pastries. And as they set about arranging the silver and porcelain on the low table between the fireplace and the sofa and wingchairs, the Duke and Duchess had time to restore their equilibrium, the flush of desire on their cheeks masked in the low light.

If Vallentine noticed anything amiss, he did not comment. And as he was committed to satisfying his hunger, he vacated the sofa and concentrated on filling his plate. The couple joined him, though both declined the repast and chose only to have a dish of coffee. On this, His Lordship made an observation.

"I'm guessin' you both had enough to eat at Louis's table," he said before sitting in the wingchair opposite them and chomping into a large slice of pheasant pie. He had barely swallowed the first mouthful when he stabbed several slices of ham with his silver fork adding, "No sooner had I tasted a drop of your chef's cream-of-celery soup when Estée went green and took to her bed—"

"She is unwell?" asked the Duke, silver spoon hovering over his coffee dish.

"And the baby—?" Antonia muttered, the breath caught in her throat.

Vallentine swallowed, shaking his head vigorously. "No! No! No need to panic! Both are well. Her physician prescribed a tonic and bed rest. It is his considered opinion—though I'd already told her —that an entire day at Court on her feet was too much for her, in her delicate condition. I stayed until she fell asleep." He made a sound in his throat, but thought better of saying anything further and went back to concentrating on his plate.

"I imagine it required all your considerable skills to bring her down from a high passion," said the Duke without sympathy, sipping his coffee. "By which time you had lost your appetite."

Vallentine glanced across at his best friend. "Aye. Somethin' like that. But in her defense, dealin' with the likes of those Salvan cousins, particularly your waspish aunts, is exhaustin', and enough to make me want to take to my bed and stay under the covers!"

"Then it will please you to know that after you play attendant at Montbelliard's wedding, there is only one other—er—matter where your assistance is required, and once that is dealt with, you have my best wishes to avoid the Salvans ever after, like the contagion they are."

"I'll take you up on that offer! What matter?" Vallentine added, intrigued. "Whatever it is, you have my assistance, no questions asked."

"It can wait. Save what little strength you have for the wedding ceremony. Today we all rest."

"I intend to spend the entire day sleeping, reading, and in my bath," Antonia announced. She looked sideways at the Duke, saying sweetly, "You are welcome to join me, Monseigneur."

"I would have been bitterly disappointed had I not received an invitation, *mignonne*."

Antonia chuckled and kissed the back of the Duke's hand. "That makes me happy!"

"Though perhaps our son will protest if you do not extend your invitation to him…?"

"Do not worry, I will make certain the *nourrices* they suckle him before bringing him to our apartment. He Julian can join *sa mère et son père* this time after our bath, but not before it, so he does not end up in it."

"Very wise," commented the Duke, suppressing a smile.

His Lordship felt an eavesdropper on such intimate conversation, and choked on pastry crumbs, yet managed to blurt out, in an attempt to change the subject, "Hey! You're not wearing your court gown!"

"Your observational skills are second to none, Lucian," drawled the Duke, setting his coffee dish on its saucer.

"Those ridiculous panniers were only needed for my presentation," Antonia explained. "And so after I made my curtsy to Her Majesty, I replaced my court attire for something more suitable for the King's supper. I did this in the apartment belonging to the Duc du Touraine, which Monseigneur he often used for his dalliances when his cousin he was away with the army. And as M'sieur le General Duc is almost always with the army, those rooms they remain unoccupied." She smiled at the Duke. "Our trunks and servants had a place to linger while we were at the supper with the King. Which was most convenient for us, was it not, Monseigneur?"

"Ah! So that's why you had a procession of carriages to the palace," Vallentine commented. "No need to return home for a change of clothing! Clever."

Antonia was about to relate to Vallentine an amusing incident which had occurred at the supper with Louis of France, but was diverted when the Duke's distracted gaze lingered on the wingchair opposite. Martin Ellicott occupied that chair, sitting with his fists on his knees, eyes closed. It was not this that surprised her, as she had seen Martin almost the moment Vallentine made his presence known in the library. It was the fact that the Duke seemed unaware that Martin was not ignoring them but was indeed asleep.

"Monseigneur, you did not know that he Martin can sleep in that way?" she asked curiously.

"I did not."

"Astonished me too," stuck in Vallentine, scraping morsels of chicken onto his plate, and taking up his silver fork. "Said he learned the trick years ago from a former soldier turned manservant he met when we were guests at the *castello* of the Marchesi Del Monte—"

Roxton was genuinely taken aback. "That was over ten years ago."

"Dare say it was," replied His Lordship matter-of-factly. "Your memory is far superior to mine. I can't remember what I ate yesterday!" And as he went about making himself a dish of coffee, it was left to Antonia to provide further explanation, which was a revelation to the Duke.

"Martin he confided that being able to rest anywhere and at any time, and in any position was how he managed sufficient sleep to carry out his duties. In those first years as your valet,

Monseigneur, when you and Vallentine were on the Grand Tour enjoying yourselves, he said he had to make many adjustments."

"He did indeed," the Duke quipped.

"I trust he didn't divulge anythin' about those years to you, chit?" Vallentine asked darkly.

"Martin would never break M'sieur le Duc's confidence," Antonia replied, affronted. "He only told me about his sleeping habits when I questioned him. I learned of his trick when M'sieur le Duc sent me away, and Martin he escorted me to England to my *grand-mère*. I could not sleep at all on the journey, and he could sleep at any time."

"How do you wake him out of this—er—trick?" enquired the Duke.

"Didn't tell me," confessed His Lordship. "He'll be mortified to be sleepin' in your presence, if I've learnt anythin' of the man!"

"I will do it," Antonia announced, and hopped off the sofa.

She went over to Martin, and with her back to the Duke and Vallentine she woke him with the simple technique he had shown her. He had confided in her only after she promised never to reveal the secret to anyone else. He woke almost instantly and blinked up at her. When she smiled at him, he suddenly realized where he was and who had woken him from a deep sleep. Looking past her, he saw Lord Vallentine sprawled out in the other wingchair, and on the sofa sipping coffee was the Duke with his steady gaze upon him.

"Mme la Duchesse! M'sieur le Duc!" he blurted out and attempted to scramble out of the chair. "Forgive me—I—"

"It is unnecessary," Antonia told him, pressing a hand to his shoulder to keep him still. "You are among friends, and Monseigneur and I, we are late home." She smiled. "But we are pleased you waited up for us."

When she glanced over her shoulder, then back at him with a glint in her lovely eyes, a look he had come to know well, Martin relaxed and returned her smile, wondering what she was about to say next. He was not disappointed.

"There is a supper—oh! what is left of it, because Vallentine he has eaten enough to fill the stomach of an elephant—"

"Steady on!" whined His Lordship, taking the bait as always. "You'd be as famished as an elephant, too, if you'd not eaten a crumb since breakfast. I'll wager Ellicott is just as ravenous."

"I am certain he must be," agreed the Duke. "But unlike you, Lucian, Martin has not only learned the art of falling asleep at will, but I suspect has trained his stomach over the years to only require sustenance when he was certain I was otherwise—er—occupied, or had retired for the night and was no longer in need of his services." He stared straight at his former valet and stated without a hint of sarcasm, "Your overriding desire was not to inconvenience me."

"Yes, Your Grace," Martin confessed awkwardly. He looked to the others and then back at the Duke. "But always of my own voli-tion," he added earnestly, "not out of servitude, and because I am by nature a creature of discipline and-and of orderliness."

"Of that I am assured, and exceedingly grateful, and a little bit in awe," stated the Duke, in a tone that did not invite argument.

"Martin he is full of surprises, is he not, Monseigneur?" Antonia observed with a smile and eased the tension in the room by adding cheekily, "Unlike Vallentine who has none."

"Hey! Now that's unfair! I have m'secrets!"

"How can I know that," Antonia argued placidly, "when they are secret? Name one for me to believe you."

His Lordship waggled a finger at her. "I'll not fall into that trap! If I did, then it would no longer be a secret, now would it?"

Antonia turned to the Duke. "Does Vallentine have any secrets, Monseigneur?"

"Why ask him? If I have a secret, it's mine—"

"But M'sieur le Duc he knows everything, so if you do, he will know it."

"Ha! So you think!"

"I do. And he does."

Vallentine chewed his lower lip in thought, then sat up straight and snapped his fingers, as if he had suddenly remembered something vitally important. "Aha! I've got one! And I don't have to blurt it out to prove it to you because it's a secret we both share."

Without changing her expression, Antonia said calmly, "You are mistaken, M'sieur. Think again."

TWENTY

As luck would have it (although Antonia was sure it was by design), the Duke took that moment to turn away to hand off his coffee dish and saucer to a hovering footman, affording Antonia the opportunity to glower at His Lordship, green eyes wide, conveying to him without speech that he had made a glaring error of judgment with his declaration.

She knew very well that the secret he was alluding to was the Comte de Salvan's pleading letter sent to her via her grandmother, which she had subsequently put to the flame out in the garden, after sharing it with Lord Vallentine and making him promise not to tell the Duke of its existence.

It bothered her that she had withheld the letter from the Duke, but not so much as to keep her awake at night, because telling him would trigger a series of events, not least of which would be the Duke making good on his threat and honoring his word to kill Salvan. She did not want him to travel into the provinces to duel with the Comte, who was not worth the Duke's time or energy. More importantly, what if something were to befall him upon the journey, or he made a tactical error in his swordsmanship and was injured, or worse, killed! Ignoring Salvan and keeping the letter to herself was the lesser of two evils, and Vallentine had agreed with her, which gave her the confidence to continue to keep the secret between them and from the Duke.

"Come to think on it, you're right, Mme la Duchesse," Vallentine announced, as if thinking it over, adding with a sigh, feigning resignation. "Blame the lateness of the hour. Lack of sleep has befuddled m'brain, and for that I apologize."

"Are you apologizing to Mme la Duchesse for letting the—er—cat out of the bag," the Duke enquired of his best friend, turning back to face the fireplace, and meeting His Lordship's gaze without a blink. "Or because you genuinely do not have any secrets to keep?"

"I don't have any cats in any bags, if that's what you're askin'."

"I am relieved to hear it. But, no, it was not what I was asking, was it?"

"It wasn't?

"No."

"Then what were you askin'?"

"If you are keeping any secrets."

"I just said I wasn't."

"No. You said you had no cats in any bags."

Vallentine pulled a face and shrugged. But his palms had begun to sweat and mentally he was quaking. "Same difference."

The Duke paused, stare leveled at his best friend. Finally he said, "If you suddenly remember that you do have a secret worth—er—sharing, now would be the perfect opportunity to confess all."

Vallentine squirmed on the seat cushion then sat forward to place his coffee dish on the low table. He did not once allow his gaze to flit to the Duchess, but looked across at the Duke with a hangdog expression, mouth parting to make comment. To his great relief he was saved by a timely interruption. It caused him to slump and run a hand down his face.

"I do not know why you think Lucian he could keep a secret

from you, Roxton," Estée announced with a huff of incredulity, coming out of the shadows to join the family by the fireplace. "If he cannot keep a secret from me his wife, he certainly cannot keep one from my brother!"

"Hey, lovedy! What are you doin' out of bed at this hour?" Vallentine exclaimed with an unconscious sigh of relief, quick to jump up and offer an arm to his wife.

Estée had arrived at the library with two of her women following close behind, one carrying a porcelain bowl, the other with smelling salts and a handkerchief. Disheveled from a restless sleep, she wore a nightcap, thick, long, black plait over her shoulder tied off with a fat silk ribbon, and over her nightgown was buttoned a flowered silk robe which did little to hide her growing belly.

"Do you think your son will allow me to sleep through the night?" she grumbled, and let His Lordship ease her into the wingchair. Seeing the remnants of supper spread across the coffee table, she pressed a lace-bordered handkerchief to her nose and mouth before saying on a heaving breath, "Please to have this food removed at once before I turn green!"

Lord Vallentine hesitated, knowing Martin Ellicott had yet to taste any of the dishes, but Martin politely set aside his clean plate, and instead crossed to the tea trolley to pour himself a dish of coffee. The Duke signaled for the low table to be cleared and then dismissed the footmen.

Madame's arrival and the ensuing servant activity provided Antonia with the opportunity to regain her composure, unsettled that Vallentine was about to blurt out a confession about Salvan's letter. She rejoined the Duke on the sofa, kicking off her mules and tucking her stockinged feet up under her petticoats. And when he set a tapestry cushion at his side, inviting her to snuggle in, she eagerly took him up on his offer. Yet, if she was not mistaken, behind the smile that accompanied his invitation there was a hint of disappointment. It made her feel wretched, and certain he did indeed know Salvan had written to her. Why had she thought for even a moment that he would not? She was not only abject, but knew herself for a little fool. But the Duke's next comment broke her out of her reflective self-castigation and pushed Salvan's letter to the back of her mind, at least for a little while.

"I presume there is a particular reason you are grinning at us, Lucian?" Roxton asked.

His Lordship was unable to wipe away his silly sentimental smile.

"If anyone had said to me ten years ago—no! two!—we'd be cozy by the fire, both of us married, both of us with sons—well, you with a son and heir, and me, God-willing, soon to have one, too—I'd have declared 'em fit for Bedlam! But here we are!"

"Perhaps it is me who is fit for this Bedlam," Estée complained, "to get out of a warm bed and come down here at this hour."

"Why did you, lovely? If our son is keepin' you awake, better to be pacin' the rug in our room, where it's warm, than risk the stairs."

"If Roxton had bedchambers situated on the ground floor like all Frenchmen, I would not have needed to use the stairs."

"Pardon, Madame," Antonia countered. "But if our bedchambers they were here and not up there, then the library it would be upstairs and you would have had to come up not down, and so the stairs they are still required, yes?"

"Can't argue with that!" announced Vallentine with a laugh.

Estée threw up her hands in annoyance. "I do not want to argue at all. Or talk about bedchambers or libraries or-or *stairs*. And if I could have waited until morning, I would have stayed in my room. But I knew that come breakfast time, there was no guarantee either of you would be there." Her reproach swept from Antonia to the Duke and back again. "You have this habit, at the oddest of times—I cannot put a finger on a pattern or circumstance —of disappearing into your apartment without warning, and we— your own family—are not permitted to see either of you for days! It is most inconvenient."

"It must be," the Duke replied without sympathy. "But as we do not intend to alter our habit, you will have to bear it as best you can."

"It is true, *ma très chère belle-sœur*. We like keeping our own company. But if there were a matter of which M'sieur le Duc should be made aware, the servants they would bring it to his attention *immédiatement*." She turned her head on the cushion to look at the Duke. "Is that not so, Monseigneur?"

"Just so, *mignonne*," agreed the Duke.

"But I do not understand why you must disappear at all—" Estée started to complain, only to be cut off by her husband when he squeezed her hand and spoke at her ear.

"What newly married couple don't want time to themselves, eh?"

Estée blinked at him with incomprehension then frowned across at the ducal couple. As they offered nothing further, she blurted out on a huff, "What you do with your time when you are private is your affair—"

"It is," stated the Duke.

"—but what you do in public is of concern to everyone," she continued with a self-satisfied smile. "That is what is of interest to me, because already I have received two letters this evening, and I do not know which is to be believed."

"That's what's keepin' you awake?" His Lordship asked, incredulous. "Gossip about y'brother?"

Estée put up her chin. "It is not gossip if it is true."

"It is if it is none of their concern," countered her husband, "and your correspondents are spreadin' it about!"

"That is why I need to know if it is true or not so I may write my reply before it spreads further."

"Allow me to hazard a guess as to the identity of one of your correspondents," stated the Duke. "My dear—er—friend Armand, Duc d'Richelieu…?"

Estée was so surprised all she could do was nod.

"I am sure he was eager to give you his version of events, in the hopes it will be the one that is repeated."

"May I tell them all about our supper with the King, Monseigneur?" asked Antonia, sitting up and placing her hands in her lap.

"By all means, *ma fée*. It will be far more enjoyable to re-live the evening in your skilled hands."

Antonia's eyes sparkled. "I do not think M'sieur le Duc d'Richelieu he will agree with you, Monseigneur. In fact we know he did not, did he?" She turned to address the Vallentines and Martin, saying earnestly, "I will say at the outset that Monseigneur he did warn M'sieur le Duc d'Richelieu, but he would not listen and insisted on joining in the game of bullet pudding with Madame de Pompadour and me."

"Bullet puddin'?" Vallentine's ears pricked up. "That game with a pile of flour and a bullet and everyone tryin' to dig it out and gettin' covered in an unholy mess?"

"The very one!"

"But ain't bullet puddin' a Christmas game?" asked Vallentine.

"As Christmastime is almost upon us, I thought it an excellent amusement to introduce to His Majesty and the court," Antonia explained. She smiled at the Duke. "And Monseigneur he agreed with me."

"Mon Dieu!" breathed Estée, shocked. She looked to her brother. "You did not allow her to play that game with the King?"

"Not with the king, but *for* the king," corrected the Duke.

"Armand he did not mention this in his letter," said Estée. "Only that there was a supper and afterwards cards."

"M'sieur le Duc d'Richelieu would like nothing better than to have his participation in the game of bullet pudding—er—erased from the collective memory."

"But we cannot allow that to happen, can we, Monseigneur?" Antonia replied with a beaming smile.

"No. We cannot. Particularly when *Sa Majesté* declared the evening one of his most enjoyable—"

"—because his First Gentleman of the Bedchamber ended the evening covered in flour, yes?"

The Duke smiled at a memory in his mind's eye. "No doubt Armand's—er—difficulties contributed to His Majesty's *bonne humeur, ma vie.* But do not discount your effect on the king—"

Antonia was genuinely surprised. "But I did little more than put His Majesty at ease."

The Duke gently squeezed her hand. "You are too humble, *mignonne.* So many courtiers have tried and failed at that simple but also exceptionally difficult task."

Antonia included the others in her reply when she said confidentially, "M'sieur le Duc told me that His Majesty he bores very easily, which is why I chose to introduce him to the game of bullet pudding."

"Mme la Duchesse, perhaps you would care to set us the scene where the game took place, and who was in attendance…?" Martin suggested

"Oh yes! Forgive me, I am racing on ahead of myself," agreed Antonia. "But please do not interrupt me, as it is late and there is the possibility I may forget something important if you do. But if I do, you must tell me, Monseigneur." When the Duke nodded, she turned to her audience and told them all about their evening.

TWENTY-ONE

"I AM CERTAIN you know this," Antonia continued, "but perhaps, Martin, you do not: Everyone who wishes to sup with the King applies for an invitation and goes on a list, from which the King then chooses with whom he wishes to share his dinner table. And while there is no guarantee your name it will be called by the usher, everyone waits expectantly on the back stairs, by the door to the apartment where the supper is to be held. It is very crowded, and footmen are forever running up and down and flapping their hands about to have quiet and order. Monseigneur and I we already knew we would be called, because the King he wrote to Monseigneur a few days before to invite us to supper."

"Which is why we were prepared for the evening."

"By which M'sieur le Duc means, we took with us our servants and change of clothing, and everything necessary to entertain His Majesty with a game of bullet pudding after supper," Antonia explained. "Madame de Pompadour she too already knew this was the entertainment I had chosen. And after the game and its rules were explained to her, and what contingencies I had put in place to ensure we would not get covered in flour from head to foot, she agreed to play the game with me."

"I was not expecting that," Estée interjected, pulling a face. "For Pompadour to readily take part in such a silly activity surprises me. But perhaps that is because she must always be front and center with the King and so could not allow you to take the stage without her."

"Armand would have you believe the Marquise to be that way inclined," stated the Duke. "But she is surprisingly humble."

Estée snorted her contempt. "And so she should be, as one of the bourgeoisie!"

"M'sieur le Duc d'Richelieu's jealousy of the King's mistress is so unbelievable as to be embarrassing for him," confided Antonia, ignoring her sister-in-law's supercilious slight at the Marquise. "And I will tell you more about that later, but to continue on with the first part of our evening…

"M'sieur le Duc d'Roxton and I as the Comtesse de Roucy were called by the usher into the King's supper room. And here is something I am certain that only those invited to these private rooms are aware, and are surprised to discover. I myself was astonished. The rooms of His Majesty's private apartments are well-appointed and have every comfort, but they are so very small. Oh la la! Smaller than the rooms here at this villa. It is true, Madame. If His Majesty were to know how we live, the size of the rooms at the hôtel, or if he were ever to visit Treat, he would be envious beyond belief. So it is as well that he remains ignorant of M'sieur le Duc's houses and great wealth. Though I think what would upset him most is the freedom we have to live as we please, that he does not." She cocked her head. "Monseigneur, you are king of your own dominion without the necessary burden of the public life His Majesty must endure. Which pleases me because although you would make a very good king, I would not wish it upon you."

A slight flush of embarrassment to his cheeks, the Duke said evenly, "If I were king, I would of course have you as my queen—"

"Pardon, Monseigneur, but I do not want to be your queen. I would be your mistress—"

"Antonia!" admonished her sister-in-law, shocked. "Do not be foolish. Of course you must be his queen."

Antonia shook her head. "No, Madame. The queen she lives a very different life from the one I would want with the king. But as his mistress, we would spend our time together in the private apartments, as Louis does with Madame de Pompadour. To see them in such an intimate setting is to know that they are truly in love. Is that not so, Renard?"

"It is. The supper, *ma fée*?" coaxed the Duke.

"There were sixteen of us squashed around the King's supper table, and the King he became very animated and witty, and told a good many jokes. I will say this about Louis of France. When he is with his friends, he is quite another being from the one that is on display in the big public rooms. It is true that he is shy with strangers, and he was a little shy with me, too, at first. But to see him with M'sieur le Duc, who always puts him at his ease, is a privilege.

"After we had eaten, the King he dismissed the servants and—you will have to believe me when I tell you this—he went into a little room off the supper room, and there he prepared the coffee for all of us himself—"

"He supervised the servants?" corrected Estée.

"No, Madame. There were no servants. The King he made the coffee with his own hands."

"*C'est vraiment incroyable!*"

"Indeed it was, Madame. With the coffee, there were plates of macarons and nougat and fruits of the season. The macarons were delicious, so delicious I asked the King for the recipe—"

"Of course you would," quipped Vallentine, adding with a laugh, "Don't tell us: Louis not only makes coffee, but he bakes as well!"

"Not these particular macarons, no," Antonia replied seriously.

"But he did confide in me that he watched his chef make them. There is a kitchen attached to the private apartments, and sometimes His Majesty he also bakes. He says he finds to do so is soothing."

"Well, if ever your chef takes ill, Roxton," Vallentine stuck in, smugly, "you know who you can call upon!"

"In exchange for the recipe for his macarons," Antonia continued in the same serious tone, "I offered *Sa Majesté*'s chef the recipe for Vallentine's favorite *nougat aux amandes*."

"Did you indeed?" His Lordship put up his chin. "No doubt when he heard the premier swordsman in all France and England has a favorite nougat, His Majesty jumped at the chance to have the recipe."

"He did not so much as—er—jump," the Duke replied with a twitch of his lips, "as splutter into his coffee."

"Why would he do that?"

"Antonia felt compelled to warn His Majesty how that particular nougat affects you."

Vallentine turned white. He stared at Antonia, mortified. "You did no such thing!"

"But of course, Lucian," Antonia replied. "I could not in good conscience offer His Majesty a recipe for nougat without telling him that when you eat it, you suffer terribly from *ballonnements*, because it might affect him in the same way." She turned to the Duke and asked, as if it had never occurred to her, "That was the right thing to do, was it not, Monseigneur?"

"Naturally. Everything that the King eats and drinks, and experiences, is of vital importance, not only to his physicians but to the country, and it has been that way since birth. France must have a strong and healthy king, and not one that suffers in any capacity—certainly not from *Ballonnements et flatulences*. He would have appreciated your concern for his welfare, *mignonne*."

"Appreciated it?" Vallentine grumbled. "So much so that his physicians must've thought he was sufferin' from an apoplexy when he spat into his coffee at my expense! I'll never be able to look him in the eye again!"

"But you have never looked *Sa Majesté* in the eye at any time, Lucian," argued his wife, blue eyes brimming with tears of laughter. "In fact you only attended court today because Antonia was being presented. Otherwise, you said, nothing and no one would drag you there!"

"Your skills as a swordsman are not in question," stated the Duke, adding with a crooked smile, "Though… if I were an opponent and wanted the—er—upper hand, I would certainly offer you some nougat before an encounter."

"First supper with the King and it's *my* reputation that's in tatters!" Vallentine sulked, a sidelong glance of recrimination at the Duchess. He looked across at Martin. "If you have any ailments to foodstuffs, I suggest you keep 'em to y'self or His Majesty could come to hear of it!"

"I do not see at all what is the difficulty with family, and others, knowing that Martin he has an aversion to asparagus, just like Monseigneur," Antonia volunteered. "It is the taste that bothers them. Is that not so, Martin?"

Martin inclined his head. "Just so, Mme la Duchesse."

The Duke raised an enquiring eyebrow. "Is there nothing Mme la Duchesse does not know about you?"

"If she don't now, she soon will!" announced His Lordship with a roll of his eyes before Martin could respond. "She'll wheedle every last surprise out of us, eventually!"

Antonia shrugged and was smug. "I will, but only if you wish to tell me."

"Touché, my love," Estée applauded.

"Now don't you encourage her, lovedy!" Vallentine replied darkly, but the mirth in his blue eyes belied his annoyance.

"Vallentine, please do not worry about the King or those at the supper remembering about the nougat," Antonia soothed. "M'sieur le Duc d'Richelieu he came off far worse for his encounter with the bullet pudding, and that is what everyone will remember about the evening." She looked to the Duke. "Did you not say that His Majesty laughed a lot harder when we were playing at bullet pudding than at any other time during the evening?"

"He did. And M'sieur le Duc d'Richelieu's public—er—outrage at his embarrassment was definitely the high point of any of the King's suppers I have had the pleasure of attending. I have never been so entertained. Thank you, *ma vie*."

Antonia beamed. "That makes me happy."

"Although I think we will find that, in his capacity as First Gentleman of the Bedchamber, Richelieu will ensure bullet pudding never features on the menu of any of His Majesty's entertainments."

Antonia sighed, but was not disappointed. "Monseigneur, you did warn M'sieur le Duc d'Richelieu several times against participating in bullet pudding. But the more you advised him against it, the more he was determined to join us in the game."

"Hahaha!" Vallentine shook his head at the Duke. "I've no doubt you were very insistent on him *not* gettin' involved!"

The Duke appeared disconsolate, but his dark eyes were bright. "I assure you, Lucian, I tried my very best to—er—warn him off, but alas to no avail."

"I will tell you about it from the start," Antonia announced, and waited for her family to settle to begin.

TWENTY-TWO

"I BROUGHT SMOCKS for Mme de Pompadour and me to wear over our clothing so the clouds of flour would not fall all over us and ruin our gowns," Antonia told them and smiled smugly. "That was very clever of me, yes? And we removed our shoes and played in our stockings. We tied caps over our hair, so that all that was visible were our faces. We looked like washerwomen, but His Majesty and Monseigneur they complimented us and said we looked very fetching. Of course we knew they were being polite, because we saw ourselves in a looking glass, and Madame giggled like a girl at our foolish appearance. Neither of us were worried in the least how we presented, as we were both excited for the game."

"I wish we'd all been there to see you," commented Estée with a sigh of disappointment. "Please. Tell us the rest!"

"His Majesty had no inkling as to what was to come," Antonia continued. "But Monseigneur did because I had already told him about playing at bullet pudding with Theo at *Grand-mere's* at Christmastime. So when Monseigneur advised His Majesty and the rest of the supper party to have their chairs moved to the perimeter of the salon, His Majesty was reluctant at first because he wanted to be as close to the pudding as possible. But when he realized that there was the possibility of being covered in flour from our antics, he soon had the footmen move everyone to the walls.

"Madame and I were left in the center of the room with the flour piled in a mound on a tray that was placed on a pedestal. This meant we were able to move freely around the pudding, and everyone could see us clearly. On top of the mound a bullet was lightly placed so that it sat there in view. We each had a butter knife and took it in turns to cut away a slice of the flour pudding, with the object being that the bullet remain at the top for as long as possible, without it being disturbed.

"But once the bullet it fell into the flour by the actions of the knife cutting into the pudding, the person who disturbed it then had to poke about in the flour and retrieve it, not with the knife or their hands, but with their teeth."

"*Mon Dieu*! I cannot believe you could do such a thing as put your face into a pile of flour," Estée commented breathlessly.

"No small wonder the flour went up in clouds," Martin added with a chuckle.

"Precisely!" agreed Antonia. "But what you must imagine is that by the time we had cut away a large part of the flour pudding—Madame and I—we were in a great state of agitation trying our best not disturb the bullet! The smaller the pudding became and the more precarious the bullet on what was left of the mound, the more nervous and clumsier we became. We may have shrieked in our nervousness—I do not remember exactly. I do know we were giggling, which made the process all the more hazardous but all the more thrilling." Antonia beamed, adding proudly but unnecessarily. "We were being very silly, were we not, Monseigneur?"

The Duke nodded, shoulders shaking with mirth at the memory. He coughed into his fist to clear his throat and said shakily, "Before the bullet dropped, we were all laughing along with you. His Majesty and I were in tears and could barely speak."

"But where was Richelieu, eh?" His Lordship asked. "I thought he inserted himself into this game?"

"Oh he did, Vallentine," Antonia assured him. "But before I told you how M'sieur le Duc d'Richelieu came to be covered in flour, you needed to know how the game was played, and how much Madame and I were enjoying ourselves." She smiled at the Duke, adding confidentially to the others, "It was as well His Majesty's physicians were not present, for I am certain they would have stopped the game for fear their royal master was having a pain of the heart!

"But to tell you about M'sieur le Duc d'Richelieu… Madame de Pompadour and I had carved the flour pudding to a third of its size, and while doing so had managed to keep the flour from puffing up into clouds. This was before we were nervous and giggling. But this was when Richelieu he decided to join in. Monseigneur says he did so because the King was enjoying himself, and the bullet pudding was a huge success, and this entertainment was not of Richelieu's doing. Also, and probably most importantly, he is very jealous of Madame de Pompadour's influence with his king.

"As we told you, Monseigneur did warn him against joining in because he did not have a smock or a cap. But Richelieu he is also very proud and said he did not need such ridiculous coverings because he was not a feeble female. He boasted that as a gentleman, he would retrieve the bullet without so much as disturbing one speck of flour."

"Naturally I encouraged him to honor his boast," drawled the Duke, "as a gentleman, and because as His Majesty's First Gentleman of the Bedchamber, he had a duty to ensure all the King's entertainments are appropriate."

"I am certain you expertly set the snare for M'sieur le Duc," Martin said with a laugh.

"Snare?" Estée snapped with a huff of dismissal. "Hunting has nothing to do with—"

"Particularly when his arrogance requires he step into it without a second thought," Roxton replied to Martin, then said to his sister in an aside, "When out of your depth, keep your claws sheathed, my dear." And to Antonia he continued in a gentler voice, "*Mignonne*, please tell us about M'sieur le Duc d'Richelieu's attempts at winning at bullet pudding."

"We had managed to keep the bullet atop of what was left of the pudding," Antonia continued. "And then M'sieur le Duc d'Richelieu he stepped up with his own knife and proceeded to circle the pedestal, looking at what was left of the pudding from every angle, sizing up the best possible way to insert the knife to make a cut and retrieve the bullet at the same moment! Madame and I we stepped back. We also read each other's minds, because we came together and held hands, anticipating the outcome of M'sieur le Duc's posturing without a word spoken! I chanced to glance at Monseigneur then, and I could see that he was of the same mind! He was laughing along with the King, and Madame and I were so happy to see them in such a good humor that we began to giggle. And then—*C'est arrivé*!

"M'sieur le Duc d'Richelieu was so confident that as he approached the pedestal he tripped over his own feet and went face first into the pudding. Poof! Instantly a cloud of flour went up into the air and rained down upon him. Not only did his face disappear into the flour, but his silk mourning frock, which was mourning black and beaded as magnificently as Monseigneur's frock, became covered in a dusting of flour, so that he looked dressed all in gray—"

"*Oh là là*! Poor Richelieu!" exclaimed Estée, half laughing, half gasping, and with little sympathy for the King's first chamberlain.

"In his shock of tripping, he forgot to close his mouth and instead breathed in as he fell forward into the flour," Antonia continued with an intake of breath to add to the dramatic effect. "And when he came up for air, spluttering and choking, he dug his knuckles into his eye sockets, and snorted clumps of flour from his nostrils!"

"I'll wager by this time the entire room was in an uproar!" exclaimed His Lordship, slapping his knee. "I wish I'd been there to see it!"

"I wish you had been, too, Vallentine," replied Antonia. "There was a great deal of shrieking and laughter from our audience, but Madame and I we were so intent on finishing the game that we rushed past M'sieur le Duc, who continued to stagger about as one blind, to get to what was left of the bullet pudding. Without hesitation, we dropped our faces into the flour, but with our eyes and mouths closed, determined to be the first to retrieve the bullet between our teeth!" She sat back, hands in her lap. "And there you have it! Our evening of playing at bullet pudding before the King." She turned her face up at the Duke, smiling. "We had such a wonderful evening, did we not, Renard?"

"We did. Everyone did. Thanks to you."

"Well? Who got to the bullet first?" demanded His Lordship. "And what happened to Richelieu after he'd rubbed the flour out of his eyes?"

"Madame de Pompadour claimed the bullet. She presented it to His Majesty to a round of applause," Roxton told them.

"You let her have it!" Vallentine accused Antonia.

"No, Vallentine. I wanted the bullet very much," Antonia countered. She shrugged. "But perhaps Madame wanted it more so that it did not fall into the possession of M'sieur le Duc d'Richelieu."

"But he was unlikely to get it, was he, what with him blinded by flour and havin' made an unholy mess of his suit!" reasoned Vallentine. "Fool!"

"Presenting the bullet to His Majesty in front of his closest friends, and with Armand looking on, was Madame de Pompadour's *coup de grâce*." The Duke smiled and winked at Antonia. "For which she will be ever thankful to her good friend, the Comtesse de Roucy."

"Monseigneur, I like her very much and so I am glad she found the bullet and put Richelieu in his place."

"The feeling is mutual, *ma chérie*. You have gained a powerful ally in the King's *maîtresse-en-titre*."

"I wonder how the Queen will view your wife's friendship with La Pompadour," Estée asked the Duke with the raise of a perfectly arched brow. "*Tante Philippe* will certainly have something to say about a member of the family taking up a post as lady-in-waiting to the Queen and being on intimate terms with that bourgeoise upstart. The two are surely mutually exclusive?"

Antonia looked from her sister-in-law to her husband and back at Estée.

"There is no need for *Tante Philippe* or the Queen to worry, Madame, because I do not intend to be a lady-in-waiting."

Estée was dumbfounded.

"How can you not?" she argued, a wary glance at her brother. "Surely Roxton told you your title of Comtesse de Roucy comes with obligations and responsibilities. The Queen will expect you to perform these duties, just as any other courtier must." She scoffed. "You cannot simply say *no* to Their Majesties."

"But I have, Madame. Not one hour will I spend as lady-in-waiting to the Queen, because it would mean an hour away from Monseigneur and Julian. And that would be *insupportable*."

Estée looked from Antonia to the Duke, astonished. "Roxton! Tell her. She cannot flout her duty!"

The Duke was unmoved. "I cannot do that. Nor do I want to."

TWENTY-THREE

"OF COURSE, as a duchesse you think you can do as you please," Estée argued. "And why wouldn't you believe it, when Roxton he indulges you. But I must remind you both of what happened the last time a member of our family flouted a royal command—and I speak of my mother, not Jean-Honoré—which ended in her disgrace and banishment—"

Vallentine stifled a yawn, and said at his wife's ear, "The chit don't need a lecture at two in the mornin'—"

"Perhaps you have managed the impossible once again," Estée continued, ignoring her husband, and addressing her brother. "I hear you gave quite the performance in the hall of mirrors to put Duras-Valfons in her place—*tant mieux pour vous*—I am certain Louis forgave you those breaches of etiquette because he too wishes Thérèse to be brought to heel. But *La*! Not even your great friendship would see him bend court obligation for your wife…"

The Duke stared at his sister without a hint as to his thoughts, and after accepting a snifter of brandy from Martin, said to her before taking his first sip, "When you are tired and overwrought, your Salvan blood, it—er—boils up and over like scalded milk and sours the air…" He sipped the golden liquid and lifted his gaze to his sister once again. "Did you truly believe I would put my wife and family through such a tedium as we endured today, if I did not already have an answer to that conundrum?"

"I will tell them all about your cleverness," Antonia announced cheerfully.

"By all means, *ma fée*. I am in a better humor already for your intervention."

After exchanging a loving smile, Antonia turned to the couple across from her, and included Martin in her explanation when she told them, "There is an oft-used custom at court whereby a place is filled, not by the office holder, but by a family member. It is this family member who performs the duties, and for a stipend." She looked to the Duke then back again at the couple. "This is how a court position remains within the same family for generations. What is most important is that the task is performed, not who is performing it. Everyone is then satisfied. Only if there is no one to fulfil the duties of the office and it falls vacant can the King, if he is so inclined, confiscate and resell it to the highest bidder."

"Pardon, Mme la Duchesse," Martin asked, curious. "But the position held at court by your grandmother—the previous Comtesse de Roucy—it has remained vacant until now…?"

"That is so, Martin," Antonia replied. "*Grand-mère* she passed away ten years before I was born, and so there was no female relative to take up her position."

Estée scoffed. "And I suppose it just so happens that no one at court, least of all the Queen, noticed that since your grandmother's passing, she has one fewer ladies-in-waiting?"

The Duke smiled thinly. "She did not. No one did. Louis was still only a boy and yet to marry Marie Leszczyńska when the Comtesse passed away."

"That solves that then!" Vallentine proclaimed confidently, with no idea as to what had been solved. Then he managed to ask something relevant that surprised everyone, "What excruciatingly important task does the Comtesse de Roucy perform as a lady-in-waitin' to Her Majesty, chit?"

"Oh, it is *très important*, Vallentine," Antonia said gravely, her tone at odds with the sparkle in her green eyes. "The Comtesse de Roucy is in charge of Her Majesty gloves—"

"*Glove handler*? I knew it!" Vallentine fell back on the sofa and clapped a hand to his forehead. "Dear God! Waitin' around all mornin' so you can slip a pair of gloves onto the royal hand, and then havin' to race back in the evenin' to take 'em off again! If that ain't the definition of mind-numbing, I don't know what is!" He winked at Antonia. "I'll wager you've come up with a cunning plan that means you won't be handlin' the royal gloves anytime soon."

"*C'est* ça. We will continue on with our lives, and not a single hour will I need to be present at the palace. I told you. Monseigneur he is very clever. Everything it is arranged, and to everyone's satisfaction, even Sa Majesties are pleased. Mme de Pompadour too. *Voilà!*"

"You intend for your duties as the Comtesse de Roucy to be carried out by another member of the family?" Estée stated slowly, taking a moment to digest what Antonia had just explained to her.

"Yes, Madame."

"Can always count on your brother to find an answer," Vallentine announced, raising a brandy balloon to the Duke. "And why would you want to spend a single moment away from each other, eh? Still I'm intrigued how you managed to convince any relation I know with noodles for brains to take up such a mind-numbingly tedious post—"

"How can you say that, Lucian," demanded his wife, instantly riled. "The position of lady-in-waiting to the Queen is one any female at court, indeed any female of the nobility, would give their best eye-tooth to possess—"

"If only they had teeth," muttered His Lordship sitting back. But the points of his shoulder blades had barely nestled against the deep velvet upholstery when his wife's next words had him bolt upright, brandy sloshing about wildly.

"—and one I will be honored to accept."

"Eh?" Vallentine swiveled about to face his wife, the color draining from his cheeks at her smug smile. "What? You?" He shook his head back and forth. "Oh no! Oh no! No! Over my dead carcass!"

Estée battered off her husband's dramatic reaction with a wave and rolled her beautiful eyes. "Do not be so surprised, Lucian. Who else is most suited to take up such a prestigious post if not M'sieur le Duc's sister, and the Comtesse de Roucy's sister-in-law?"

"Prestigious?" His Lordship's voice was high-pitched and thin. "There's nothin' prestigious about bein' a glove handler!"

"That is how little you know about it," Estée replied smugly. "Glove, stocking, ribbon, or fan. The object and task are of less consequence when weighed against the female's proximity to Her Majesty's little ear. And you cannot get much closer than glove handler. Is that not so, Roxton?"

Before the Duke had time to respond, Vallentine turned on him, and jumping to his feet he stabbed a long bony finger in his direction. "Whatever did I do to you to deserve this?" he snapped.

"Is that a rhetorical question, Lucian?" the Duke replied coolly.

"Vallentine! It is impolite to poke a finger at M'sieur le Duc," Antonia complained, frowning.

"Antonia is right. Do not poke at my brother," Estée demanded of her husband. "I do not understand why you are angry, when this great honor bestowed upon me has nothing to do with you!"

"*Nothin'* to do with me, eh?" Vallentine repeated, grinding his teeth. "So you think! It has *everythin'* to do with me!"

"Sit down, Lucian," the Duke ordered softly.

"All that nonsense earlier about cats in bags, and now would be a good a time as any to tell you if I have a secret! Ha!" Vallentine continued, ignoring the order to sit, arms now flapping about, furious gaze riveted to the Duke. "I see what you're about! You'll let y'sister continue on with this foolish notion of takin' up a court position for as long as it takes to wear me thin, and I'm made miserable enough to confess all to you—"

"Lucian, you cannot accuse my broth—"

"No! No, wife!" His Lordship snapped, a finger to his lips before throwing out a hand for her to be quiet. "You've had your turn, now it's mine. I know how this is goin' to play out. Your brother always wins—in the end." He turned back to the Duke. "But I want you to know, Roxton, that Ellicott had no part in this little drama—none!"

The Duke glanced across at Martin, who remained as stone by the tea trolley, brandy decanter in hand striving to be as inconspicuous as possible. Returning his gaze to Vallentine, the Duke said softly, "I am aware of that, but thank you for stating it."

His Lordship smiled crookedly. "A'course you are! As you are aware of everythin' else!"

The Duke bowed his head in acknowledgment of the truth in this declaration, and resumed sipping his brandy, but he made no further comment.

Estée dabbed at her moist eyes and looked across at Antonia, confused, "I do not understand at all what is going on, *ma très chère belle-sœur*. Are we still discussing your position as lady-in-waiting, or are they talking about something else entirely? Me, I am lost!"

"I think we have moved on from that, Madame," Antonia confessed in a whisper. "Though Vallentine he seems convinced there is a connection between the court position and what he is about to confess to Monseigneur."

His Lordship swallowed a lump in his throat and forced himself not only to look at Antonia, but to meet her clear green eyes. They were without guile, and his face flooded with guilt. He made her a small bow, feeling wretched. "I beg your forgiveness, Mme la Duchesse, but I am about to betray your trust…"

TWENTY-FOUR

W HEN ANTONIA sat up, eyes widening and her mouth forming into a silent *oh*, he knew she understood, and his despondency increased. But it did not stop him turning to his best friend and making his confession.

"It's late. In fact it's early mornin', and I'm certain we'd all like to be in our beds before sunup, so I'll come straight to the point: I have kept somethin' from you." He let his gaze dart to the Duchess before again addressing the Duke. "That's because I made Mme la Duchesse a promise not to tell you about-about—Salvan's letter. I shouldn't have done that. But we both thought at the time—if you can believe me—that it was the right thing to do."

He sighed and he let his hands fall to his sides.

"But you knew this already, didn't you? You've probably known almost from the moment she showed it to me, and I made her that promise. But y'know what?" He put up his square chin. "While I regret keepin' a secret from you, I don't regret makin' her a prom-ise." He looked at Antonia, and then stabbed a finger in the air in Roxton's direction. "And I did it for you. She—I—*we*—were hopin' to protect you. That's right! Protect *you*. And what do you think of *me* for doin' that? That I'm a traitorous scoundrel, that's what!"

"I think no such thing, Lucian," countered the Duke, and in a tone that suggested he was offended by such an accusation.

"What letter from Salvan? What are you blathering on about, Lucian?" Estée demanded, looking from her husband to her brother and then to her sister-in-law, and then back at the Duke. "We were discussing Antonia's court position, but now Lucian he is talking about something that is ludicrous in the extreme! Salvan he would have to be a-a *lunatic* to write to Antonia when he knows to do so means honoring your word to kill him. No! I do not believe it! He would not risk it. Someone else signed his fist and wants you to think it was him. There must be any number of relatives, not least the ancient aunts, who would do such a wicked thing. After all, if you kill Salvan, then Montbelliard will be comte, and that would suit the family very well indeed. No. Salvan is a pathetic weak creature, but surely he is not an idiot. Lucian! Antonia! You have both been duped. Lucian! Sit beside me this instant or I truly will be ill, and that will wake the baby, and we will have no peace!"

"You're wrong, wife. Salvan *is* an idiot, and he *did* write to Antonia," Vallentine stated, still seething. "And I won't sit until I have your brother's word he ain't sendin' you to court as a royal lackey to punish me for my treachery!" He turned away from his wife and looked to the Duke. "And now I've confessed all, and apologized, you'll have done with tauntin' me and assure me you've chosen one of your lunatic Salvan relatives to take up Antonia's court position."

"Vallentine," Antonia said quietly, "all of this is my fault entirely. You must not be angry with M'sieur le Duc, but with me. He is entirely blameless, and if you think he would send his sister to court, all to punish you, you do not know him at all! *Et c'est tout ce qu'il y a à dire là-dessus.*"

She scrambled up off the sofa and in her stockinged feet, turned to the Duke, back to the others, and put her hands on his crossed knees. She lifted her gaze to his dark eyes and there again was that glint in his eye—disappointment. She felt wretched as she shuddered in a breath, but she kept her chin level and said simply, "Monseigneur, you cannot blame Lucian. He only did what I asked of him. I know now that I should not have put him or you in such a difficult position. But he speaks the truth when he says all we wanted was to protect you. So he you must not chastise, only me." Her smile was tremulous. "You know—you must know—there was no other reason for keeping Salvan's letter from you other than I love you beyond words."

The Duke covered her hand with his and took a moment to master his emotion, then said quietly, "I know that, *ma vie*. But you and I—we cannot keep secrets. Marriage has made us one. Which means we share *everything*. To keep secrets would take us down a path neither of us wants. There are those who will always cause mischief, who will try and come between us. If not today, then tomorrow, or the day after.

"Today was a prime example of that. The Comtesse Duras-Valfons attempted but failed to drive a wedge of doubt between us. She could not because we have always been candid with each other where she is concerned. That gave you the confidence to deal with her when she confronted you, secure in the knowledge that there was nothing she could say or do that could cause a schism in our marriage. I am exceedingly proud of how you handled her. But equally, having secrets from each other can hurt those we love."

"Such as making Vallentine choose between us?"

"Just so."

She nodded. "I see that now. I had not thought of it in that way, but you are right." She looked up from playing with his fingers. "No one will ever come between us, friend, or foe. I will never allow that."

"We—together—will never allow that." He drew her closer and said so only she could hear, "We will talk further in private. But first I must put Lucian out of his misery and correct my sister's grand presumption about your court duties." He smiled into her green eyes. "And then we can go to our bed and sleep in each other's arms past noon."

"I would like that very much. Monseigneur! It was the Spymaster-General who told you Salvan had written to me."

It was not a question, and the Duke did not hesitate to bow his head in acknowledgment of her statement. "I was also informed it was your grandmother who was the intermediary in that correspondence. I will deal with Augusta at the right time, too."

"Why did you not tell me before today that you knew?" she asked curiously.

"And spoil your presentation and the memories of this day? I could not do that."

"Ah, Monseigneur, you are so thoughtful," she replied in a small voice, and sniffed back tears. Before she stepped away, she leaned in and lightly kissed his cheek. "I did not mean to disappoint you, but I know I have, and I am truly sorry for it."

"No more secrets."

"No more secrets," she repeated with a smile, adding brightly, "And as it is tomorrow, the memory of yesterday will remain untouched, and we shall remember it that way always, yes?"

"Always."

She nodded and said nothing further on the matter, resuming her seat beside him and placing her hands in the lap of her voluminous black silk petticoats. She apologized to the others for turning her back on them, adding needlessly, "But it could not be helped, because it had to be said between us here and now."

TWENTY-FIVE

"WELL I'M GLAD you're both feelin' better for your *tête-à-tête*," announced His Lordship with a crooked smile, "but that still leaves the rest of us no less miserable and wonderin'!"

"Lucian, we have known each other since Eton," said the Duke. "Yet there are times when you act as if you do not know me at all. Antonia is in the right. You should know me well enough that the last thing I would do is make you miserable. Nor would I ever rescind my edict forbidding my sister from taking up a position at court. As I explained to you, Antonia's presentation was a formality that had to be endured because I wished for her to attend Louis' little suppers with me. I have no desire, and neither does she, of being at court in any other capacity."

He looked to his sister. "While your lineage is impeccable, and no doubt Their Majesties and your Salvan relatives would approve of you being a lady-in-waiting to the Queen, you are not and never have been—er—battle-hardened for such a role. I care too much for you, and for Lucian, to ever throw you into that viperous pit. To thrive in such a poisonous environment unscathed requires an acute intelligence, and a cunning that is beyond your capabilities—"

"You think me a fool!" Estée pouted and sniffed.

"No. What you possess is an—er—acute fragile sensibility," replied the Duke at his most diplomatic, "better suited to being a grand hostess of a Parisian salon, than a noble servant of the crown, caught up in the backstairs machinations of a palace entresol."

Estée was mollified by this. While she would enjoy the prestige that came with being a lady-in-waiting to the Queen, she was pragmatic enough to know that the novelty would wear thin within the week, and be miserable thereafter. And when she gave it further thought, she agreed with her brother that the French nobility were little more than glorified lackeys to their king. He had told her once that the present king's grandfather, Louis XIV, had enticed his nobles away from their landed estates by giving them prestigious but mundane positions at court, effectively castrating their power, adding that the English nobility would never fall for such duplicitous behavior from their monarch. The last time a Stuart king attempted something similar, he was sent packing across the Channel, the English nobles offering the throne to his daughter and son-in-law.

At the time, her French noble blood had been deeply offended by his summation but thinking about it later, she grudgingly had to agree with him. Rational when it suited, she was glad only half her blood was French, and she could claim kinship to an English ducal house. Besides, the notion of being anyone's lackey—even royalty —was beneath her.

Yet it niggled that she had not been given the choice to refuse the position of glove handler to the Queen, passed over by whomever her brother thought more suitable to take on the duties of the Comtesse de Roucy. Which is why, even though she was prepared to acquiesce, and no longer argue the point with him, she continued to pout and asked spitefully,

"So which half-wit Salvan cousin in dire penury begged to be given such a menial position in the Queen's household?"

The Duke smiled thinly, not surprised by her rancorous response, but relieved there were to be no more sisterly histrionics. Still, he was prepared for her to be anything but placid when he put a name to the Salvan cousin. Thus, for the benefit of Vallentine and Martin, who were still in ignorance, he made sure to provide a full explanation before a name.

"She is neither a half-wit nor poverty stricken. She did not beg. In fact, it was a surprise to her when Mme la Duchesse and I asked if she would be interested in the post. While the position might appear menial—handing Her Majesty her gloves is indeed facile—the very closeness to the Queen puts the lady-in-waiting in the center of the royal household. From such a vantage point she is in the unique position to report on everything she sees and hears—"

"A spy?" interrupted Estée. "For you?"

"For me, and others—"

"For our old school chum Ned Shrewsbury, I'll wager—" stated Vallentine with a click of his fingers.

"Ned?" interrupted Estée, none the wiser.

"Edward, Lord Shrewsbury, is England's newly minted Spymaster-General, lovely. And he was at Eton with Roxton and me. We called him Spaniel—for obvious reasons."

"It is not obvious to me," Estée stated seriously.

His Lordship touched his nose and said in a voice heavy with meaning, "Always had his ears close to the ground—"

"He has big ears?"

"No—well, yes! Come to think on it, he does have large ears. But that's not why we dubbed him spaniel. Spaniels dig about in the muck, discover things hidden before you do, which makes Ned well-suited to rooting out people's secrets, *compris*?"

As Estée's eyes widened in understanding, Martin Ellicott thought it an ideal opportunity to seize the moment.

"Pardon, M'sieur le Duc, but would a Frenchwoman willingly spy for the English?"

His question ended the couple's preoccupation, and Estée swiveled about to glare at Martin, outraged. "A Salvan would never betray his king!"

"That is an excellent question. All I have asked of her is to send me factual reports of court life," the Duke explained, ignoring his sister's outburst. "What I do with those reports—written in code and left unsigned—is my affair, and she does not wish to know."

"And in return for these—um—reports, she is content to be the Queen's glove handler?" questioned His Lordship. He leaned into Roxton and jabbed his temple. "Are you sure she ain't a little bit simple?"

The Duke smirked at the absurdity in this, and after a wink at Antonia, said to Vallentine, "Mme la Duchesse will concur that the woman in question is not only one of the most intelligent I have met, but that she is related to me by blood is gratifying. I have every confidence that with her abilities, she will make a success of her new role, or she would not have been offered the post."

"Well it's gratifyin', as you say, to know not all Salvans are a roll short of a baker's dozen!"

Estée was instantly riled. "Lucian! You forget that I and my brother are both Salvans."

"I've said it a hundred times—you and he are the best of 'em. And you're not a Salvan, you're a Hesham. Of English blood that's been polluted with a drop of French—"

"If I may ask a further question?" enquired Martin, ignoring the arguing couple. When the Duke waved a hand, added, "I cannot imagine that an intelligent woman would jump at the chance to be in service to the Queen, who by all reports is a sweet but dull and pious creature. Thus sending you reports will no doubt provide her with mental stimulation. But what does she personally hope to gain from such a position?"

"Ah! *Le parrain de Julian* he is astute, is he not, Monseigneur,"

Antonia answered brightly. "May I answer this?" And when the Duke nodded, said to Martin, "A position at court will bring her into close daily contact with Mme la Pompadour and the King, and their friends. Her great wish is to become Madame's intimate, and through their friendship further her family's, but mostly her father-in-law's, ambition. He has a great desire to be a friend of the Marquise, too." She smiled up at the Duke. "We have every confidence in the Queen's new glove handler being a great success in all her endeavors, for us and for her family's advancement, do we not, Monseigneur?

"We do. I predict she and the Marquise will indeed become great friends. She may have been born a Salvan, and her father a General-Duke, but Madame Haudry's father-in-law is a Farmer-General, and thus she has great empathy for the King's mistress. La Pompadour needs an ally at court who understands the hostile environment in which she finds herself. I foresee the King offering M'sieur Farmer-General a senior government post before the summer."

"And I predict—*no*! *Tante Philippe* detests the King's bourgeoise mistress," argued Estée. "So I cannot see her allowing one of her Salvan relatives to befriend the creature—"

"*Tante Philippe* will do as I bid her," stated the Duke with finality. He looked across at His Lordship, a glance at Martin to include him. "You have a wedding to attend tomorrow, so you need a few hours' sleep before that—er—ordeal."

He made motions to stand, shaking out his large, upturned velvet cuffs—signal the evening was at an end. On his feet, he held out his hand to his Duchess. But when his sister made a noise in the back of her throat, as if she were choking, he turned to her with the raise of an eyebrow.

"Haudry? *Michelle* Haudry?" Estée rasped out in shock, eyes wide in disbelief, the name finally penetrating her consciousness. "So this is your-your *devious scheme* for the disgraced daughter of the Duc du Touraine—to be a lady-in-waiting to the Queen—and she has agreed to-to *spy* for you?" She was incredulous. "*Tante Philippe* and our Salvan cousins may be forced to fall in with your plans, Roxton, but not even you in your great arrogance can truly believe you hold such sway over the Queen and her ladies-in-waiting that she will accept your candidate for the position of her glove handler!"

"But he does, Madame," Antonia responded cheerfully as she hopped off the sofa to slide her stockinged feet into her velvet mules. She tucked her hand into the Duke's warm clasp. "And you are not to worry needlessly. It is all settled, and to everyone's satisfaction. After I was presented to the Queen, and before our supper with the King, M'sieur le Duc and I were invited to the Queen's private *salle*, and there witnessed Madame Haudry graciously accept the position as Her Majesty's lady-in-waiting. *Bonne nuit, très chère famille.*"

And with that she and the Duke disappeared into the small dark recess of the stairwell leading up to their bedchamber. On the second step she turned and threw her arms about his neck and was gathered up in a loving embrace.

"Alone at last! And you, *mon homme adorable*, are long overdue to discard these clothes to flaunt your great arrogance just for me."

TWENTY-SIX

WHEN HIS LORDSHIP and Martin Ellicott were set down under the villa's *porte-cochère* the following afternoon, they were returning from attending the wedding of Hubert Gabriel Louis Hyacinth Salvan Montbelliard to Elisabeth-Louise Salvan Gondi Touraine.

The butler directed them to the library where they found the Duke seated at his desk. He was in at-home undress, chinoiserie silk banyan thrown over a crisp, white linen shirt secured with a cravat of similar fine cloth, black silk waistcoat, and velvet breeches, stockinged feet in a pair of soft-kid Moroccan slippers. He was fastening the folded pages of a letter, ducal seal pressed into warm wax. When done, he placed this letter, with half a dozen others, on a silver salver held by a liveried footman who then took his leave to have the letters dispatched by his master's swiftest courier. The two footmen standing to attention by the double doors were dismissed, leaving the Duke alone with His Lordship and Martin.

They sat by the fireplace, where the coffee urn and trolley had been placed earlier. In need of sleep, Vallentine leaned his cheek on a fist to prop up his head, and briefly closed his eyes. He calculated that he'd had less than three hours of slumber, and it was less than ten hours since he had been seated in this precise spot that same morning. But what made him all the more tired were the four cups of strong punch he had downed at the wedding breakfast. Thus, strong black coffee was essential to keep him awake.

A hand lightly to his shoulder, and he opened his eyes to find Martin had poured him a dish. And while he silently savored the brew, he was grateful to his fellow wedding attendee for also conveying to the Duke all that had transpired earlier that morning —at the ceremony held in the Church of Notre-Dame on the *rue de la Paroisse*, and afterwards, at the small wedding breakfast held across the street at M'sieur Haudry's elegant townhouse on the *rue Hoche*, used infrequently by him when he was in town on business or visiting family.

"The only Salvan relative to attend the ceremony was Mme Haudry, as you directed, Your Grace," Martin told him. "And as Montbelliard's sisters live many leagues distant, His Lordship's presence was greatly appreciated by the groom. Although—and I am sure he will concur—the young couple was so happy to finally be up before the *curé*, they barely noticed who was in attendance."

"An hour and forty minutes! One full hour and forty minutes, damme!" Vallentine groaned. "That's not countin' the befores or the afters at the weddin' breakfast. I don't know about you, Ellicott, but by the time we escaped from the church, I was ready to down more than my fair share of the punch!"

"Your appraisal of the wedding breakfast?"

Vallentine pulled a face and rallied himself enough to reply.

"As far as I could tell it was the usual avaricious relatives, come to put their stomach worms out of their misery and stick their noses where they're not wanted. The Salvans bein' under a Farmer-General's opulent roof must've come as a novel experience and turned 'em all green with envy!" He looked sideways at Martin. "A fair appraisal, wouldn't you say, Ellicott?"

Martin smiled. "I would, my lord—"

"Hey! Hey!" Vallentine waggled a finger. "What did I tell you."

"I would—*Vallentine*," Martin corrected and blushed.

"Better," replied His Lordship, and closed his eyes as he settled deeper into the cushions.

The Duke addressed himself to Martin, saying confidentially, as if his best friend was not in the room, "It may surprise you to learn —which I discovered about Lucian when we were still at Eton— that when he has imbibed beyond levels intolerable to others, he is at his most clearheaded."

That did surprise Martin, but then he made an observation of his own. "It was as well you had each other for company when your friends overreached, for I have never known you, Your Grace, to drink to dissipation."

"Don't think we didn't try and get him drunk!" Vallentine commented from deep within the wingchair.

"The irony, my dears," drawled the Duke with a crooked smile and a heightened color to his lean cheeks, "is that—er—dissipation in all its forms is best savored sober." Returning the conversation to what was uppermost in his mind, he enquired of Martin, "From Lucian's estimate of the number of guests at the wedding breakfast, I must conclude that M'sieur Haudry did not apply my edict beyond the ceremony. He invited the entire Salvan miscellany to partake of his largesse…?"

"Select members, Your Grace," Martin replied. "Mme Haudry was at pains to assure me—she was aware I was attending as your representative and therefore was speaking to you through me—that her father-in-law's invitation to the bride's family made no mention of the wedding and was for her closest blood relatives. It was their grandmother Madame Touraine-Brissac who made certain her relatives kept the invitation to themselves. It must be said, from my observation of those present, that your aunts appeared not to know why they were there, and were very much, as the saying goes, *fish out of water*, to be in the house of a Farmer-General. It only became apparent once the bride and groom arrived—the last to enter the salon and with the *curé*—and M'sieur Haudry made a toast to their good health and happiness."

"I almost envy you your presence at this auspicious gathering," the Duke commented with a satisfied smirk. "The ancient aunts would have summoned the shield of four-and-a-half centuries of nobility to protect themselves from the opulent surroundings provided by M'sieur Farmer-General. That the invitation was kept from their wider family and friends saved them from complete humiliation. I trust *Tante Philippe* was suitably chastened. That she showed both granddaughters the proper respect. After all, one is now the wife of the heir to the Comte de Salvan, and the other is now the only Salvan with a court position—" He caught Martin frowning. "What is bothering you?"

"Not so much me, Your Grace, as Mme Haudry. She commented that Mme Touraine-Brissac was not herself… that her grandmother's spirits were unusually buoyant."

"In what way?"

"Mme Haudry said her grandmother arrived at the reception with a glint in her eye and a smile plastered across her face, as if she were privy to a secret of significance known only to her. She said the Marquise had an air of—and these were her words—*secretive smugness*."

"Did she postulate a reason for this—er—air?"

Vallentine roused himself enough to comment.

"Havin' her unmarriageable granddaughter finally married and to the Comte de Salvan's heir, might account for it."

"Very true, my lor—Vallentine," agreed Martin, but said to the Duke, "Mme Haudry overheard her grandmother enquire of M'sieur Haudry—and in the most charming manner—if he would extend his generosity to the couple by permitting them to stay at his townhouse for a week, possibly two. They were only to spend the wedding night and one more before setting off for Arles."

"*Tante Philippe* made this request directly to the Farmer-General?"

"She did, Your Grace."

"How mortifying for her," replied the Duke unsympathetically. "What reason did she have for the couple postponing their journey and remaining here?"

"She told M'sieur Haudry she was expecting news in the coming week, news the couple should hear firsthand, and not from the depths of the provinces," Martin told him. "M'sieur Haudry agreed to her request without hesitation, and put the townhouse at the couple's disposal for as long as they wished. He enquired if the news might be that the bride's father—M'sieur le Duc du Touraine—is to pay the newlyweds a visit. To which the Marquise responded with a polite laugh that while her son was caught up in his military duties, there was the possibility that when he, too, heard the news she was expecting, he might very well apply to *Sa Majesté* for a leave of absence to personally offer up his congratulations to his daughter and new son-in-law."

"Congratulations?" Roxton repeated with mild surprise. "That was the word she used?" When Martin nodded, the Duke sat back and ruminated for a moment. "I wonder…" Then he voiced his thoughts. "Having the couple delay their journey to Arles makes perfect sense if my aunt knows about Salvan's letter—"

"What?" Vallentine blurted out and sat up, more alert than he had been since entering the library. "How could she possibly know that festerin' worm wrote to Antonia?"

"She is not unintelligent, and she is politically astute," the Duke replied mildly. "In her son's absence she has acted as head of the Touraine family for years. And since Salvan's banishment, she has acted on his behalf here and in Paris—"

"Would Salvan confide his intention to write to Mme la Duchesse?" Martin wondered. "Surely Mme Touraine-Brissac would advise against such a suicidal venture."

"Or encourage it," replied Roxton cryptically. "But she has other—er—surreptitious means of obtaining information."

"Means?" asked Vallentine. "How?"

"Members of the French secret police are in her pay," explained the Duke. "I know this because I pay more handsomely. I am also on better terms with the Lieutenant General of Police for Paris, M'sieur de Marville. While he is yet to confirm this to me, we can safely assume that it is through these contacts that *Tante Philippe* found out about Salvan's letter."

"She might know of its existence, but would she know what the weasel wrote?" Vallentine asked.

"The point of paying the secret police is to ferret this out," the Duke replied. "Once the letter left Salvan's possession and reached Paris, it would find its way to the desk of a flunkey working in the police department, whose specific duties are to examine the correspondence of the nobility, and others whom the King deems of interest.

"And as a disgraced courtier banished by a *lettre de cachet*, Salvan is such a person of interest. Secret police open these letters, read them, and those they consider worthy of reporting are copied out. These copies are then bound and sent daily to M'sieur le Marquis de Maurepas, who as Minister of the King's Household, is responsible for reporting this information to *Sa Majesté*. The original letter is expertly re-sealed and sent on its way, the correspondents none the wiser.

"The irony is, the secret police are no secret and neither are their methods. It is presumed all letters going through the Parisian postal system have the potential of being opened. Which is why I employ my own couriers, and have informants within their ranks to inform on others.

"To return to Salvan's letter… Once it was read and copies made, it was resealed and sent on to England, to Antonia's grandmother, for her to then include in her own correspondence to Antonia—"

"Pardon, Your Grace," interrupted Martin, digesting and making sense of all that Roxton had told them. "As the English also have a sophisticated network of spies and a department within the government that deals with espionage, I presume a letter from a disgraced French comte to the grandmother of the Duchess of Roxton, would alert the relevant flunkeys."

"It did. And that is how I came to—er—discover Salvan had written to Antonia."

"It should have been me and not Spaniel who told you," Vallentine said sheepishly, an embarrassed sideways glance at Martin. "Damme, Roxton," he growled, thumping the padded arm of the wingchair. "M' gut churns every time I think of how I didn't warn you!"

"How comforting that at least one of your organs is penitent," drawled the Duke. He let out a breath and sat up. "But it will churn for only a little longer; you are soon to redeem yourself, as I require your services—"

"Name anythin' and I'm your man!"

"I know that, Lucian. Thank you."

"A pity a flunkey in the Parisian secret police didn't tell you about Salvan's letter before it left for London," His Lordship remarked casually.

"A pity indeed," purred the Duke, setting his teeth. "Be assured, it is but a hiccup in my network of informants. The—er—lapse is being dealt with as we speak."

"Good. Nothin' worse than an incompetent sluggard!"

"You are troubled, Martin," said the Duke. He smiled crookedly. "I won't have the—er—incompetent sluggard slain, merely removed from his post."

"I was not thinking of that individual at all, Your Grace," Martin admitted. "Incompetence should be dealt with swiftly, and disloyalty harshly—"

"Bravo to that!" interjected Vallentine.

"I was struck by your earlier remark," Martin continued. "That Mme Touraine-Brissac might encourage Salvan to write to Mme la Duchesse, aware that such a perilous action would start a chain of events leading to his demise."

"Do you always rattle on in that way, Ellicott?" His Lordship asked wonderingly

"He does," stated the Duke, with a smile of satisfaction.

"I think I understand what you're gettin' at," said Vallentine. "But let me get it straight: You're sayin' *Tante Philippe* likely put the notion into Salvan's skull to write that letter knowing full-well that if he did Roxton would make good on his threat to kill him?"

The Duke bowed his head. "Precisely."

Vallentine and Martin looked at each other at the same moment, smiled at their similar responses, with His Lordship asking bluntly, "Why? Why would she do that? He's a festerin' worm, but he's still her nephew."

"Think, Lucian," said the Duke. "When Salvan dies by my sword, Montbelliard inherits not only the title of Comte de Salvan, but he also restores the family's fortunes, and their court appointments. He is also young, and *Tante Philippe* believes she can manipulate him, much better than she ever could Jean-Honoré."

"You said she was politically astute," said His Lordship. "And if she's behind this letter then she's more cunnin' than I'd have given her credit! And I'll tell you somethin' else—I've yet to meet a grandmother I like!"

TWENTY-SEVEN

"*T*ANTE *PHILIPPE* and Augusta Fitzstuart share commonalities, which is true," the Duke responded. "They are both intelligent and cunning. But whereas the former used hers to sail through the halls of Versailles to advance the family fortune, the latter cultivated her vanity and carnal appetites, allowing her intelligence to stagnate and her cunning to fester into jealous spite. Both are utterly ruthless in the means justifying the ends. *Tante Philippe* will do everything in her power for her family, Augusta everything for herself. Neither gives an ecu for those who stand in their way.

"But I digress. Lucian, you will be accompanying me to Limoges, specifically the Chateau D'Ambert. I have written to M'sieur le Comte de Salvan and sent the letter by my swiftest courier. He will know soon enough that I am coming to honor my word and put an end to his life. I want you as my second—"

"Of course. It will be my privilege," stated His Lordship. "It's goin' to be a one-sided contest, and over before it begins. A swift end is not what I had in mind for Salvan, but he'll be quaking in his stockings once he reads your letter, and be in a state of abject terror until it is all over. I'm satisfied with that. But what has me mystified is if there is a gentleman in France who would willingly step forward to act as that weasel's second. Unless someone can be found, how do you propose to bring this affair to a satisfyin' conclusion? And that's assumin' Salvan will meet with you."

"He will. He has no choice. And do not despair. A second will be found. I have written to the Duc du Touraine, requesting his presence to officiate at the encounter. His battalion is presently only half a day's ride from Limoges. I have charged him with finding a soldier amongst his men who will act as Salvan's second, someone with impeccable honor that matches his own. In this way, all will be conducted, recorded, and reported without bias and blemish. I will not have my good name besmirched, nor Salvan's death at the point of my sword glorified."

When the Duke stood, so did Vallentine and Martin. His Lordship rubbed his hands together.

"When do we leave?"

"The day after tomorrow. Preparations are well underway for our journey, and for our wives to return to Paris." Roxton looked to Martin. "I want you to keep company with the Duchess. She will need you; even more so if the—er—unthinkable were to happen. And Lucian," he added quickly before either man could interrupt, "I fear tonight and tomorrow will not be pleasant for you, once you tell Estée what is afoot—"

"Ain't you tellin' her?" asked Vallentine, instantly filled with dread at the picture in his mind's eye of his wife's overly dramatic reaction. There would be tears, lots of them, and cushions thrown, and names called. "You're the head of the family and her brother, and the one fightin' the duel with Salvan."

"I could not deny you a husband's right to inform his wife of his intentions to act as my second," drawled the Duke. "Nor be so overbearing as to pull—er—rank on you."

"You certainly chose your moment to find some humility!" Vallentine grumbled.

"And that is my right, as head of the family," the Duke replied, and made his brother-in-law a polite bow. He then clapped him on the shoulder and said without artifice, "I have two nights and one day with my wife and son before you and I set off. I wish to spend that time with them, alone and without interruption. Is that too much to ask?"

Vallentine shook his head. "Not at all. I'm a selfish sot."

"If I may make a recommendation, my lord?" Martin Ellicott said quietly. When Vallentine nodded, suggested, "To lessen Lady Vallentine's anxiousness and stop her mind from wandering to imagining the more shocking of possible outcomes of her brother fighting a duel with her cousin, steer her thoughts to the upcoming extensive renovations of your apartments at the hôtel. You may then avoid an extended period of soothing her fears and macabre fancies. Did you not tell me that you have yet to agree on a final selection of colors for—"

Vallentine's blue eyes widened in understanding. He snapped his fingers. "The swatches! Damme! That's an excellent notion!"

He strode over to the Duke's desk and yanked open a bottom drawer. He pulled out a velvet bag stuffed with swatches and color cards and held it up, as if it were a prize stag he had just brought down.

"I know what I'll do. Tell her the news about Limoges, and in the next breath, while she's still thinkin' that through, and before she can conjure all sorts of flights of horrible fancies, I'll make a *counter-riposte*—pull out this bag and tell her I'm still in two minds about the colors she's chosen. I might even become stubborn and while she's *parryin'* about that, I'll make a *fleche* by declarin' her selections are not mine." He let out an uneasy chuckle. "She'll make a *lunge* for me, but I reckon she'll be suitably diverted—No! She'll be infuriated with me—hopefully until we leave for Limoges. That will keep her from worryin' unnecessarily. Thank you, Ellicott. You're priceless."

"And you, Lucian, are a braver man than either of us," quipped the Duke.

Lord Vallentine beamed. "I am, ain't I!"

And with that declaration and the velvet bag slung over a shoulder, His Lordship wandered off to verbally cross swords with his wife.

WITH VALLENTINE GONE from the room, the Duke returned to his desk and sat behind it, offering Martin the chair opposite. On the blotter in front of him was the tooled and gilded red-leather *portefeuille* emblazoned with the ducal coat of arms. The Duke splayed his long fingers over this symbol of his rank and fortune and looked across at his former valet.

"There are several documents I wish you to keep safe for me while I am away—one being a copy of my last will and testament —should the—er—unthinkable happen and only my mortal remains are returned to Paris—"

"Your Grace, please! There is not the remotest possibility of that happening!"

"I have every expectation that it will not, but we know Salvan is not honorable. He will do whatever it takes to save his mortal carcass at the expense of his immortal soul. Thus, anything is possible." Roxton's smile was lop-sided. "And so one must plan for all and any eventualities—real or imagined."

"And you want *me* to be the custodian of these documents? Why not His Lordship, or-or an esteemed relative—"

"And why not you? I trust you—"

"Thank you, Your Grace. But Vallentine, he is your best friend!"

"I have many friends and esteemed relatives, but I can count on one hand those I trust. And you forget—Vallentine will be with me." The Duke removed his fingers from the leather satchel and sat back. "If Antonia had shown you Salvan's letter and asked that you not say a word to me, what would you have done?"

Martin did not hesitate in his response. "I would have advised against such action and done my utmost to convince her to take the letter to you."

"And if she had not taken your advice, and still burned the letter?"

"That would not have deterred me from telling you, and telling Mme la Duchesse of my intention to do so."

"That is what I thought. I believe that had she confided in you, she would have taken your advice—" The Duke inhaled deeply and settled again in his chair. "—and this situation in which we find ourselves would have been resolved more expediently and with fewer—er—complications. But I am mindful that she will always follow her heart, and for that I am forever grateful. Thus I am not overly perturbed at how matters have arranged themselves."

"You knew a day would come when you would make good on your threat to kill Salvan?"

"Indeed."

"You have told me the *portefeuille* contains your last will and testament, Your Grace, but may I know what other documents you wish me to keep safe?"

"As well as my will and several letters, there is a document—a list of instructions if you will—for the Duchess. It concerns several unencumbered properties, relatives and retainers who enjoy my munificence, certain members of my household here in France and in England who are to receive particular gifts. And there are my wishes concerning my—*our*—son's upbringing..."

Roxton stopped himself and a long silence followed. Martin knew the Duke was struggling with an inner turmoil, and that it had everything to do with the Duchess and their infant son. In the event of his death, the Duke would leave behind an inconsolable young widow with an infant. It was not lost on Martin, and he was certain the Duke either, that were that to happen, it would be family tragedy repeating itself.

In his position as valet, Martin was used to the Duke keeping his own counsel, and he not speaking until spoken to. But in his new role as friend and confidant he needed to move the conversation forward so the Duke could recover his sangfroid.

"Your Grace, you mentioned letters…? What would you have me do with those… send them—?"

"No. You may hand-deliver them. Two are for the Duchess, the other is for my son, for her to give to him when she thinks him old enough to read its contents. By the by, you may as well know now that the executors of my will are Mme la Duchesse, the Duc du Touraine, Lord Vallentine, and your esteemed self—"

"Good God! Me?"

The Duke's lips twitched.

"You look horrified. I have overwhelmed you yet again. But I make no apologies." He sighed, and added in a tongue-in-cheek drawl, "The price you pay for being part of such an illustrious family, and the trusted friend of its illustrious head. A heavy burden for you, but not for me—"

"I am—I am truly honored, Your Grace," Martin replied, ignoring the sarcasm. "I won't disappoint you, or Mme la Duchesse."

"I know that, Martin or we would not be having this conversation. If you would not interrupt, I have more to say—"

"Of course—pardon!"

"The executors have jurisdiction over the substantial property and income that will remain in trust until my son reaches his majority," the Duke explained. "And to Antonia, I have given free rein over the rest of my affairs and estates that are not entailed. This will not please anyone. That is understandable, given she is young and female. I am already thought by many to be in my dotage for marrying her. But I do not give a groat for the opinions of others where my marriage is concerned. And as you know, in everything, I aim to please myself, and I do.

"But in giving her this—er—freedom, should she become a widow, means she will face opposition and obstacles from almost everyone. To overcome these, she needs a confidant, someone she can trust implicitly, who is loyal to a fault but who will not shy away from telling her the truth, and who has her best interests, and those of my son, at the core of their being—their heart. And for my own peace of mind, I must know she has that someone in her life —always. I believe you to be that someone, Martin… Are you?" When the man blinked, choked back tears, and dropped his head, nodding, he added softly, "I need to hear you say it."

"I am! I am, Your Grace. With-with every fiber of my being."

The Duke stood. So did Martin. But with Martin's next words the Duke sat again.

TWENTY-EIGHT

"As you have so graciously confided in me, and honored me with these responsibilities, should the unthinkable come to pass, I wonder if Your Grace would permit me to tell you what I have decided about my future." Martin smiled diffidently. "It will take but a few moments."

When he did not follow the Duke's lead and resume his seat, Roxton was compelled to ask, "You wish to remain standing to say your piece?"

"I do, Your Grace."

At that the Duke sat back and waved a hand for him to continue.

Martin coughed into his fist to clear a dry throat. He was nervous, not only because he wondered if his proposal would be accepted, but if the Duke might consider it a grand presumption. But he would never know if he did not lay out his plans.

"After you and Mme la Duchesse changed my life forever by making me a gentleman of independent means, you remarked that I might curse rather than thank you for doing so. That with the necessity to be gainfully employed removed, and able to live as I please, you wondered how I would fill my days. I pondered this ever since and have an answer."

"So soon?"

"Yes, Your Grace." When the Duke said nothing further, Martin continued. "I asked myself how I could repay you for your kindness and generosity—"

"The Duchess and I do not want that. You have wasted your time." The Duke smiled crookedly. "But as time is yours to do with as you please, you may—er—waste it however you please."

"My wish is to be of use to you and Mme la Duchess," Martin continued earnestly. "And I believe I have found a way."

"Go on."

"My proposal, if acceptable to you both, would allow me to make a contribution to this esteemed family, and to spend my days gainfully occupied." Martin could not help a smile. "I do believe I shall never be bored again. Every day will bring new challenges and interest, and no doubt surprises."

"Ah, and now I am intrigued."

"You possibly have not yet thought to the time when Julian is breeched. But I have. I know that when my godson puts on his first pair of breeches, he will leave the nursery and the exclusive company of female servants and start his long path to manhood.

"As your heir, he will have his own household in a part of the many houses you occupy, where his needs specific to being your heir will be met: Academic tutors, a fencing master, another for deportment and dance, one for music, for horsemanship, and all the other many and varied instructors necessary for the education and nurturing of a future Duke of Roxton. And then there are the servants required to run such a household from the valets to the cooks, to the footmen, and a tailor. I do not have to tell you, Your Grace, but I mention them so that you know I have given it all my considered thought, and to allow you to think over my proposal."

"Which is…?"

"As Julian's godfather, I would be honored to take on the role of majordomo of his household," Martin stated. "Naturally, I would never presume to make any decision regarding his welfare without consulting Your Graces, but the decisions requiring the day-to-day running of his house, dealing with servants, menus, juggling the time of competing masters and tutors, I would gladly spare you— most particularly Mme la Duchesse.

"As his mother, it is natural she will fret once Julian has his own establishment, regardless that her son still resides under the same roof. And—pardon me for making such a presumption—but as the daughter of a—some have branded—*radical* physician who permitted her a boy's education and a unique upbringing, Mme la Duchesse may not appreciate that Julian as your heir must be reared in a particular way so he is fit to take his place as the sixth duke. I am confident Mme la Duchesse will bring her own special perspective to her son's education, and Julian will be all the better for it. But I believe that if I am the majordomo of his household and the one she consults on day-to-day matters, she will be less inclined to worry, you will have less to concern you, and the tranquility you expect under your roof will be maintained."

"Dear me, Martin, you certainly have thought deeply on this matter. May I ask what you intend to do in the interim—though of course it is none of my business. You may do as you wish when you wish. But I am sure you have calculated it will be four or five years before you could take on the responsibility for my son's household."

"I have indeed considered that, Your Grace," Martin replied, unconsciously perching himself on the end of the seat and smiling across the desk at the Duke. "In those handful of years there will be, God willing, more children added to your nursery. I hope I can be of use to Mme la Duchesse, in whatever capacity she requires, as she juggles her children's needs while they are infants. And— pardon the presumption—I can smooth her concerns, so that when the time comes for Julian to leave the nursery, she will be reassured knowing I will be the one in charge of her son's household."

Martin took a breath. Undaunted by the Duke's inscrutability

—a characteristic he had dealt with for two decades, and one that left lesser men quaking in their boots—he continued.

"I know Your Grace will enter into any and all discussions with Mme la Duchesse where your children are concerned, but as you have other matters to attend to regarding the estates and affairs of state back in England, my involvement would at least relieve you of some of the necessity to participate in any of the preliminary discussions regarding your nursery."

"And this would sufficiently and satisfyingly occupy your time?"

"It would, Your Grace. I may, from time to time, spend a few months a year at Moran Hall. But other than that, I have no plans but to be part of this family."

The Duke believed him, and yet he felt compelled to ask, "And it is your sincere wish to be majordomo of my son's household?"

"It would be my great honor, Your Grace."

The Duke stood, and so did Martin.

"I will talk over your proposal with Mme la Duchesse, but I think I know what she will say—"

"I truly hope she will find it agreeable—"

"Agreeable?" Roxton repeated, and breathed a small sigh of gratitude. "She, like me, will be overjoyed, knowing our son's welfare could be in no better hands."

"That is very gratifying, Your Grace. Thank you."

The Duke extended his hand across the desk to have it warmly taken.

TWENTY-NINE

Earlier that afternoon, the Duke had left Antonia soaking in her bath, with her *femmes de chambre* washing the powder from her waist-length honey curls, and scrubbing her clean of the perfume, powder, and paint necessary to attend court. Now returning to their apartment after speaking with Martin, he expected to find her drying her hair by the fire, reading.

Instead he entered their bedchamber to discover her birthday sedan chair parked by the full-length windows. It was without its poles, and the door was wide on the view of the royal parkland. He heard his wife and son before he saw them. She was reading aloud, and their infant was squealing with delight.

They were not alone. Two chambermaids were gathering up into a basket the last of the damp toweling strips, having bound the Duchess's hair a second time, and a footman was busy arranging the coffee things and a silver urn on its pedestal. Seeing the Duke they all scurried away.

Roxton stooped under the sedan's doorway and took a moment to commit to memory the enchanting scene of his wife and child closeted away from the world.

Antonia was curled up on the velvet upholstered seat, leaning against the silk-wallpapered wall with knees drawn up. She was in undress, a silk banyan over her chemise and stockings, and wrapped in a cashmere shawl. Her hair was arranged in one long thick plait over a shoulder, wound tightly with fresh toweling strips to aid in drying. On her lap was their infant son.

In one fist he flapped about a length of fat satin ribbon which was tied around the ends of his mother's plait, and in the other was a silver-handled teething stick of coral encircled by a ring of tiny silver bells. Every time he moved his hand, they tinkled, and he squealed his delight.

"*Bonjour, ma très chère famille.*"

"Monseigneur! You have returned to us at last! And just in time. Celeste or Cecile will soon be here to put Julian to the breast again." She frowned. "He did not sleep at all well last night. Celeste she did not say so, but me I can tell. He is not in a pleasant mood, despite his squealing. I think the toothing is keeping him awake."

"No one who has toothache is ever in a good mood," he replied. He took his son in his arms and stepped back to allow Antonia to scramble out of the chair. "Need I wonder why your town conveyance is in our bedchamber?"

"I had Julian brought to me in it," she said matter-of-factly as she slipped on her brocade mules. "In this way he will not forget he enjoys riding in his maman's chair." She tilted her chin up to receive a kiss. "Thank you. We missed you."

"And I you," he said, dropping a further, lighter kiss on her forehead.

He walked with her to the sofa by the fire, and when she was settled, put their son back on her lap. He glanced at the book she had discarded on the low table, a small, sealed letter tucked between two pages to hold a place, and asked conversationally, "Which particular story from *Les Contes des Fées* were you reading to him?"

"Monseigneur, I am not convinced Madame d'Aulony's stories are suitable for children," she replied with a heavy sigh.

This made the Duke turn from organizing the coffee things, and regard her pensively, porcelain milk jug in hand.

"I agree. Some of her tales are not fit for adults. And this one, *ma fée…?*"

"*Le Mouton*. I had not read it before. It is about a prince who is turned into a ram by an ugly fairy, and a princess whose father, the king orders her death. But the woodsman he cannot carry out the king's orders. So one of the princess's animals, her dog, sacrifices his life to save her. There is a lot more to the story, but I cannot bear to tell you the rest, only that the ram he falls in love with this princess, and when she is late returning to him, he dies of a broken heart."

"That is indeed distressing, *ma belle*. But you must take comfort in the fact that our son is too young to understand what you are reading. He merely enjoys the sound of your voice."

"Which is why I made myself be happy while reading it, for his sake. I wanted to cry because the dog reminded me of poor Tan… Renard, I so wanted the story to end well—"

"—for the ram to transform back into the handsome prince so he and the beautiful princess could live happily ever after?"

Antonia kissed her son's rosy cheek and smiled up at the Duke. "Yes! Just like us!"

Roxton let out an involuntary chuckle. "Just like us."

He went back to making their coffee, and brought it over on a silver tray that had upon it two dishes and a small plate of delicate pastries. He placed this on the low table before the sofa and sat beside her. He then took his infant son onto his lap so Antonia could drink her coffee.

"I think I will return to reading to him from Tacitus," Antonia announced. "Or Suetonius, or Livy—any of the ancient authors would be better than these gruesome fairytales."

"The Julio-Claudian are far less ghastly," the Duke mocked.

"Monseigneur, you said so yourself. Julian he will not mind

what I read aloud, only that I do it." She smiled impudently. "So I will please myself." She sipped at her coffee and on a thought said emphatically, "I do not think your father he would have read Mme d'Aulony's tales to you."

"I do not recall that he did, only that he read to me, and often."

"They are lovely memories to have. But no, he would not have read from *Les Contes des Fées*."

"You are convinced. Why? Because the stories they are—er —unpleasant?"

"Most everyone would say because they are only fairytales and not to be believed, it does not matter if they are horrid," Antonia argued. "But there is always an element of truth in every story. But these particular ones are not only the stuff of nightmares, they are very sad." She met his gaze. "And for your father, they would have been even more unpleasant because they would have reminded him of his father."

"How so, *mignonne*?"

"Because your grandfather, he inhabits these fairytales in many terrible guises."

"Then we shall consign Madame d'Aulony's tales to the library to gather dust."

Antonia could not help herself… she giggled behind her hand. "Pardon, Monseigneur. But you will not be happy to learn that is where Jean-Luc he found this book. Amongst the dust!"

Roxton pretended to be shocked. "*Mon Dieu*, there is *dust* in my library?"

"It is the dust that horrifies you more than the fairytales."

"But of course, *ma vie*." His mouth twitched, but he said perfectly seriously, "My grandfather was a monster, but even he had —er—standards. Ah! And now it is time for my heir to return to the nursery," he added in an altogether different voice, and in English, spying a *nourrice* and one of the nursery maids lurking by the tapestry *portière*. "And for his parents to have some time to themselves—at last."

THIRTY

THEY FINISHED their coffee in companionable silence, Antonia saying as she set aside her empty dish, "With your permission, I wish Jean-Luc to come to Paris with us."

"Is there a particular reason for his company?"

"It is so he can spend a little more time with the *nouricces* and their children. They are all fond of him, and he enjoys their company. He reads to the children. He is also anxious to reshelve all the books we brought with us, and perform the tasks your librarian may require of him. To leave him here alone in an empty and silent house I do not think would be good for him."

"Then he must go with you."

"Thank you, Monseigneur. That will please—oh! Everyone!"

"Martin will also be accompanying you and Estée back to the hôtel while Vallentine and I are away."

"I am glad Lucian will be with you, but Madame she will not be pleased by his absence."

"An understatement, *ma fée*. She will howl all the way from here to the *pont neuf*. Which is why you will be traveling in separate carriages. I have also ordered the furniture and luggage wagons and the servant carriages to be between you in the convoy."

Antonia smiled. "That is very thoughtful of you. Martin and I may have a pleasant journey after all." She sighed heavily. "But in truth I do not think I will notice Madame's howls because I will be too preoccupied with worry over you."

"Come here, *ma belle*," the Duke coaxed. When she had slid down the sofa to be gathered into his embrace, he said gently, "I cannot tell you *not* to worry. Of course you will. All I ask is that you not allow your mind to wander to imaginings that are the stuff of Madame d'Aulony's fairytales. I will return to you and Julian, unscathed. I give you my word. And I always keep my word, do I not?"

"I know in my heart you will come back to us. But nothing is ever straightforward with Salvan. He is like one of the wicked mythical beings found in the pages of *Les Contes des Fées*. He is capable of great evil. Which is why I worry. And as we are talking of him, I have something for you."

When she shifted in his arms, he let her go and she reached for the book on the low table. She removed the place holder and held it out to him. It was a small, sealed note.

"I found it in the box with the handkerchiefs *Tante Victoire* sent me for my birthday. I did not break the seal when I recognized it. At first I did not know what to do with it, so I left it in the box and tried to forget it was there." Her smile was tremulous. "But our promise to each other to have no secrets reminded me I still had it, and so here it is for you to do with as you please. No secrets, *mari bien-aimé*."

The Duke turned the note over. Pressed into the red wax was the seal of the House of Salvan. His jaw locked. His first thought: That he could not wait to cross swords with his cousin to finally put an end to his insidious interference in his life. And then he quickly quelled his anger for he would not allow his fury with

Salvan to intrude into this most precious time spent with his wife. Nor would he spend another second thinking about his cousin until it was time to set off for Limoges.

To this end, he stood and held out his hand.

They stepped over to the fireplace, and there the Duke consigned Salvan's note, unread, to the fire. They stood watching the tight folds of parchment blacken and curl and burst into flame. When it had turned to ash, it was Antonia who broke the silence. She put her hands to the front of the Duke's silk banyan and looked up at him. What she said next was surprising because it was the last thing on his mind.

"Renard, I do not think you will find a spy amongst our household, because it is not a spy in the true sense of the meaning of that word."

The Duke gave this consideration and then said, "If not a spy, then whom do you suppose has been providing reports about our lives, not only to my ancient aunts, but to your *grand-mère*?"

She smiled brightly and taking his hand led him back to the sofa. "I knew you would understand *immédiatement*!" Curling up on the cushions facing him, she continued, just as animated. "I did not know this, but I am certain you must! Most, if not all of our servants are the sisters or brothers, aunts, or uncles—of some relation or other—of other servants in other great households. I knew your former coachman Baptiste is the brother-in-law of our butler Duvalier, but I did not ever imagine how complex is the interweaving of servant relations employed by the nobility here in France. It must be the same in England, yes? Oh! And not only the nobility, but the houses of the Farmers-General, too." Her eyes widened. "I discovered this when Gabrielle she told me that *all* her sisters are maids in noble households here and in Paris! It is *incroyable*, yes?"

"Gabrielle? How many sisters does your personal maid have in service?"

"Three. Yvette is the eldest. She is personal maid to Madame. Giselle is next and she is the maid of Elisabeth-Louise Salvan Gondi Touraine—oh! Who is now Madame Montbelliard. Rose is the maid of Elisabeth-Louise's sister Michelle—Madame Haudry. And then there is my Gabrielle, who is the youngest. Gabrielle she told me that it is no coincidence Michelle Haudry lives in the villa next to ours, because it was she who told her sister Rose, the personal maid of Mme Haudry, that the house it was for lease."

The Duke thought this over for a moment, and then said, "Estée would have consulted her personal maid when I requested she engage a maid for you, when I first brought you to the hôtel—"

"—and Yvette would have recommended her own sister Gabrielle for the position!" Antonia exclaimed with satisfaction. "*Et voilà!* That is how everything it arranges itself."

Her enthusiasm made him smile. He kissed her palm, saying over the top of her fingers, "So tell me how you think these sisters are involved in the reporting of our lives to others?"

Antonia frowned in thought. "Renard, I do not think it was done maliciously, or even deliberately, but in the way gossip travels from one mouth to another." She shrugged. "They are sisters. I never had a sister, but I know sisters they talk amongst themselves. It would be an easy thing to do for Yvette and Gabrielle, who are here in the same house. Would they not eat together in the servant hall, and pass each other on the stairs?

"And they both have the opportunity to see more of Rose because she resides next door with the Haudry family. But I do not think they would see much of Giselle. I met her in the house of *Tante Philippe* when you found me there suckling the Comtesse's distressed infant. She is circumspect, which is more than can be said for her mistress Elisabeth-Louise!"

"So we can discount Giselle as the sister spreading—er—gossip about us?"

"Yes! But I have never met Rose, so cannot comment on where she fits in this little mystery."

The Duke mentally smiled, but kept a neutral expression for fear she might think him insincere and not taking her musings seriously. When in fact he was impressed that her hypothesis about the identity of the spy in their midst could very well be the right one.

"As Giselle and Rose do not reside under our roof, they would only be the receivers of this gossip—"

"But could they not then pass it on?"

"True. Yet, as Giselle is circumspect, and Rose serves Mme Haudry and thus would not move in the same circles as the sisters who are employed in noble houses, I believe we can dismiss her too. Which leaves the other two sisters—Estée's personal maid—Yvette?" When Antonia nodded, he continued, "Yvette, and your Gabrielle. But which one is the unwitting—er—spy? Or is it both?"

"Monseigneur, I also do not know Yvette, but Gabrielle I do know. She is young and naïve, but she is no spy."

"What is your reasoning, *mignonne*?" he asked lightly, but this time he could not hide his grin, because Antonia's personal maid was several years her senior.

She seemed to read his thoughts when she said with a pout, feigning offense, "I do not forget Gabrielle she is older than me. But she has little experience of the world, other than her home, and our households here in France, and in England." She lost her pout and her eyes sparkled. "Whereas my experience of—oh! almost everything, I owe to M'sieur le Duc d'Roxton."

"And your esteemed father, who cultivated your intelligence, insatiable curiosity, and delightful forthrightness—"

"—all of which M'sieur le Duc greatly appreciates," she responded cheerfully. "Perhaps curiosity most of all."

"So you think?"

Antonia gave him a sidelong look. "Most certainly you do—in the bedchamber."

Roxton gasped, pretending shock. Then he pulled her into his arms. "And any other room of your choosing," he murmured, and kissed her.

"I am very curious about this room…"

"Vixen."

She giggled and he chuckled as they sunk ever deeper into the sofa cushions.

THIRTY-ONE

WHEN THEY FINALLY came up for air, disheveled and sated, the Duke was stretched full-length on the sofa, a hand under his head, Antonia cuddled up to him. She lifted her chin off his chest, returning to the topic of spies.

"Renard, when we speak in private, we often do so in the English or Italian tongue, so Gabrielle and our servants they can have little idea what we are talking about."

"I do not think your maid is the least interested in what tongue we discuss the Julio-Claudians, or the causes of the Peloponnesian wars, or whose side we take in the conflict between Scipio Africanus and Hannibal. It is our daily lives and our—er—interactions which are of interest. And I believe I know how it is being done—"

"I knew you would!" Antonia exclaimed happily, and snuggled back in. "Please explain it all to me."

"We know that our lives—and I speak in a general sense about the nobility—provide those who serve with a surfeit of gossip. This gossip is exchanged with their fellows, mostly for sheer titillation, which is harmless if kept amongst themselves. And then there are those who are less loyal and more mercenary who seek remuneration for providing these morsels of fascination to others. They sell them on, the buyers of this gossip with their own reasons for wanting to harm us."

"For *grand-mère* it is because she is spiteful and jealous. And for the Salvans, they wish to puncture your oh-so-great arrogance for sending the head of their family into exile, yes?"

"Just so, *mignonne*… And some take offense merely because I am the confidante of the King. Ambitious courtiers have often attempted to humiliate me, hoping I will lose favor with Louis—"

"But you have never cared about the opinions of others, so how then can they humiliate you?"

"But I care deeply that *you* not get caught up in their repellant intrigues. Such unsavory methods are now being used on Louis's mistress. Pompadour appears fragile—"

"She is very beautiful and delicate," Antonia stated.

"Not nearly as beautiful as you, *ma fée*, and she lacks your spirit—"

"Ah, I love you for saying so, *mon amour*. Her beauty and fragility must confuse her enemies, who think her fragile of mind too?"

"They will learn soon enough, to their detriment, that such fragility hides nerves hewn of marble. The Marquise will need to employ her shrewd intellect to outwit her opponents, but she will prevail."

Antonia frowned. "But, Renard, surely none of our personal servants would betray us?"

"I certainly pay them enough for their loyalty," quipped the Duke.

"Madame would scold you and say that is the thinking of a merchant," she teased. "Merchants pay for loyalty, but dukes are of noble blood and that should suffice for any man to want to serve you."

"My noble brethren, who live on credit, using their good name and title as surety, expect those who serve them, and the merchants who seek their custom, to be grateful to have their patronage. Settling their accounts is the last thing on their mind, and often it is their heirs who are left with an enormous debt. I won't allow that to happen to our children—"

"—because you are a good master and a good father," Antonia stated. "And a most wonderful husband."

The Duke smiled and gave her a hug. "Thank you for believing in me, *ma vie*. In truth, I have ever been pragmatic. I won't be indebted to anyone. I have always paid well and on time for exceptional service, so I am assured it will be prompt and well performed; loyalty is a secondary consideration, though I expect that, too."

"You are too harsh on yourself, Monseigneur. Your servants are loyal because you are a benevolent master, like your father before you. After we married, I asked about him, and discovered there are servants here at the villa, and at the hôtel, who served him, and they speak of Lord Alston with great fondness."

"He certainly was the antithesis of *his* father."

"I am glad we named our son in his memory, and they are too. They say it is a sign that he too will be a kind master, like his grandfather, and a benevolent one like his father."

"They are one and the same thing, *ma chérie*."

Antonia sat up, smiling brightly, and kissed him. "Yes. And you are both. So do not argue with me!"

"I would not dare!"

When they resettled, comfortable on the sofa facing one another, the Duke returned to the question of spies in their midst.

"I believe you are correct about the sisters. Our daily lives are being recounted indirectly through the conduit of their gossip… And I believe *my* sister is—"

"Estée?" Antonia gasped. "*Vraiment?*"

"—the common thread which entangles all the sisters."

Antonia's green eyes widened. "*Oh là là*! But of course! You are very clever. I should have thought of that."

"I have dealt with her ways and means for a great deal longer than you, *mignonne*. When she is—er—vexed, she is exceedingly carefree with her opinions, and without a care in the world who is within earshot."

"That is true," Antonia replied glumly. "I do not think she notices her servants until she needs them. And you are right, she never worries about voicing her thoughts at any time. Monseigneur!" she added in a rush on a sudden thought, "Perhaps Yvette felt the need to complain to her sisters about Madame's beh—"

"—tantrums? For that is what they are. Yes. Who wouldn't want to garner the sympathy of a sister after one of Estée's particularly energetic invectives."

Antonia sat back against the cushions in frowning thought, unconsciously fiddling with the ends of her long plait.

"Even if Yvette learned particulars about us through Madame, and she spoke with Gabrielle, how does this gossip then arrive in the ear of an ancient aunt? I do not believe Gabrielle would repeat it. And if Giselle is circumspect? She would not say a word…"

The Duke pulled a face and shrugged, as if he, too, was just as perplexed. But Antonia was not fooled. She saw the glint in his dark eyes, and the hint of a smile that lifted the corner of his mouth, and she scrambled across the sofa to snuggle up to him.

"I think you have been letting me wander up the garden path!" she scolded playfully. "You may agree with me that the sisters are gossips and gossip about us, and that Madame is reckless with her opinions when she is in one of her belligerent moods, but you do not believe that is how your ancient aunts or my *grand-mère* have discovered intimate details about us! You know, do you not, Monseigneur, and have always known, and you were merely humoring me all this time! Tell me! I do not want to wander anymore!"

"Oh? But what a lovely wander through the garden of possibilities we've been having, *mon adorable petite fée*. And it has allowed us to forget, even if for only a little while, what we both are to face in the coming days." He gave her plait a playful tug. "We will not wander any further today. To be entirely truthful, I had not entertained the notion that any of my servants would betray us. I assumed all along that it must be a servant of a Salvan who had ingratiated himself into our household. And my aunts in turn had passed on what they learned to your grandmother." He lightly kissed her forehead. "But you have shown me that the simplest explanation is often the right one. It makes sense the sisters would gossip, and perhaps they were often overheard by others, and they then gossiped beyond the walls of our houses. But even then, I do not think they are to blame."

"If you wish a simpler explanation, I believe it is Madame who is gossiping with your ancient aunts—"

"—and in her correspondence with Augusta," said the Duke, finishing her sentence. "And you would be correct. Your grandmother has a knack for extracting even the most minute detail from her correspondents, and thus I am confident Estée unwittingly told her everything she wished to know."

"Thank you for telling me," Antonia replied softly, "I, too, have enjoyed wandering *and* wondering in the garden of possibilities with you. But then," she added with a loving smile, "I could sit here in silence with you all day and be content."

"Why don't we do just that until dinner?"

"Oh! I should like that very much," she replied, but surprised him by hopping off the sofa and slipping on her mules. She apologized. "First I must have my hair dried and arranged."

Roxton's glance darted to the doorway. In the shadows was Gabrielle and peeking out from behind the *portière*, two of the chambermaids. He stood and pulled the silk banyan closer about his wide frame, then drew Antonia to him.

"I will collect our books," he told her, hand running the length of her plait to the fat silk ribbon. He curled her braid about his wrist. "Have them dry it by all means, but bring me your brush…"

She smiled and nodded, and after they exchanged a gentle kiss, he let her go. His gaze never left her as she crossed to the *portière*. But when she did not disappear behind the tapestry curtain but stood talking with her lady-in-waiting in hushed tones, he waited.

Antonia bustled back to him, a frown between her brows. She looked up, troubled.

"Renard, Mme Haudry is here. She says she must speak with you. That the matter is of great importance and cannot wait."

THIRTY-TWO

T HE DUKE looked over her head at Gabrielle. "Mme Haudry may come to me the day after tomorrow, at daybreak, before I set off for Limoges."

Gabrielle bobbed a curtsy and disappeared behind the *portière*. Antonia went to follow her when a commotion in the next room erupted. A door banged against the wallpaper, there was a crescendo of chatter, and other muffled noises, as if a scuffle had broken out. Finally a deep, low voice penetrated the mayhem, and all went quiet, but only for a moment.

The ducal couple looked at each other, and then back at the *portière*. The Duke drew Antonia into the circle of his arm, and they both waited in silence, wondering. Neither was surprised when the tapestry curtain rippled, then was flung out of the way. The Duke's valet, George Gerharty, strode in and bowed. On his heels was Gabrielle, and behind her a wild-eyed footman. But it was who was behind them that set the Duke's teeth.

"Roxton! Antonia! Oh, Thank God! *Mon Dieu*! What news! What shocking news! I can hardly believe it!"

It was Estée and breathing down her back was Lord Vallentine.

"Calm yourself, lovedy," His Lordship ordered soothingly. "I told you it was best if I handled this. Can't be good for the baby to get y'self worked up in this way. What if you go into labor—"

"Don't be ridiculous, Lucian! I have weeks—*months*—before the baby it will arrive! How you expect me to be calm when *Tante Victoire* sends me this news, I know not!" She brandished a single page in the air and rushed over to her brother. "Roxton! Read! You will not believe it!"

"You may leave us," the Duke said calmly to his valet, gaze sweeping over the other hovering servants, whose wide eyes dropped to the floor when their master dared to look their way.

The servants had barely shuffled from the room and the tapestry curtain fallen back into place when Vallentine said sheepishly, "Sorry for bargin' in here like this. But it couldn't be helped."

"Must I place armed guards at the doors in my own home?" enquired the Duke with icy politeness. "Furnished with pistols to stop you?"

His Lordship shrugged. "Pistols it would have to be. And the order 'shoot to kill', because Estée would have me engage them in a bloody struggle if they drew a sword—"

"—and for her you would slay every one, Lucian," Antonia interrupted with a smile.

"I would—for her, Mme la Duchesse," he replied meekly.

"Oh, Lucian! You are the bravest, most wonderful man I know!" Estée blurted out, throwing herself into his arms and bursting into tears.

"Now, now, there's no need for that," His Lordship soothed. "I know why you're overwrought, but we need to keep our wits about us to explain to y'brother and Antonia why we dared to rudely barge in on 'em."

He looked over her head buried in his chest and rolled his eyes, before turning his gaze on the Duchess. He instantly wished he had not because she was in undress, wearing a silk banyan over very little else, hair braided in one long plait. He blushed, and that deepened when he realized his best friend was similarly unclothed. The Duke was without his cravat and the ribbon that usually tied back his long black curls was loose, hair falling across his brow and about his shoulders.

Vallentine took his gaze around the room and up to the painted ceiling and made an innocuous comment. "Don't think I've ever been in this part of the house—"

"—or will be again," quipped the Duke, then let out a weary sigh. "What is so—er—momentous that you dared to disobey me?"

Estée turned her face from being buried in her husband's waistcoat to look at her brother. She thrust out the letter. "Read it, Roxton. *Tante Victoire* she says—she says our cousin he is—he is —*dead*."

The Duke stepped forward, a tightness in his throat. "Cousin? Not Alphonse—?"

"Alphonse?" Estée frowned and shook her head, and tucked the letter into his hand. "No! No! Not Alphonse."

"*Dieu soit loué,*" murmured the Duke.

When he went to the fireplace to read, Antonia, Vallentine, and Estée watched and waited. But his sister could not be silent long. She addressed the Duchess in a loud whisper.

"This is why we had to come. Why I made Lucian force his way in here. I am sorry but this letter it changes *everything*."

"I do not understand, Madame," Antonia replied. "What does it change? Who has died?"

The Duke turned and faced them. His face was white. He asked quietly, "Is Mme Haudry still at the villa?"

"She is here? Why?" It was a surprise to Estée, and also to Vallentine, who shrugged.

"Thank you for bringing this to me," Roxton said. "We will talk later tonight, at dinner—"

"You're endin' your isolation and re-joinin' the family?" enquired His Lordship.

"With this news, I must. Be good enough to send in a footman."

"I do not understand! Why are we being dismissed? I brought the letter! I need to talk about this with you now. We can't leave. We—"

"Come, lovedy," His Lordship coaxed, putting an arm around his wife's shoulders, and slowly leading her across the room. "You heard y' brother. He said we'll all talk later tonight, at dinner. At this minute he needs time to take it in, and to discover if it is indeed true—"

"*Tante Victoire* would never lie about something as prodigious as this!?" Estée argued. "Do you not understand it is a mortal sin to—"

"Oh, what I understand is that we've committed a mortal sin by bargin' in here!"

Before she knew where she was, Vallentine had his wife at the curtain. He lifted it and ushered her into the next room, still talking and arguing with her, leaving the Duke and Duchess alone again, but only for a moment. A footman appeared in the doorway.

"Bring Mme Haudry to me. If she has returned home, fetch her back. Have her wait in the library. We will join her there."

Roxton then turned to his Duchess and gave her the letter.

"It's Salvan. He's dead.

THIRTY-THREE

MADAME HAUDRY was sipping a second dish of coffee when the ducal couple finally joined her in the library.

Both had dressed in clothing befitting their preeminent rank.

The Duke wore an ensemble of softest black velvet with a waistcoat smothered in silver spangles, and low-heeled black leather shoes with large buckles encrusted with diamonds. In the folds of his white linen cravat was a gold pin and his raven hair was pulled off the stark handsome face, the long braid tied off with white silk ribbons, one at the nape, the other at the end of the queue in the middle of his back.

The Duchess was similarly sumptuously attired in a silk Robe Volante gown in tones of muted mauve and silver with delicate lace engageantes cascading from elbow to wrist. The deep V-cut to the bodice, infilled with a stomacher smothered in silver spangles, mirrored her husband's waistcoat and displayed her impressive bosom to perfection. She wore no jewelry. A radiant beauty, she had no need of it.

No wonder Michelle Haudry had been kept waiting for over an hour. It was clear that in dressing with such care and in such opulent fabrics, the ducal couple was giving the occasion the formal solemnity it warranted.

She dispensed with her coffee dish and saucer and was up off the sofa and down into a deep curtsy with all the grace required of a newly appointed lady-in-waiting to the Queen.

"My apologies for intruding on your time, M'sieur le Duc. But this could not wait."

"Is it true?" the Duke asked, gesturing for her to resume the seat opposite. He waited for Antonia to arrange her voluminous gown, before flicking out the skirts of his frock coat to sit beside her. Lifting his dark eyes to their guest, he asked. "The Comte de Salvan is dead?"

Michelle Haudry kept her gaze on his, voice steady. "I am here to inform you, *M'sieur le Duc et Mme la Duchesse*, that Jean-Honoré Louis Gabriel de Salvan, the Comte de Salvan is dead. He-he—" She faltered and stopped when the Duchess sighed and slumped against the Duke's arm.

Antonia made a quick recover, however, muttering her apologies, the Duke murmuring something to her that Michelle Haudry did not catch, before returning his attention to their visitor.

"You know this how, Madame?"

"A representative of my father-in-law was in Limoges—"

"—and happened to be there at the exact moment of M'sieur le Comte's demise? How fortuitous."

"Pardon, M'sieur le Duc, the meeting had been prearranged and was to inform the Comte of the financial provisions my father-in-law has put in place for the Chevalier Montbelliard and my sister." She smiled diffidently. "He thought it prudent to make the Comte aware of these arrangements."

"M'sieur Haudry is ever shrewd," commented the Duke, and gave a nod for her to continue.

"When the representative arrived at the chateau on the specified day and time, he found the Comte's household in a state of great agitation. The word he used was *uproar*. Their master had locked himself in his rooms three days earlier, and no one at the chateau, not even the cinders maid, had been able to gain access to the Comte's rooms since."

"Did this—er—representative discover the reason Salvan had locked himself away?"

"No one was able to provide a definitive answer," Michelle Haudry replied. "The Comte's valet confided in the representative that it was not unusual for his master to have episodic sulks, where he would refuse all food and drink—that is until his valet, or his physician could coax him around to unbolting the door. Such sulks rarely lasted an entire day, and even when he refused to see anyone, he would still shout his demands from the other side of the door. Which is why, when three days had gone by and there was no sound from the Comte's rooms, the physician had the servants employ a battering ram to break down the door."

"How medieval! And the reason for this particular—er—sulk?"

"The valet postulated that it was because several letters and packages had arrived from Paris and Versailles, wishing him *joyeux anniversaire*, and his master hated being reminded he was another year further away from the day of his birth."

"That sounds like Salvan, sulking about his birthday!"

"But, Monseigneur, sulking cannot have killed him," Antonia argued. She asked Michelle Haudry, "Does the representative know what were in the letters and packages?"

"An excellent question, *ma vie*."

The Duke and Duchess regarded their visitor in silent expectation.

"Only one letter, and a wooden box, had been opened. Both were from my grandmother." Michelle Haudry glanced at the Duchess, who was listening intently, hands in her lap, before continuing. "The valet gave my grandmother's letter to the representative, and it is now with my father-in-law—"

"He did not think to offer it to me. After all, you and he are aware, I forbade your grandmother from corresponding with Salvan, and that letter proves her perfidy—"

"M'sieur le Duc, it does and does not. To explain: You barred her from all contact with her nephew, and yes, she did write to him after she gave you her word. But in her defense, she wrote advising him that it would be the last time she would have any contact with him. The wooden box was a final, parting gift."

"And in the box?"

"Two jars of marinated figs packed in straw. The Comte had opened it the night before he locked himself in his rooms. The valet remembered this particularly because when he was attending to his master before he retired for the evening, he saw the two jars on the dressing table."

"Had they been opened?"

"Not then, no," Michelle Haudry replied, curiosity compelling her to ask, "May I know why you would say that, M'sieur le Duc?"

"As the valet was keen to inform M'sieur Haudry's representative that he remembered the figs, and this representative then told him, and now you are telling me, it would appear the figs have a vital part to play in Salvan's demise."

Antonia drew in a sharp breath. "Monseigneur! You think the figs they killed him?"

The Duke was unable to suppress a chuckle. "Not in the literal sense…"

Antonia clapped a hand to her mouth to smother a giggle, then whispered, "You are being absurd! Thank you. I feel better for it."

"My pleasure, *ma fée*," he replied and returned his gaze to their visitor, solemnity re-established. "We have reached the point where you tell us—without the representative's hyperbole—precisely how the Comte de Salvan met his end."

"Very well, M'sieur le Duc. It is the opinion of the physician the Comte died of a heart attack, brought on by consuming a surfeit of figs."

"A heart attack?" The Duke looked unconvinced. "Did he consume both jars or just the one?"

Again Michelle Haudry was enquiring. "Only one jar was opened, and though the representative thought it strange that half its contents remained untouched, and thus the Comte had eaten only a small quantity of the delicacy, the physician was adamant in his diagnosis."

"Did the physician entertain the idea the figs could have been laced with poison, and it was the poison which induced a heart attack?"

Antonia sat up. "If it was poison, and the figs they were a gift from *Tante Philippe*—" Horrified, she looked to Michelle Haudry. "Pardon, Madame, I should not assume it was your *grand-mère* who put the poison in the jar of figs."

"There is no need to apologize, Mme la Duchesse," Michelle Haudry interrupted. "I am well aware of what my grandmother is capable, and it would not surprise me to learn she laced the figs with poison." She sighed, as if mustering her strength to continue. "My father-in-law believes—and I agree with him—that my grandmother already knew the Comte was dead—or was soon to be—when she attended the wedding reception of the Chevalier to my sister. That would account for her buoyant mood, and the reason for her request that the couple remain a little longer in Versailles. And that too, suggests her guilt."

"In poisoning one nephew, the Marquise Touraine-Brissac denied her other nephew the satisfaction of defending his honor. I do not thank her for that."

"You think that, too, was deliberate on her part, Monseigneur, —to deny you?" asked Antonia.

The Duke's lip curled. "It would give her a certain sort of satisfaction, to think that she has outwitted us both. That Salvan is dead is a huge relief. And it has released me from the inconvenience of traveling to Limoges. But, no, I do not believe that was my aunt's primary motivation for gifting Salvan a jar of poisonous figs."

"So why did she do it?" asked Antonia, still baffled. And then answered her own question. "So Montbelliard he could succeed to the title, and her granddaughter be the Comtesse de Salvan, much sooner than anyone anticipated."

"It does mean the Salvan family will be restored to their positions at court, Mme la Duchesse," said Michelle Haudry.

"Motivation enough to commit murder," the Duke drawled.

Antonia was unconvinced, and her brow furrowed. "But she would have achieved the same outcome had she let M'sieur le Duc meet Salvan with swords. And what of the risk of her being discovered a murderess? Committing murder is a sin from which she can never recover; her priest will tell her so."

"This is not the first time she has sinned, *ma fée*. And even she would agree that breaking the fifth commandment and adding it to her long list of sins will hardly blacken an already blackened soul." He inclined his head to their visitor. "I beg your pardon if the truth is painful for you, Madame."

Michelle Haudry was philosophical. "There is no need, M'sieur le Duc. I learned to ignore that pain a long time ago. My father confided in me the irony that his mother will justify committing any sin you care to name, if it is in the pursuit of advancing the family's honor. Honor! It would be laughable if it was not so disturbing." From a concealed pocket she produced a letter, and this she passed to the Duke. "Perhaps this contains the answers you both seek about the Comte's death."

The letter was sealed with the Salvan crest pressed into the red wax, and one word was written across the obverse: Roxton. It was in Salvan's handwriting.

It required all the Duke's willpower to take the letter, and then he did so as if required to touch something utterly repellant. He immediately slid it into a deep pocket of his frock coat and flexed his fingers, as if shaking them free of contagion.

"It was discovered on his body," Michelle Haudry told them. "The representative gave it to my father-in-law and assured him that no one knows of the letter's existence, except the physician, and he was paid handsomely to forget."

"Does M'sieur Haudry know its contents?"

"No, M'sieur le Duc. And, please, before you ask, you know as well as I, that it would have been an easy thing to have it opened, read, and then resealed. But my father-in-law is an honorable man. He left the seal intact and wanted me to assure you of that. That handing over this letter to you is a gesture of his loyalty—to you, M'sieur le Duc, and in thanks for placing your trust in me."

"His loyalty is greatly appreciated, as is yours. To that end, the Duchess and I invite your father-in-law and your family to dine at the hôtel upon our return to Paris."

"We will be honored to sit at your table, M'sieur le Duc."

"We are returning home tomorrow," added the Duchess, a smile up at the Duke. "Now all of us can do so as a family, which pleases me greatly."

"My father-in-law also offered for his representative to call on you at your convenience, M'sieur le Duc. So that you may have a firsthand account of his visit to the Chateau d'Ambert. We had hoped to inform you before anyone else, but I am afraid my grand-mother received word by a swifter courier and the family were given news of the Comte's death early this morning—"

"Which explains how my sister came to hear of it from *Tante Victoire*," interrupted the Duke with annoyance. "No matter. By nightfall the palace will be talking of nothing else, and it will be the only topic of conversation in the Parisian salons by morning."

Michelle Haudry stood and bobbed a curtsy. "I must return to my duties at the palace, and as I can offer you nothing more, I will bid you a good afternoon, *M'sieur le Duc et Mme la Duchesse*."

THIRTY-FOUR

MICHELLE HAUDRY was barely out of the room when Antonia threw herself into the Duke's arms.

"I am so very happy you are not leaving me for Limoges! Madame too will be pleased to have Vallentine to travel back to Paris with us." She frowned in thought. "But I think perhaps he would have enjoyed a few days sojourn with only you for company."

The Duke grinned.

"Can you doubt it when he will now be spending the entire time on the Versailles road knee-deep in fabric and wallpaper samples?"

They both laughed.

Antonia looked up at him through her lashes, a blush washing over her porcelain cheeks as her smile evaporated and she confessed, "Monseigneur, it is selfish of me, but I feel a huge relief you no longer need to cross swords with Salvan. I know your great wish was to have justice served, but now we can go on with our lives knowing he cannot harm any of us."

"*Mignonne*, he was a blot, an irritation, nothing more. That he can no longer interfere with your happiness is a great relief. The only satisfying consequence of not killing him in a duel is that his inelegant end has denied him an honorable death."

"But you are not entirely content. I see it. There is something about Salvan's death which bothers you still, and I think it has to do with the figs."

"More to the point, why my aunt felt compelled to—er—hurry along Salvan's demise."

"Mayhap the letter Mme Haudry gave you will offer an answer?"

Roxton was reluctant to have anything to do with his cousin's letter. Its contents could prove enlightening or cause him more angst. He wanted to toss it, seal unbroken, into the hearth. But then he would never know one way or the other, so he removed the single folded parchment from his pocket and broke the seal.

Folding the sheet out, he was surprised to discover it contained another folded note. He removed this and put it to the back of the single sheet and read what the Comte had written. He then opened out the folded note, which was in a different fist, and read that. Coming up for air, he held both out to Antonia.

WHAT THE COMTE wrote to Roxton:

Mon cousin,

All my family have abandoned me on your command.
Congratulations! You have reduced poor Salvan to living as a
trapped cockroach.

You will see from the enclosed missive that old buzzard Tante

Philippe wanted me to burn it. Why should I? Did she honestly believe I would not realize both jars contained poison? Ah! But she is a true Salvan! Pride comes before all other considerations. But I do not think she cares who knows about her treachery. What concerns her is being found out that she does indeed possess a beating heart! Je suis étonné! And you are too.

My only solace in departing this earthly existence is knowing I have made your angel of a wife happy, and when her time comes to ascend to Heaven you and she will be separated for all eternity.

I await you in Hell.

WHAT *TANTE PHILIPPE* wrote to Salvan:

Joyeux anniversaire mon neveu!

A parting gift. Two jars of your favorite marinated figs. Which one you decide to open is yours to make. But before you do, let me inform you that I will not permit, however remote the possibility, a repeat of the family tragedy that befell my sister Madeleine-Julie. She was too young, too good and kind, too beautiful, and too deeply in love with her husband to be a widow before her time. So too is Antonia Roxton.

You could face your cousin in a duel and die an honorable death, for Roxton certainly will kill you, or you can select the jar which allows you to pass painlessly into an eternal slumber, knowing you have finally done something noble in allowing that sweet girl to enjoy many more years of married life.

Burn this note or the world will see what we do—a sniveling coward. You are a disgrace to your lineage, and no one will mourn your passing. I know which jar you will choose. Savor every morsel. Either choice leads straight to Hell.

Adieu à vous pour toujours.

THIRTY-FIVE

T HE FAMILY gathered for dinner that afternoon, dressed for the occasion in their best silks and satins. They were in an unusual mood—reflective because of the Comte de Salvan's death, but also cheerful and satisfied—their stay at the villa coming to a close now that Antonia had been presented at court and dined with the King, both of which were a resounding success. There was no need to remain at Versailles. Everyone was looking forward to returning to Paris and their lives in the space and opulence to be had at the *Hôtel* Roxton.

From the head of the table, the Duke surveyed his family. The Duchess and Martin were chatting, the topic of their conversation seated on Martin's knee. A nurserymaid approached and took his little lordship to settle him in his highchair, which was placed between his mother and his godfather. The Vallentines sat opposite, heads together and deep in discussion about wallpaper.

The Duke brought all conversation to a halt before the first of the covered dishes and tureens had arrived by signaling to the butler to have the wine poured. And while crystal glasses were being filled, he announced calmly,

"I have decided that it would be for the best if you were to remain here at the villa for a few weeks."

The Vallentines looked at one another and then at the Duke, both so startled neither spoke.

The Duke picked up his wine glass, mouth twitching. "I am gratified to have no argument from either of you—"

"Wait up! You haven't said why we should."

"Would it make a difference?"

"No. But—"

"Of course it would make a difference!" argued Madame.

"Then I will let the Duchess tell you," the Duke replied smoothly, and winked at his wife.

"Monseigneur, you are teasing them unnecessarily," Antonia complained without heat.

The Duke smiled. "I am."

"Hey! That's unfair!" complained Vallentine.

"I believe M'sieur le Duc is in an uncharacteristically jovial mood," Martin ventured to explain. "Which is why he is teasing you."

"*Exactement*, Martin," Antonia agreed.

The Vallentines looked at one another, Estée shrugging her acceptance of this explanation. Vallentine threw up a hand and grabbed for his wine glass.

"Fair enough. That news we got this mornin' of the death of *he who will not be named* has put all of us in a good mood, so I'm up for anythin' you want to throw at me—us! Why are we stayin' on here?"

"I will tell you," Antonia announced. "It was entirely my idea, and Monseigneur said he wished he had thought of it. And so, you are to stay here and enjoy a few weeks of rest and *rétablissement* while your apartments at the hôtel they are renovated. Naturally you will visit to see how things are progressing, but with all the workmen crawling about your rooms, there will be so much noise, and paint and glue fumes, and activity to give you both headaches, it will be unbearable—"

"Damme! That's an excellent notion, Mme la Duchesse!" Vallentine exclaimed. He addressed his wife. "In your delicate condition, the last thing you need is noise and disruption, lovely!"

"And while Madame she is resting during the day," Antonia explained, "Vallentine you can continue to visit *La Grande Écurie* with the Chevalier Montbelliard—oh! Excuse me, the Comte de Salvan." She looked to the Duke with a smile. "We must all grow accustomed to saying the name without bitterness because now it is to be associated with a young man Vallentine tells us is of unimpeachable character."

"Capital idea!" Vallentine announced enthusiastically, then seeing his wife pouting he added in a more subdued tone, "I wouldn't want to be under your feet all day. And if you're feelin' up to it, perhaps I could invite Montbel—*Salvan* around to dinner with his bride—" He stopped and looked to the Duke. "A'course that will depend on if we have your approval to have 'em to dine."

"Lucian, you may invite whomever you please to your table, and that includes the new Comte and Comtesse de Salvan. In fact, I insist you make their acquaintance." He looked to his sister. "If you feel you have the strength, I would appreciate you representing the family at the memorial service for our cousin."

"Of course," Estée replied. "And we will have a small reception here for our cousins and the newly married couple now they are elevated to the title." She smiled at Antonia. "Thank you for thinking of us, dearest. I like your idea exceedingly. But—" She sighed and tried to appear disinterested. "Will there be enough room to accommodate all of us here? I do not wish to be an inconvenience to anyone."

Her husband gave a start, Martin suppressed a grin, the Duke's eyes shot to the ceiling.

Antonia also knew at once to what her sister-in-law was alluding—would Martin be staying on, and what of those servants and retainers who had always been at the villa? She exchanged a knowing smile with the Duke.

"There is no inconvenience," Antonia answered brightly. "Only your servants will be here, and naturally any of Monseigneur's household from the villa you need to retain for your comfort. Everyone else—including Jean-Luc—will be coming with us to the hôtel. Oh! Except Martin. But I will let him tell you his travel plans."

Vallentine was instantly upset. "What? You're not leavin' us for long are you, Ellicott?"

"For only a few months," Martin replied, visibly touched by His Lordship's disappointment. "I mean to spend a month with my mother at Alston, and then travel to Bath to inspect the improvements to Moran Hall. I also have a few errands to run for Their Graces in London—"

"But you'll be back in time for the birth?" Vallentine asked anxiously. He looked at his wife, and included her when he said, "We want you to be here. He has to be, doesn't he, Roxton."

"Of course," Martin reassured him. "I would not miss the momentous occasion for the world."

"Then it is settled," stated the Duke.

"And in the spring," Antonia said airily, "Monseigneur and I, we will return to Treat because our second son he should be born there—"

"I knew it!" Estée blurted out with smug satisfaction. "You *are* pregnant!"

Antonia appeared pensive. "Madame, I do not think so…" Her smile was secretive. "But that is not to say that by then I won't be. And there are many good reasons to spend the warmer months at Treat." She made wide eyes at her infant son and grabbed his fist, which was banging against the chair tray, and gave it a resounding kiss, before again addressing the rest of her family. "One is that as Martin he is returning with us, he can introduce his godson to his mother—"

"—and after that introduction," interrupted the Duke, looking over the rim of his crystal glass at the Duchess, not at all fooled, "you will sit down to cake with Mrs. Ellicott and talk about the weather…?"

Martin looked awkward but Antonia's green eyes were alight with mischief.

"Monseigneur, it would be impolite of me if over the cake I did not enquire of Mrs. Ellicott about her time as housekeeper up at the big house—"

"Fibber," the Duke interjected lovingly. "What you most want from her is to find out all there is to know about my—er— boyhood incarceration under the roof of my tyrannical grandfather."

"M'sieur le Duc, you are *très astucieux*!"

"And you, Mme la Duchesse, are an imp!"

The ducal couple were locked in a playful battle of wits which was baffling to the Vallentines. But nothing could distract His Lordship from the footmen hovering, their arms weighed down with covered dishes awaiting the butler's instruction to lay them on the table.

"Are there any other reasons, dearest?" asked Estée, intrigued, but still mystified.

When Antonia and Martin exchanged a knowing smile, the Duke said, "If there are, I suggest you confess all, *ma vie*, so I may give the signal, or Lucian may faint from hunger."

Antonia pretended to prevaricate, and then she laughed.

"Very well, to save Lucian." And included everyone when she said, "Naturally, my most important reason for visiting Mrs. Ellicott is for her to make Julian's acquaintance. But once she has told me everything about Monseigneur's time under his grandfather's roof, I intend for us to have a Lemuralia feast. In this way the malevolent spirit of the fourth Duke will be cast from the house forever."

"And as head of the household, you expect me to participate in the rites of this Roman feast by walking about—er—barefoot at midnight?" interjected the Duke, feigning irritation. "Tossing black beans over my shoulder and reciting the incantation: *Haec ego mitto; his redimo meque meosque fabis?*"

"*These I cast, with these beans I redeem me and mine?*" Vallentine blurted out, translating the Latin. He pulled a face. "What gibberish!"

"And you think throwing black beans about is less nonsensical?" blustered his wife.

"It impresses me very much that you know your Latin, Lucian," Antonia complimented.

"I might appear a hanktelo," His Lordship said loftily, chin up, "but I have managed to retain some of the drivel we were taught at Eton."

"Latin class was just before dinner," explained the Duke. "And Lucian is at his most alert when hungry." He signaled to his butler to start serving dinner, and said to his best friend, "My apologies for keeping your stomach waiting."

"Accepted," said His Lordship, gaze never leaving the center of the table where footmen were offloading covered dishes of various sizes. "If you ask me, this Lem-*whatsit* feast—

"*Lemuralia* feast," Roxton corrected.

"Lemuralia feast—*that*," continued Vallentine, ladling cream of mushroom soup into his bowl, "might be just what such a gloomy monolith in marble needs. I'm all for anythin' that will purge Treat of the fourth Duke's menacin' spirit."

"What you are most for, Lucian, is a feast," stated Estée, which had everyone laughing.

Vallentine grinned. "That too! But not the beans—"

"That is wise, because I am very sure beans, they would have the same effect on you as the almond nougat," Antonia stated matter-of-factly.

There was more laughter about the table.

"I'm goin' to ignore you, chit, and drink m' soup!"

"Mme la Duchesse, may I enquire how many times M'sieur le Duc is required to repeat this incantation while he is throwing—um—beans over his shoulder?"

"Martin, stop encouraging her," the Duke cautioned mildly.

"Nine times! And Martin he must encourage me, Monseigneur, because he too wishes to see you perform the ceremony to banish your grandfather's spirit."

"That I do, Mme la Duchesse," agreed Martin, avoiding the Duke's eye. "I am very sure my mother—and those who served under the fourth Duke—would also appreciate the gesture."

"Why not ask her—in fact, all the old retainers—to join us?" drawled the Duke. "I am certain Mme la Duchesse will make sure there are enough—er—beans to go 'round!"

"What a most excellent idea, Monseigneur," Antonia replied sweetly, ignoring his heavy sarcasm and exchanging a smile with Martin Ellicott. "I will do just that!"

She then looked about the table at her family, who were busily plying their bowls and plates with food, and then at her infant, who was happily flapping his arms and making gurgling noises, and with a contented sigh returned her gaze to the Duke.

"And as Vallentine and Madame and their infant will be joining us at Treat, the rest of your family can be involved in the ceremony too. So you cannot object and say you will be alone in your bare feet throwing the beans," she argued cheekily. Her gaze went about the table again. "While M'sieur le Duc he is tossing the beans about the rooms and repeating his incantation," she explained, "we will all be following him in our bare feet, too, bashing bronze pots together and repeating—oh! Let me say it in French, so we all understand —*Ghosts of my fathers and ancestors, be gone!*"

There was a clatter of metal on porcelain when the Vallentines dropped their silverware and stared at her in horror.

"Monseigneur, did I translate the phrase correctly?"

The Duke nodded, napkin pressed to his mouth to hold in his laughter, all self-control lost at the image in his mind's eye of him and his family barefoot performing the Roman rites of exorcism, he tossing beans over his shoulder and inadvertently pelting his family in the process.

"You see, JuJu!" Antonia announced to her infant son, kissing his fist and then his chubby cheek. "Your papa he and your family, they are already much happier just at the prospect of purging the ghost of *ton arrière-grand-père* from our home!" She sat up and looked about the table before addressing the Duke. "I am determined Treat will be a happy home for all of us!"

The Duke, eyes still moist with laughter, raised his glass to her —the others followed his lead—and said tenderly, "Of that, *mignonne*, I am utterly convinced. To Mme la Duchesse!"

"Mme la Duchesse!"

BEHIND-THE-SCENES

Explore the real people, places, objects, and
history in *Their Graces* on Pinterest.
www.pinterest.com.au/lucindabrant/roxton-foundation-series